THE LEATHER MAN'S JOURNAL

MATT BANNISTER WESTERN 14

KEN PRATT

Published in the United States by Wolfpack Publishing, Las Vegas

CKN Christian Publishing
An Imprint of Wolfpack Publishing
5130 S. Fort Apache Road 215-380
Las Vegas, NV 89148

cknchristianpublishing.com

Paperback ISBN: 978-1-63977-434-0
eBook ISBN: 978-1-63977-433-3
LCCN 2022939666

THE LEATHER MAN'S JOURNAL

Dedication

This book is dedicated to my friend
Andrew Worley. He'll know why.
May the Lord use you brightly!!

Chapter 1

It was Thursday, July 3rd and the Independence Day preparations had the city of Branson as busy an ant hill with all the people running here and there, setting up booths and getting ready for the most anticipated celebration of the year. The excitement was high as the many community events promised a fun-filled day. There were games, foot and horse races, raffles, vendors coming to town to sell their goods, and a special one-day appearance by the Chatfield & Bowry Fun Circus and Amazing Sideshow. It was the first time a renowned circus company had come to Branson. Two weeks prior, a package of Thirty-Two colorful posters advertising the circus arrived at City Hall for the Branson Planning Commission and Jessup County Commissioners to spread out across the city and valley to promote the event. Despite the growing excitement for the circus, the Annual Independence Day Community Dance held in the city park, followed by the fireworks show, was still the grand finale that everyone looked forward to. It promised to be a fantastic Independence Day celebration.

Like everyone, the Branson Sheriff Tim Wright could feel the excitement in the atmosphere clear down to his bones. However, his good mood soured after listening to a vagrant who wandered into town dressed in rawhide leather. The vagrant was the strangest looking man Tim had ever seen and the story he told made him the craziest man he'd ever met. Tim had no tolerance for a lunatic invading his town, especially when the streets would be full of hard-working citizens celebrating. A man like the one that stood in front of him could make the Independence Day celebration most uncomfortable for many people. There was no doubt the man was crazy, which meant he could be dangerous. Tim did not want him wandering around town begging for food or money.

The sheriff gazed at the strange man with a perplexed expression that transformed into an uneasy grimace. Tim spoke bluntly, "Get out of my town. You are about as crazy as a..." he looked to his deputy Bob Ewing for help. "As a what?"

Bob chuckled while peering at the stranger. "About the craziest loon in the sanitarium. Did you escape from there, Leather Man? Or are you a part of the circus sideshow? I know some folks are excited about you freaks coming to town, but couldn't you wait until showtime and make a buck?"

The stranger shifted his eyes from Bob to Tim, annoyed. "Can you help me or not? You are the

2

marshal, right? Your brother in Willow Falls told me you could help find my wife."

"No, I'm not the marshal," Tim answered sharply. "Can't you read? The sign says Sheriff's Office. Listen to me. We don't take kindly to people like you. I suggest you keep walking right out of my town. If not, I'll throw you in my jail long enough to get through our Independence Day celebration and then send you to the sanitarium in Salem."

"But I've done nothing wrong," the stranger argued.

"I don't care!" Tim snapped. He took a threatening step closer to the stranger. "You're not welcome here. If my deputies or I see you in town, I will have you arrested until you get that one-way trip to Salem. Now, get out of my office and keep walking straight out of town."

The strange-looking man frowned. "I was told the marshal could help me. I can't leave without my wife, and there are miners here."

Bob licked his lips with a bit of a humored grin. "By all means, Tim, let him go knock on the doors out at Slater's Mile. You'll probably find her there."

"Where is that?" the stranger asked.

Bob answered, "South of town a couple of miles. You can't miss it. If you find her or save her, bring her by. I've never met a middle earth broad."

"Will you arrest the men that took her?"

"Sure, we will. Good luck, your majesty," Bob said, shaking his head with a chuckle. It wasn't every day that he met a person claiming to be a king from the middle earth.

3

The stranger shifted his eyes back to Tim. "I don't know how to read. We have no use for it in the land below."

"I don't care!" Tim shouted. He was irritated with Bob for suggesting the man walk through town to Slater's Mile. "Just get out of my town. If you go to Slater's Mile or the mine, just keep walking south. Don't come back to town. Understand me? I don't want you here and you will be sorry if we catch you in town again," Tim warned.

"I must stay for a few days, but I will be no trouble."

"No, you're not staying a few days! Now leave."

***

He stared straight ahead without a glance to the left or right as he walked up Main Street. He ignored the many strange looks, laughter and snide comments directed his way. It was nothing he wasn't used to and expected nothing less. His homemade clothing was fashioned out of rawhide and creaked like stepping into a saddle as he walked. Beads of sweat blotted his forehead and soaked into his bangs that barely touched his eyebrows. He kept a pair of scissors in his bag to cut his hair when it got in his eyes. His dark brown hair was slightly longer on his right side, where it covered his earlobe, while the hair on his left side was cut at mid-ear. The hair on the back of his head was about as choppy and lopsided.

His homemade rawhide hat stood six inches

above his head with a flat top and stiff sides and a two-inch flap of a bill on the front. It was a ridiculous-looking hat, sweat-stained and stiff as a board, but it fit his head snugly, and not even a high wind could blow it off. He could bet a dollar that there was no other like it since he had made it himself. His oblong face was thin and covered with an unkempt beard about three inches long. Dust was smeared across his nose and cheeks, where he had wiped the sweat away. His eyes were blue, and a narrow straight nose protruded outwards just enough to become a prominent feature.

The stranger's long sleeve shirt was two pieces of rawhide cut to size and sewn together into a single piece pulled over his shoulders. Around his neck was a black obsidian arrowhead necklace with turquoise, blue and red beadwork on a deer hide string. His rawhide pants were made the same way as his shirt, with both pieces stitched together with leather cordage. They were tucked into a pair of homemade rawhide knee-high, pull-on boots with wooden soles. Many things were odd about him, but the clicking sound of the wooden soles against the boardwalk was one of the audible ones.

He wore a heavy, knee-length coat made from random pieces of rawhide sewn together with leather cordage. Random fragments of rawhide were stitched onto his coat to keep handy for patches or perhaps a new garment if he could think of one.

A large rawhide bag with a rawhide strap over his head and shoulder was worn across his back.

He was used to ridicule and drawing people's attention. He didn't say a word in return, he just kept walking, but even the way he walked drew laughter. Most people walked with their arms swinging in the opposite direction of their legs. As one leg moved forward, the arm came back. The stranger's steps were in unison with his arms. His right leg moved forward simultaneously with his right arm, and then his left leg stepped forward in line with his left arm. His clothing, hat, wooden soles, lop-sided hair and the way he walked were all oddities that invited attention whether it was meant to or not.

It was hard to see the signs on Main Street as he walked in the shade of the awnings above the boardwalk. It was a hot day and the clothing he wore was heavy, which added to the heat and caused him to sweat all the more. He walked under the awnings to keep in the shade as much as possible. A large bay window with *U.S. Marshal Matt Bannister* written in gold paint caught his attention. He opened the door and heard a cow bell ring above his head which drew the attention of a young, clean-cut deputy marshal.

"Hello, can I help you?" Phillip Forrester asked slowly. The expression on his face showed his uncertain reaction of what to think of the man before him.

"Are you the marshal?" the stranger asked curtly.

Matt was sitting at the table by the woodstove with Truet Davis and Nate Robertson eating a pie Nate's mother made. Matt stood and wiped his face clear of any crumbs or apple pie from his beard and mustache. "I am," he said, approaching the strange man clad in leather. The other two men stood and followed to get a closer look.

Matt reached out a hand to shake over the partition. "I'm Matt Bannister. How can I help you, sir?" He already had a good idea of what the stranger wanted. His brother Steven had warned him that the man could show up some time, but that was weeks ago.

The stranger stared at Matt awkwardly. He was surprised to see such a young and handsome man. Matt was tall with broad, muscular shoulders. He had a full beard and mustache kept neatly trimmed and long dark hair worn in a ponytail. He expected Matt to be much older and more grizzled. "I was told to come to see you. I hope you can help me find my wife. She was taken by two miners."

Nate Robertson, familiar with the story Steven had told Matt, bit his lip tightly to keep from laughing.

"If I can. Do you know who took her?"

The stranger explained, "Two miners. They mined through your world into mine, slid down a rope, grabbed her and went back up the rope. I followed, but I can't find her."

"I see," Matt said, slightly annoyed at Nate for snickering behind a hand that hid a smile he couldn't resist. Matt continued, "And your world is…?"

"Underground." He sighed irritably with a coarse glance at Nate. "My name is Napoleon the Great. I am the King of Ziarria. My queen is missing. You have miners in this town and I'm sure she's here. Can you help me? I don't want to bring my warriors up here, but if I have to, I will, to find her."

Matt frowned. "We don't need you doing that. I'd love to help you find her, but I don't know who I am looking for. I don't know what she looks like or her name. Can you describe the miners?"

"Her name is Josephine. Empress and queen of Ziarria..."

Truet whispered something to Nate and nudged him with his elbow. Nate burst out laughing uncontrollably and waved a hand towards Matt as he staggard towards the steel door of the jail and stepped inside, closing the door behind him. Truet grinned as his cheeks reddened slightly to have Matt's disapproving eyes on him.

"I apologize for my deputies. You'll have to forgive them. Your story is a little bit different than most we hear around here," Matt explained. "Please continue. How would I know her if I saw her? Does she wear a crown?"

"Don't patronize me," Napoleon said irritably. "Her crown fell off when they took her up the rope. She has long dark hair and is as beautiful as the sunset. She'll be wearing a beautiful dress."

"There are a lot of women wearing beautiful dresses around here. Is it red? Purple? Can you be more specific?"

"She's dressed like me, but it's a dress."

Truet forced his smile away. "That must be a gorgeous dress."

Phillip snorted. "Excuse me," he said and left his

desk quickly to walk to the jail. He opened the door and started laughing as the door closed.

Napoleon watched Phillip with a scowl. "Your deputies don't believe me. I ask that you do because I need your help."

"I understand. Well, Napoleon, where is Ziarria? We don't have kings in America."

He sighed. "There is a world beyond this world, called the middle earth. Some of the lava tubes are access points to and from the middle earth. I thought all of you toppers knew that."

"Toppers?" Matt asked.

Napoleon spoke slowly to explain the obvious, "Those of you who live on top of the earth. I understand the explorer Jules Verne wrote about his exploits in our land. We live down there just like you do up here. The water's better down there, though. It's newer and younger than up here. It keeps us more youthful."

Matt nodded. "That would make sense, wouldn't it? Well, I'll tell you what I'll do, the manager of the mine married my cousin, so I know him well. I'll ask him if any of his employees have a new wife named Josephine and wears a rawhide dress. If any do, he'll know."

"She's not their wife!" Napoleon spouted. "She is my wife, and I'm taking her home!"

"Of course. If I find her, where can I locate you to let you know?"

Napoleon hesitated. "I'll have to let you know. I just got to town and will make a camp outside of town somewhere. I discovered a tannery in another town and got this," he lifted a six-inch scrap of rawhide with a single stitch of leather string connecting it to his coat. "That's a nice piece, right?"

Matt raised his eyebrows admiringly. "Beautiful. Well, let me know where you'll be staying. And, Napoleon, I will warn you, if you see the two miners, you let me confront them. Don't you do that. Understood? I'm afraid they may not treat you well. I don't want you getting hurt."

"I will. Thank you."

"You bet."

Napoleon held up a dirty finger with black dirt under the fingernail. "One more thing, the sheriff told me to leave town or he would arrest me and send me to the sanitarium. Can he do that?"

Matt shrugged his shoulders uneasily. "I suppose he could arrest you for vagrancy. But I believe he would need a court order to send you to the sanitarium. In all fairness, I will tell you that Jules Verne's book, *Journey to the Center of the Earth*, is considered fiction..."

"Fiction! Who considers it fiction?"

"Well, just about everyone. That makes your story a little hard to believe, Napoleon. Most folks don't believe there is a middle earth."

"Well, there is!" He was adamant. "Are you telling me I don't know where I'm from? You toppers are so arrogant that you probably think you're the highest life form among all the stars too. Are you aware that there is life in the ocean? I swear, all you toppers are the same. Those men took my wife and you're telling me you don't believe in the middle earth. Prove it doesn't exist," he challenged.

"I'm not going to argue with you about it. But you know some people will say the mine outside of town has dug nearly a thousand feet down and hasn't reached it yet. Other mines around the country and world have gone much deeper and still nothing. That must've been a long rope those miners used."

Napoleon scowled. "I told you not to patronize me! It just goes to show you know nothing. Ziarria is on a mountain top, so it's closer to your surface. I'll let you know where I make camp."

Matt watched as Napoleon left the office and walked along the boardwalk. His strange appearance was made odder by his walk, swinging his arms and legs in unison.

Truet laughed. "Sorry about that. I knew it! I whispered to Nate that his wife's name was probably Josephine and sure enough," he laughed.

Matt grinned. "Well, there's your assignment for the week; find Josephine."

"A dollar says, if Christine wore a leather dress, he'd want to fight whoever was dancing with her."

"I doubt she'd wear a rawhide dress. Besides, she has enough love-struck admirers without you pointing him her way," Matt said with a grin.

The jail door opened, and the two deputies were still laughing. "I bet that is a pretty dress," Phillip laughed at Truet's words.

"You are all terrible," Matt said with a slight smile. "Nate, in your opinion, what are the chances we can find his wife?"

"Zero to none," he snickered.

"I think you're right."

"Matt, you should have asked him what his last name is. I'll bet it's Bonaparte," Truet said.

"When he comes back, I'll ask. I bet you it's not."

"A dollar bet?" Truet asked.

"No, let's make it hurt. Phillip wants Saturday and Sunday off. How about the loser works both days to babysit John." John Painter was a prisoner staying in the jail but was laboring at the granite quarry during working hours.

"Oh..." Truet groaned. "That would hurt. I'm supposed to spend the weekend in Willow Falls with Annie and the family. But I'm feeling confident, so deal."

Chapter 2

Premro Island was a large basalt land mass that separated the Modoc River as it dropped in elevation just outside of Branson's city limits. The island was surrounded on both sides by channels of fast-moving water that hurled down the natural shoots over a series of turbulent waterfalls and rapids. The current created a perfect power source for water wheels to power the equipment of the Premro and Sons Milling Works, Seven Timber Harvester Lumber Mill, a small flour mill, and others that took advantage of the natural power source of the river. A heavy wooden bridge was built from Branson across the twenty-foot-wide rapids that fired down the channel separating the island from Branson. Another bridge crossed the far side of the island where the main torrent of water was broader and fell down a steep incline of roaring power. The whitewater dropped sixty feet in a short distance as the river came out of the Blue Mountains and entered Jessup Valley. The two water forces came together in a deep pool at the island's western end.

The pool was where almost everyone gathered to swim in the summertime and the June weather was drawing a crowd of people to the cold refreshing water. The sound of the rumbling falls, the rotation of the sawmill blades cutting through a log, and the turning waterwheels added to the atmosphere of a long-awaited perfect summer's day. The winter had been long and cold, but now that the temperature was just over a hundred degrees, the cold water coming off the mountain was a reprieve from the day's heat.

Children with their mothers played with delight in the shallow water of what was known as the beach. It was an area of level ground beside the pool at the base of a short hill where folks picnicked and rested on the grass while enjoying the river. Some people dove off the rocks of Premro Island into the deep water, or for the more daring ones, riding down the rapids on their hind ends, even though such acts of bravado occasionally ended in tragedy.

Teenagers were frequently at the river and to-day, being the hottest day of the year so far was no exception. Nick Griffin stood on the last boulder protruding from the water at the end of Premro Island. He dove for the third time into the deep pool and resurfaced with a refreshing shout as his feet paddled to keep his head above water. "Ollie, jump in!"

Ollie Hoffman stood on the bank, shaking his head. "I'm talking to Linda." He was talking to an attractive teenage girl with thick light-brown hair that fell freely over her shoulders. They stood about fifteen feet away from another group of teenagers. "Nick, come here," Ollie called to his friend. He left Linda alone and walked down to the water as Nick swam towards him.

Nick walked out of the water in a pair of cut-off brown pants and no shirt. Nick was tall and lean. He had black hair that reached the mid-ear in length. He could grow no facial hair, but acne plagued his face and back more heavily than any other teenager in town. His dark-brown eyes and dark eyebrows were attractive on his oblong face, but there was a menacing undertone to them that made some people feel uncomfortable. "The water feels great," he said, refreshed and ready to go back in.

Ollie drew close and spoke quietly, "Nick, everyone's parents will be at Slater's Ball tonight. I was talking to Linda, and she wants to get some alcohol and meet us down around the bend on Cabbage Island when the dance starts."

Nick was skeptical. "You mean Linda and her friends want us to join them tonight? No, she doesn't. She's just pulling your leg as those rich girls do."

Linda Fowler was of a much higher social standing. She was the seventeen-year-old daughter of Larry Fowler. Larry was the Slater Silver Mine's chief geologist who reported to Wally Gettman in the mine's engineering and geological sciences department.

Linda was upper society and being so, she made best friends with Elizabeth Chalkalski and Paulina Sorenson, both of which were daughters of two of Branson's Elite Seven and lived in large homes on King's Point. Elizabeth nor Paulina had ever given Nick or Ollie the time of day, let alone wanted to know their names. Nick doubted Linda and her friends wanted to spend the evening with two younger boys from the poor side of town, that lived in the Dogwood Flats Apartments.

Ollie continued, "Believe it or not, she invited us to join them. She said all their parents will be at the Slater's Ball until late." Ollie was of average height and build, with a round face and soft blue eyes. His straight blond hair reached the ear lobe. There was nothing overly handsome or special about Ollie, except his sincerity was plain to see in his eyes.

Nick didn't believe it. "It's got to be a joke. Those girls don't even talk to us."

"Ask her." Ollie turned around. "Linda," he called, "Nick doesn't think you're serious. Were you joking?"

Linda Fowler was a pretty girl with blue eyes and high cheekbones on a square-shaped face. Her light brown hair with a reddish tint hung thick and frizzy over her broad shoulders. She was taller and larger boned than her friends, but her father was also a large man and she had inherited his body build. However, her smile was brilliantly white and pretty. She questioned, "Why would you think that I'm joking?" She left her friends to speak to Nick, "You don't believe we want to invite you to our party?"

Nick shook his head lightly. "No, I don't. Why would you invite us? You and your friends have never once spoken to Ollie or me. I thought Josh Bannister, Chester Hatfield and boys like that were more your crowd."

"Our crowd?" she asked skeptically.

"Yeah. You know the more well-to-do than us."

Linda wrinkled her nose. "They're certainly our friends, but I don't see why we can't invite Ollie and you. It's not that big of a deal if you decide not to come. I'll try to bring a bottle of something from my father's bar that he won't notice if it goes missing. My parents are not big drinkers. Elizabeth and Paulina are going to try to bring something too. I thought you two might be able to bring a bottle or two of something in case we chicken out. We three girls could get in a lot of trouble if our parents found out."

Nick's eyes narrowed pointedly. "If you get drunk tonight, you'll be hungover tomorrow when everything is happening here."

Linda scoffed. "Do you think I haven't been drunk before? It's going to be fun. The band will be playing in the park, and we'll be able to hear the music so we can have our own dance without our parents' eyes prying on us like they will be tomorrow night."

"Won't your parents be upset if you rich girls come home drunk?" Nick asked with a sarcastic tone.

Linda's lips rose just enough to imply rebellion.

"They would, but Paulina's and my parents think we are spending the night with Elizabeth. Elizabeth's parents think she's spending the night at my house. All our parents are going to William Slater's ball and won't be home until late and will come home drunk and go straight to bed. We're staying the night down here and going home in the morning. Our parents will never know."

A slow, thoughtful smile appeared on his lips. "Yeah, we'll join you. I'll bring a bottle of whiskey or two. It'll be fun."

"Great. Then we'll see you tonight when the dance starts."

Nick looked at Ollie. "Let's go to my place. My Pa has a few dollars on his dresser. Today is his payday, so he won't miss them. Maybe I can get an advance on my pay too."

***

Ollie Hoffman could get very nervous when Leonard Griffin came home from work in a bad mood. It made Ollie glad he didn't have a father. He lowered his head and kept his mouth shut as his chest filled with an uncomfortable fear for his friend, Nick.

"Pa, I didn't take it! I didn't do it!" Nick shouted. His father had thrown him to the floor and sat on Nick's chest with his arms pinned under his father's knees.

"Then who did? Ollie?" The cold and angry empty sea of blue in Leonard's eyes glared across the room at Ollie suspiciously. Leonard worked at the sawmill and although not a big man, his forearms were massive from moving heavy planks day after day. He was a muscular man with short black hair and a triangular face that he kept clean-shaven. Wrinkles on his forehead were permanent fixtures, as well as the scowl that revealed his bitterness towards life. The only time Ollie had ever seen Leonard smile or laugh was when he was drinking and had a woman he was trying to impress. The women had never stayed long, but Leonard was not a loving man.

Ollie shook his head like a frightened puppy cowering in a corner. "Not me, sir."

"No!" Nick exclaimed. "It was probably that whore you brought home."

Leonard's rough right hand flashed downward, followed by the shrill, high-pitched sound of Leonard's calloused hand striking the soft skin of Nick's cheek. It was followed by a left-handed slap that mimicked the same painful sound, followed by another harsh right. All three were hard and immediately reddened Nick's cheeks.

Leonard shouted, "She might become your mother! Don't ever refer to her like that again." He grabbed Nick's hair with both hands and began pounding the back of the boy's head against the floor. He hissed through gritted teeth, "You should've learned to keep your mouth shut a long time ago! You cursed your mother, and I won't have you cursing Ruth now." He released Nick's hair and squeezed the boy's cheeks to open his mouth. Leonard glared down at his son with wrath burn-

19

ing in his eyes. "I know you took the money off my dresser because you are the only thief I know!" He released the boy's cheeks and then slapped his son again with a hard right. The high-pitched sound of his weathered hand hitting Nick's cheek made Ollie cringe.

"I don't know where it went," Nick replied with watering eyes that refused to release a single tear. An angry sneer twisted his lips. The money was in his worn-out shoe. "Ask your whore!"

Ollie watched Mister Griffin's open hand slowly close into a fist as he glared down at his son. The fist struck fast and hard, spinning Nick's head to the left. Leonard snorted in through his nose and sucked up the mucus of his summer allergies. He spat the thick phlegm onto his son's face. "That's what I think of you – snot! I wish you were never born, Nick." The man stood and looked at Ollie. "Why do you waste your time with him? The kid is worthless! I suppose you're not any better, but at least you had a mother to raise you."

Nick stood immediately, humiliated and angry. He wiped the mucus off his face with his shirt sleeve. "I wish I was never born!" he shouted in a loud voice.

"Me too!" Leonard screamed in Nick's face. His cold eyes, wide and harsh, carelessly glared at his sixteen-year-old son. His expression turned to disgust. "Are you going to let me spit in your face and get away with it?" He shook his head with disgust that Nick stood still and lowered his eyes. "Really? You make me sick."

Nick's chest heaved with his heavy breaths. His dark brown eyes, which looked like his mother's, lifted to glare at his father.

Leonard snickered and moved his face closer, intentionally taunting Nick. "I'll even close my eyes so you can try to hit me with your soft little hands. You're such a damn girl. I wish your mother was alive to show you how to wipe your..."

Nick swung his right arm with every ounce of fury he could muster, but his father blocked it with ease. Leonard drove a right fist upwards into Nick's abdomen, bending him over, forcing the air out of him and dropping the boy to his knees. He fell face forward onto his forearms, trying to get a breath; it would not come easily.

Leonard chuckled spitefully. "I'm going to the saloon. I suppose you two girls are going to the dance tonight. Maybe you could stop by Bella's Dance Hall and ask if any ladies will lend you a dress. Have fun, girls." He walked out the door.

Ollie exhaled, relieved to see Mister Griffin leaving. They all lived at the Dogwood Flats Apartments; Ollie lived with his mother a few apartments over. It was interesting how he and Nick could walk all over Branson neighborhoods and not hear the same kind of fighting, arguing and violence they heard daily in their apartment complex.

The Dogwood Shacks was a single-level housing complex with twenty small apartments. It was shaped like a horseshoe with six apartments on one side leading back away from Second Street, eight apartments stretching across the center, and six more leading back to Second Street. The design left a courtyard with a single willow tree in its center. Initially, it was an unusual design with benches under the tree and a beautiful little place to live for the hardworking people of Branson. But, over the past twenty years, it had become a cockroach-infested, rat-filled, nearly debilitated complex for the poorest citizens, barely able to keep a roof over their heads. The property was owned by Big John Pederson, the owner of Ugly John's Saloon, and as long as he got his ten dollars rent per apartment a month, he couldn't care less what happened there. Maybe that was one reason why there was so much yelling, fighting and violence.

"Are you okay?" Ollie asked his best friend.

"Yeah," Nick squeaked out. He slowly got to his knees and then to his feet. He looked at his friend. "I hate him."

"I don't like him either."

Nick sat down at the small kitchen table. "There's not a thing to eat in the house and he got paid today. He's going to have steak for dinner, no doubt at the saloon and I'll be begging your mother for scraps."

"We don't have much ourselves, but she'll feed you. She always does."

"I know. I wish the store was open when we stopped by, but I get paid next week. I'll give your ma some money for always feeding me then. I have to hide my pay from my father. He takes my money, you know. He'll hit me for taking his, but he takes mine without asking every other week." Nick worked a few hours a day delivering groceries for

C & A Culpepper's Grocery Store. It didn't pay him a lot of money, but it was better than nothing and the tips from customers usually earned him a few dollars a week.

"It's too bad your pa won't let you just move in with us," Ollie said.

Nick gave a discouraged sigh. "He wouldn't have anyone to beat on if I wasn't here. I think that's the only reason he wants me here."

Nick turned sixteen two weeks before without a single mention of it by his father. It was just another day of being thrown around. Leonard moved Nick to Branson two years before from California. When Nick was nine, a cholera outbreak took the lives of his younger brother and sister, and his mother was quite sick with the terrible disease. Angry at his father for not letting him leave the house while they were quarantined, Nick spouted the words, "I hope Mother dies!" He didn't mean it. He was just a nine-year-old boy angry at his father for not letting him have his way. Unfortunately, Nick's mother did die a few hours later.

That day had changed his father and it had only gotten worse over time. Nick had mourned the loss of his mother and repeatedly apologized for saying those words. Leonard considered those words a curse and believed Nick cursed his mother to death. It was Nick's fault that she died, and his father had never forgiven Nick for it. Nick's father reminded him of it often enough.

Ollie Hoffman was fifteen and Nick had become his best friend. Ollie's mother had courted many men, including Leonard. The most prolonged courtship was with Richie Thorn, which lasted approximately four months. Richie was abusive, but it ended when Richie beat Ollie's mother badly enough to need medical attention. Ollie was furious enough to want to kill Richie. He would not stand a chance in a fist fight against Richie Thorn, and he knew it. Nick retrieved his father's revolver and gave it to Ollie to get his revenge. Ollie confronted Richie on Main Street, but it was ended by the marshal, Matt Bannister.

Matt had sent one of his deputies home with Ollie to check on his mother and then took her to the doctor to have her wounds treated. The marshal was kind enough to pay the doctor's bill without even meeting his mother. Ollie wished Matt would become his father. He respected the man that much. Knowing Richie was afraid of Matt was perhaps enough to satisfy Ollie's rage because Ritchie never came by the apartment again. It was moments later that Ollie and Nick watched Matt shoot and kill Bloody Jim Hexum by the door of the Monarch Hotel. Witnessing a man get shot drained the murderous intention out of Ollie.

On the other hand, Nick wasn't so quick to let the outrage for Ollie's mother go. He had an idea and stole two axe handles from a barrel of the hardware store and drove two long nails through the two axe handles so they could beat Richie to death late at night as he left the saloon. Ollie declined to participate in any such action knowing the consequences would be facing Matt Bannister and the law eventually.

Nick sat at the dirty small, round dining table and looked at Ollie with a growing grin. "Those girls want to get drunk tonight. I know Elizabeth is engaged to Chester Hatfield, but he's away at college. I'll bet you that I can end that engagement tonight if she gets drunk."

Ollie shook his head doubtfully. "Elizabeth didn't even look our way when we were talking to Linda."

"Doesn't matter. She will tonight. I'll bet you."

Chapter 3

Bella's Dance Hall would not be closing for the community dance in the city park tonight, but they would be closed tomorrow night for the dance until after the fireworks display. One thing Bella had always done well was promote her business. Allowing her dancers to mingle with the community's citizens always brought new customers. It was like throwing bait into the river before casting in your line to hook unsuspecting men with the lady's beauty, elegance and class. Men who had never been tempted to come into her establishment would become enamored with one of the girls and want to dance with them. The agenda was for the ladies to seek out new faces and dance with men who had never come to the dance hall. Of course, the girls were instructed to remind the men that the dance hall would be opening after the fireworks display.

Christine Knapp was at peace. Almost four years ago, her grandmother sold her farm and gave Chris-

tine and her husband, Richard, the money to leave
Indiana and buy a farm in the fertile Willamette
Valley of Oregon. Crossing the Kansas plains, their
young daughter Carmen died of sickness. She was
buried on the Kansas plains with a bare wooden
cross to mark her grave. Christine knew then that
she would never be able to revisit Carmen's grave
once the wagon continued westward. In Denver,
Richard was stabbed to death in a saloon. Left alone
and mourning two tragic losses, Christine was devastated. With the wagon train to Oregon anxious
to leave, she was pressured to decide if she would
continue with them or not. Across town, Bella
heard of the young beautiful lady's circumstances
and sought her out to offer her a place to stay and
mourn in safety, and if she chose to, stay and dance
as employment. Christine sold her wagon and most
of her family's goods and moved into Bella's Dance
Hall in Denver. She saved enough money to purchase a tombstone for Richard's grave, but she had
always regretted not having Carmen's name etched
into the granite stone.

May had been her planned wedding month, but
sometimes blessings come when you least expect
them, occasionally even when it is most inconve-
nient. A second cousin she did not know had paid
a detective company to track her down and offered
to pay her fees to take Christine back to Indiana
to visit her grandmother. The opportunity was a
blessing above any she had ever dreamed of, and
she got to spend the last few weeks of her grandmother's life with her. On her original wedding

date, her beloved fiancé Matt Bannister walked through the door. He had traveled to Indiana to be with her on that special day. He met her grandmother and received her blessing to marry Christine. Her grandmother passed away shortly after.

Together Christine and Matt rode a train west and stopped in Denver. They visited Richard's grave and hired a stonemason to add Carmen Lucille Knapp and her birth and death dates onto Richard's tombstone. They did not have time to see the finished work, but Matt paid a photographer to photograph the gravestone when it was finished and mail Christine the picture.

Christine now held the photograph of her husband's tombstone with her little girl's name beautifully engraved on it. Carmen would never become a nameless cross on the Kansas prairie to be knocked down, stepped on and lost. Carmen's name was etched in stone for Christine's future grandchildren and following generations to see.

Christine sighed as a slightly sad smile lifted the corners of her lips. Two of the greatest desires of her past four years were now completed and the peace she felt within her heart was satisfying. She had moved on, but Richard and Carmen would always be a piece of her life. Christine put the picture inside of her bedside dresser drawer and closed it.

On top of her bedside dresser was a framed picture of Matt and her taken at the Spring Fling Dance. She loved Matt. The image of him alone could make her heart skip a beat and she had come to love and appreciate him all the more since he supported her in postponing their wedding to see her grandmother. For him to travel three thousand miles to spend that date with her showed how deeply committed his love for her was. Coming home, Matt understood why she wanted to visit Richard's grave while they were in Denver. He insisted on paying for Carmen's name to be engraved and it was his idea to have a photograph taken and sent to her. Again, it showed how much love he had for her. To be loved by the man only built the foundation of her love for him all the stronger.

Like a campfire surrounded by stones in the dark of night, their love could light up the darkness with a bright reflection and feel the warmth on the coldest night. However, too often, the roaring fire is neglected, and the flames slowly dwindle, perhaps not noticed as the fire still burns but day by day, the flame lowers as the charcoal pieces drop away, weakening the very pieces of oak that once blazed. The reflection in the shadows draws closer to the firepit and soon, only a flicker of flame and fading coals tell the story of a fire that once burned bright. By morning the coals are damp with the dew and the fire becomes a memory of what once was.

Christine refused to let their love fade away over time and lose the passion and excitement of falling in love. She didn't need to buy him anything or be the best cook. She only needed to do what she always had, be his friend. Listen to him with a kind heart, encourage him in his endeavors, offer wise advice and make him feel important because he was. The greatest way to douse the flames and lower the temperature of the fire is with criticism. Christine had committed not to criticize even if she was angry. Anger is an emotion that everyone experiences, but what is said or done in anger can leave lasting impressions that, like a handprint in cement, harden into solid walls that may never be broken down. Barriers like the stones around a fire are meant to protect the flame from escaping its confines; walls caused by hurt are like taking a stone away and opening a gateway to destruction.

Christine knew the temptation of married men to seek new ground; she saw it every night at the dance hall. Most of the married men that came into Bella's were not content at home. Whether the fire died, dwindling down or now a bed of burnt-out coals, the story was usually the same; the walls from harsh words sabotaged the foundation that once encircled a blazing fire.

It wasn't just women; the same could be said for men. A negative word begets a negative word and criticism on either part builds walls that separate one burning piece of oak from the other. When the space between expands with every charcoal piece that falls, both pieces of oak try to survive on their own and the flames that once burned bright fades. Firewood seldom burns well alone.

It would not happen on Christine's part. She was determined to keep the fire burning and enjoy her chosen man for the rest of her life.

They had made a new wedding date. It would be at the end of the summer on a Saturday afternoon on August 30th. They could have gotten married at the end of June or later in July, but June was too soon as invitations needed to be resent and Phillip Forrester's wedding was in July. Christine wanted to dance through the summer to save as much money as possible to help Matt purchase the hill where she wanted to build her home. Being raised on her grandfather's farm, Christine knew one thing: if a dream is worth having, then the work needed to make it happen needed to be done. Her dream to watch the sunrise and sunset with Matt on their wrap-around porch wouldn't come for free. She would do her part to help make that dream come true.

Chapter 4

Napoleon the Great walked down the middle of Main Street, watching people set up for the Independence Day celebration. The energetic atmosphere was contagious, and everyone seemed to be jovial as they nailed booths together and hung red, white and blue banners across Main Street from one building to another. Salesmen, tinkers, businessmen, food of various kinds, and raffles of items from a pie to a new wagon were advertised. The sound of musical instruments could be heard as the city quartet practiced for the parade in the morning. The city was alive with busyness to prepare for the grand festivities of the following day.

No one said a friendly word to Napoleon as he slowly walked along, gazing from side to side at the people like a lost child looking for a home. It was hard not to notice how the people caught a glimpse of him and then stared. Most either began to laugh or thought he was too strange and tried to avoid making eye contact.

One young lady outside a pottery shop glanced over and stared as he approached. She was a charming lady with long curly black hair and a young son clinging to her dress. Her husband, a man with a missing lower leg, was trying to climb a short ladder to nail an advertisement for their pottery shop seven feet up on a corner post. The ladder was braced against the post, and the man insisted that he climb the ladder because his wife was pregnant. Unfortunately, he was trying to carry a hammer in one hand with the sign under his arm and a crutch under his other arm, while trying to hop to the second step of the ladder. He was having difficulty maneuvering his one good leg up the ladder with his hands full.

"Excuse me," Napoleon said. "I'm looking for my wife. Have either of you seen her?"

Lucille Barton shook her head as she stared at him, not knowing what to think except the reddened cheeks and beads of sweat were easily explained by the uncomfortable leather he wore. The weight of the clothing had to be a tremendous burden on such a hot day. "I wouldn't know. Aren't you hot?" she asked compassionately.

"Yes, Ma'am. A couple of miners took my wife. I followed them from the middle earth and cannot find her. She is beautiful, like you. She should be wearing a dress made of the same material as my clothes. Have you seen her?"

Lucille put a protective arm around her son.

Lawrence Barton's brow rose curiously. "The

middle earth?"

"Yes, sir. I am from the kingdom of Ziarria. I am King Napoleon the Great. My wife, Queen Josephine, was taken."

"Oh." Lawrence Barton said awkwardly. "I suggest you talk to the marshal, Matt Bannister, about that. I hope you find her." He turned to try to maneuver up the ladder again. His balance kept pulling him back as he tried to navigate with one leg.

"Be careful," Lucille spoke to her husband with concern.

Napoleon offered, "Young man, let me nail that up there for you. Please."

Lucille's appreciation was quickly expressed. "Thank you. My husband lost his leg in the mine. He's getting around pretty well, but he's never tried climbing a ladder since then."

Lawrence backed away from the ladder and shook his head with frustration. "It's hard to climb a ladder with all the stuff I have to carry. If you would nail the sign up there, I'd be appreciative. My wife is pregnant, and I don't want her falling."

Napoleon smiled understandably. "Of course. Let me help." He climbed the ladder as the sound of the hot rawhide creaked as he moved. The leather clothing seemed to double the afternoon's heat. He nailed the sign quickly and stepped down. Sweat dripped down his face.

"Thank you so much," Lucille said. "Can I get you some water? You appear very warm."

"I'd like that. Thank you."

"Do you want to come inside the shop and get out of the sun? I'll get you some water and something to eat."

Napoleon had not eaten yet that day and was starving. "I'd like that. Yes."

They began to cross Main Street when Deputy Bob Ewing made a direct line towards Napoleon. He had noticed the leather-clad man standing above the crowd, nailing up a sign for the Barton's Pottery Shop. "Hey! You, circus freak. What did the sheriff tell you? You're under arrest, Leather Man. Do I need to shackle your wrists or are you coming peacefully?"

"What has he done, Bob?" Lawrence asked.

"That's none of your concern," Bob replied curtly. "Let's go, freak." He pushed Napoleon to get him walking.

Aggravated to be missing a free meal, Napoleon asked, "Why are you arresting me? I didn't do anything illegal."

"Because we don't want your kind here. Now get moving or I will shackle your hands and drag you to jail like a dead cow if I have to."

"But I have broken no laws."

"Vagrancy. We don't need crazies like you walking free in our town. You were told to leave, and you didn't. Go!" Bob shouted and pushed the man, forcing him to start walking towards the sheriff's office.

"Stay here with your father. I'll be right back," Lucille said to her young son and walked away quickly. She hurried to the marshal's office and entered. "Matt?" she spoke urgently. "Is Matt here?"

"Yes," Phillip Forrester replied. Truet Davis and Nate Robertson stopped what they were doing to pay attention. Matt came out of his private office at the sound of her urgent voice. "What's wrong, Lucille?" he asked.

"Matt, Bob is arresting a man for doing nothing wrong. He helped us hang a sign and now Bob's arresting him. The man asked what he did wrong, and Bob said he doesn't want him in town. The man is strange, but he shouldn't be arrested without a crime, should he?" Lucille asked.

Matt glanced out the window in time to see Bob shoving Napoleon forward on the street. Matt stepped outside, followed by his deputies and Lucille.

Bob glanced at Lucille irritably as they came out of the marshal's office. He had watched her hurry to Matt's office like a spoiled child running to her parents to get someone else in trouble. "Matt. Gentlemen," Bob greeted them.

"Why are you arresting him, Bob?" Matt asked.

"Vagrancy. The sheriff warned him this morning to leave town. He knew what would happen if he stuck around. I'm just doing my job."

Matt grinned with a shake of his head. "How many people will you arrest this weekend because they don't live in town? People are coming from all over the county to celebrate Independence Day. Are you going to arrest them all for vagrancy? If this man hasn't broken a specific law that you can name, you need to let him go. Half of the city will be vagrants this weekend if you want to be technical. Have you seen all the people setting up camps on the edge of town? If you arrest him, you better be arresting them all."

"The sheriff told him to leave town."

"Tim Wright does not make the laws and what he says, without a cause, does not matter. Has this gentleman broken a law that all those other campers aren't doing?" Matt asked, pointing at Napoleon.

"Vagrancy."

"Let him go. There is no law saying he can't come here to celebrate Independence Day. There are lots of folks doing the same thing. Napoleon is no different."

Bob gasped and asked loudly, "Have you spoken to this man? He's crazy! We don't need a crazy person staying in town! It's dangerous."

"Until he breaks the law, you have no reason to arrest him. Tell Tim to leave this man alone unless he has a good reason to arrest him. Napoleon has every right to walk around town without being harassed by the law."

"Fine, but if anything happens, it's your fault." He took his hand off Napoleon's arm. "Stay out of trouble or I'll be your worst nightmare, Leather Man. You freak," he added.

"Thank you," Napoleon said to Bob. "Have either of you seen my wife?" he asked, looking between Bob and Matt.

Bob laughed spitefully. "Have you heard about the middle earth, Matt? Talk to him and you'll understand why we want him locked up. The man is as looney as they come. He needs to be locked up before someone gets hurt. But that being said, he's your problem now." Bob wiped his hands together to simulate wiping the dust off them. He walked away frustrated.

"Thank you," Napoleon said to Matt. "Perhaps we could talk in private?"

"You already told me about your wife. We'll keep our eyes out for her. Enjoy your day," Matt turned to go back into his office.

Truet Davis couldn't help himself. "Napoleon, what's your last name?"

"Pickle," he answered simply. "Marshal, I need to talk to you privately," he called after Matt. "Please."

Matt turned around. "Follow me."

Napoleon spoke to Lucille. "Miss, thank you. I have to talk to the marshal. Can I stop by afterward and take you up on that meal?"

"Hi, Uncle Matt," Hannie Longo said with a light-hearted snicker as Matt reached for his office door. She was Matt's cousin Karen's daughter. Technically, she was a second cousin, but she started calling him her uncle after listening to her cousins calling him Uncle Matt. Hannie was fourteen years old and was with her best friend, Rose Fowler.

"Hi, Hannie. How are you?" Matt asked with a welcoming smile.

"Good." She and Rose both held a half-eaten large cookie in their hand. "Uncle Matt, we bought a cookie, but now we're thirsty. Do you have a couple of nickels we can have for some lemonade?"

"I do. So, tell me, are you two excited about the

circus tomorrow?" Matt asked as he reached into his coin purse.

"Yes! I can't wait. Are you going with Christine?"

"I am." He handed the two girls a nickel each.

"We should all go together. Uncle William says he's going too. Thank you, Uncle Matt," she said sincerely.

"Thank you," Rose said.

"You're welcome. Have fun, girls," Matt said as the two young ladies hurried to get a lemonade.

***

Napoleon entered Matt's private office, removed the large bag off his back and set it beside the chair in front of Matt's desk.

"Okay, Napoleon Pickle, what can I do for you?" Matt asked as he closed his private office door and took a seat behind his desk.

The dirty and sweat-covered face of Napoleon was reddened from the heat. He spoke frankly, "You can take me out to a place called Slater's Mile and search every house until we find my wife."

"No. I cannot do that."

"Can you keep a secret?" Napoleon asked. "Seriously, can you be trusted not to repeat what I'm about to tell you?"

Matt's brow lowered. "I can."

Napoleon removed his odd-looking hat and exposed a balding head with uneven hair on the sides. "Excuse me one moment, I need to get into my bag. It has a false bottom which is where I hide my stuff." He reached into his bag and pulled out his blanket and canvas tarp. A variety of pieces of scrap leather filled the bag. At the bottom, he pulled up a thin false bottom piece of wood and then revealed a leather-bound book with a leather strap to keep it closed. He set the bag down and held up a book for Matt to see.

"What's that?"

"My journal. Marshal Bannister, my real name is Avery Gaines. I am a reporter for the Monmouth Pointe Chronicle newspaper in New York. I'm not from the middle earth nor normally dress like this."

"Why are you? You don't plan to write about me, I hope." Reporters irritated him.

"If I may explain. Robert Fairchild owns the chronicle. He moved from New York to just north of here to a town called Hollister."

"The sheep man," Matt said knowingly.

"Yes. Have you met Robert?"

"No. I've just heard of him."

"He's a great man. I was in San Francisco doing an undercover investigation about the shady side of the city. I lived and worked on the docks and got a firsthand view of the filth there. I wrote my article series and thought I was going to Seattle next when Robert asked me to come here as a vagabond to write about Oregon's natural beauty and how the people of his new home territory treated me. That explains why I am here, but it does not explain why I dress like this and sound crazy."

"No, it sure doesn't."

"Bear with me. Back East, there is a man who

regularly walks a three-hundred-sixty-five-mile loop through Connecticut and New York. His path never changes, and you can count on him arriving in town every thirty days. It takes him thirty days to walk three-hundred-sixty-five miles and he is precisely on time. It is a routine that has gone on for years and still happening today. The newspapers over there have written about him since 1870. He is called the Leather Man. He is a vagabond who never asks for money and is fed along the way by the people who know he's coming. He is not violent nor speaks English. Apparently, he speaks French. No one really knows who he is or what his story is, but there are some rumors; whether they are true or not, I don't know. What I do know is he is consistent and wears a homemade suit of leather like this.

"I decided since no one in the west has probably heard of him that I would have a suit of rawhide fashioned after his as close as I could. Instead of speaking French, I decided to make up a stupid story borrowed heavily from Jules Verne's book. It was all done to record the people's reactions and how I was treated. Call it an experiment."

Matt narrowed his eyes curiously. "You were in Willow Falls over a month ago and you're just getting here?"

Avery nodded. "I visited the towns of Natoma and Willow Falls, yes. Then I went back to Portland and did a few interviews with a couple of socialites there. I make my living by writing, Marshal, and quite frankly, I hate wearing this suit. It is hot, uncomfortable and heavy. It was a bad idea," he laughed. "But the story will be worth it. I wanted to come here on Independence Day, mingle with the crowd, and record their reactions. It's deceptive but very honest as well."

"So…why are you telling me this?"

Avery chuckled. "Because the sheriff really doesn't like me! I wanted you to know the truth because you are one of the few people that have been courteous and fair. You seem like a good man, and it is my honor to meet you. I'd love to interview you for my paper. The people back east will love it."

Matt shook his head disagreeably. "I don't do interviews. I don't like being written about and, generally speaking, I don't like writers."

"I understand. I just want you to know who I am in case I'm thrown in jail and shipped off to the Salem sanitarium without being able to prove who I am." He chuckled. "I always like for at least one person to know who I am. But if you could keep that between you and me until after July Fourth, I would appreciate it. It is way too hot to be wearing this costume for long. After tomorrow, I'll be in my regular clothes and leaving town," he explained.

"I suppose I don't have to worry about you confronting miners and getting hurt then?"

"No, sir. I am playing a role and I'll admit, sometimes I might carry it too far. However, I think the temporary discomfort will be worth the story. I plan on writing a book about my western exploits when I do go back home for the winter. This necklace," he held an obsidian arrowhead necklace with delicate beadwork out from his chest for Matt to see clearly, "it was given to me by Red Shirt, an Ogalala Sioux Chief that I interviewed. He is a good man and we got along so well that Red Shirt gave it to me himself. I told you about San Francisco, but I've traveled all over collecting interesting interviews to send back home and you would be a great interview to add to my collection."

"No," Matt said plainly.

"You will be mentioned in my story about my adventure here."

"I don't care about that as long as you are truthful. Just don't write I killed six infamous gunmen simultaneously for spitting on a woman or some horse crap like the dime novels do."

Avery Gaines stood. "I promise I won't do that. Hey, it's been nice talking to you and we'll do it again before I leave town. But right now, I have to get out of this suit. So, where is the safest place for me to disrobe to the nude and jump into the river? As you might imagine, I don't wear anything underneath. It's way too hot and heavy for that."

Chapter 5

Debra Slater stepped into the marshal's office and waited for Matt to come out of a meeting in his private office. She looked pretty in a light-blue, long-sleeve dress with white laced ruffles along the arms and on the skirt. The breast had a circled crest of a pink floral design. Her blonde hair was braided upwards into a bun with a light blue hat with white lace trimming set on her head that matched her dress. It was a new dress to wear in public as it was a special day. However, the new dress she bought for the annual Independence Day Ball that her father hosted was much more elegant. She knew right away that she must have looked stunning because all three of the deputies had not taken their eyes off her yet.

"Miss Slater, would you like some coffee?" Nate asked nervously. He shouldn't have been nervous; he had known Debra since they were in school together. She was a few years older than he, but she was the one crush or, perhaps better stated, an infatuation that always made him a bumbling fool when he saw her.

"No, thank you, Nate. It is far too hot for coffee. What you should have available to offer people is sun tea or lemonade or something more refreshing in the hot weather."

Truet Davis grinned with a quiet laugh. The woodstove had not been lit for hours and what little coffee there was in the pot was from early that morning.

"That's an excellent idea. We'll have to start making that," Nate replied. "Your family is hosting your annual ball tonight, right?" The ball was by invitation only and he had always hoped to be invited, but his parents were not in the same social circle as the Slater family.

"Yes, we are."

"I'll be at the dance in the park if you want to..." he trailed off as the thought occurred to him that she would not be interested in leaving the ball to dance with him in the city park.

Debra smiled kindly. "I hope you have fun. I know we in the city council certainly tried to make it a fun and entertaining night for the community. There should be some good food too."

Truet offered, "I think Nate was trying to ask you for a dance."

Debra looked at Nate, uninterested. "I appreciate the offer, but I will be at my father's ball tonight." She turned to Truet with a giggle. "I think it's cute

45

when he blushes."

Nate had turned red.

The private office door opened, and Matt spoke as he held the door open for Napoleon Pickle to exit, "I'll keep my eyes open for your wife. Just promise you won't bring your military into our world, agreed?" Matt asked to keep up the ruse.

"You better find her, or I will bring my soldiers here, and we'll search every house in the area until I find her. If you find her, I'll give you a medallion of the King's court."

"That's encouraging. Have a good day, sir." Matt rolled his eyes at Truet as Napoleon walked to the partition gate to leave the office.

Truet rubbed his mouth to cover his growing grin.

Debra, standing on the other side of the partition, stepped back against the rail as far as possible while the strange man walked past her. He opened the door and paused to look back at Debra as if studying her. "Josephine?" he asked. "Is that you?"

Debra was startled. "What?"

Matt spoke, "That's not your wife, Napoleon. She lives here. Her name is Debra."

"You're not lying to keep her for yourself, are you?" Napoleon asked.

"No, sir. Have a good day."

"She looks just like Josephine." He stepped outside into the heat and let the door close.

"Who is that?" Debra asked, turning around to face Matt.

Truet answered, "The king of...where?" he asked Nate.

"Ziarria or something. I don't know. Somewhere in the center of the earth."

Matt waved his hand through the air. "He's just a confused man. How are you today, Debra?"

"I'm well. I wanted to come here and give this to you. It is an invitation to our ball this evening. You can bring Christine, or you can come alone. The invitation does say you can bring an adult guest. It will be on the third floor of our home in the ballroom and offers a great view of the city and the stars. I think there is a full moon tonight." She handed over a piece of paper, for him to take.

"Oh." Matt took the invitation and read it. "I doubt I'll be there. Christine is working tonight."

"That's unfortunate. I would have liked to get to know her. You can still come, though. There will be many people to mingle with and you could dance with me for free." She giggled. "Anyway, I hope you will come and have some food, at least. It's an enjoyable time."

"I won't promise," Matt replied hesitantly.

"I think you'll come. I'll see you then. Bye, boys," she said to the others with a wave over her back shoulder as she left the office.

"You were invited to the Slater's Ball but not us?" Truet asked. "Nate has had a crush on that girl since he was, how old, Nate?"

Nate was downcast. "Since the first time I saw her. And you had to mention I wanted her to dance!"

Truet laughed. "Yeah, I did." He waved a hand towards Nate and explained to Matt, "He looked like an infected pimple; his face turned so red."

"Jeez," Nate scoffed with a shake of his head. "I'd do just about anything for her to invite me."

"Would you?" Matt asked. "I have an invitation. It doesn't have my name on it, but if you want to work this coming weekend for Truet, I'll give it to you because I know he has plans to leave town. It will get you in the door; the rest is up to you."

Nate took a deep breath. "I don't have a date."

Truet threw a pencil at him. "That would ruin the point of going, wouldn't it? Go there and talk to Debra. You have one chance to make an impression outside of school, here or on the street. Wear something nice and go to the ball. What do you have to lose? Be bold and tell her you would like to dance. Tell her how pretty she is."

Nate stared at him and slowly smiled. "You just don't want to work the weekend."

"No, I don't."

"Do you want to go with me, Tru?"

"No, I don't. I want to go to Willow Falls and see my lady."

"Phillip, do you want to go?" Nate asked.

Phillip raised his brow. "I would like to see inside their mansion sometime, but I can't. I'm having dinner with Heather's family and then going to the dance in the park."

"Who am I going to take? I would feel awkward going alone."

Truet added, "Nate, you don't need a date. I'm sure there will be a few single ladies there. You're a handsome young man. Go meet someone. And if anyone looks down upon you for not being wealthy, just remind them that an honest man with integrity and the Lord on his side is worth more than anything the Slaters own."

Chapter 6

Napoleon walked over to Barton's Pottery Shop and was given a tall mug of sun tea and a cold meatloaf sandwich with sliced pickles on the side. He sat outside under the awning on a chair and ate hungrily while at the same time watching the people around him and taking note of the odd looks, stares and comments. Although he could not write in his journal at the moment, he would try to recall all his mental notes onto the pages later that night under candlelight.

"Napoleon, it is far too hot to be wearing so much leather. Would you like some cooler clothing? If my husband's clothes are too small, I'm sure I could get some larger clothes from someone at church. I'm even willing to buy you some cooler clothes if need be." Lucille Barton had been the kindest person to him so far. Her sincerity was visible in her facial expression.

Napoleon declined with a shake of his head.

"The middle earth is this warm every day because we are closer to the lava lakes. Sometimes they spit like a camel, so we must wear thick rawhide. I am most used to it. Thank you, though." One particular thing Avery Gaines enjoyed about undercover investigations was being able to make up an identity, history and life of a fictional character. The role he currently played had been found humorous by the marshal's deputies, but it humored Avery most of all. He dared not smile or laugh as it might ruin his charade, but he would thank Lucille and Lawrence for their kindness and reveal his true identity to them before he left town. He also made a mental note to send them a copy of his finished article where he would praise them and, surprisingly, the famous U.S. Marshal, Matt Bannister as well.

"Are you sure? You look hot," Lucille prodded.

"I know where I am from."

"Of course, you do. I was trying to help."

"Thank you, but I must be going to find my queen. You have a very nice shop. You obviously use good clay. Did you know the finest clay on the earth is found in Ziarria, in my kingdom?"

"Um, no. I didn't know that."

"It is. When I return, I will have a barrel sent to you. You can drop a note down a deep volcanic tunnel that I will show you if you want more."

"Okay."

Napoleon could barely stand the heat as the leather warmed in the sun and trapped the heat within his clothing. His skin was chaffed in his crotch from the heat, sweat, and skin rubbing against the leather. His underarms were chaffed as well, but the burning itch of his upper legs and crotch brought an urgency to get out of his leather clothes. The rawhide suit weighed forty-six pounds altogether and in the heat of the afternoon, it was a miserable thing to wear. It was becoming a burden and he could not wait to strip the suit off and jump into the river. Heat exhaustion was a real threat, and he knew his body was running out of sweat. He walked quickly, staying in character to move his arm and leg together in unison to create a more strange-looking fellow. He cursed the very idea of the garments that had come to him and the walk he practiced for a week to perfect. The sun was boiling his body inside of the prison of rawhide. His reddened cheeks and sweaty hair were clear indications of being too hot, but until he could find a private place along the river to jump in and cool his body, he labored to walk left arm and foot forward, right arm and foot forward. It was his character's walk, and he had to see it through to the end.

He left Main Street and walked five blocks to Rose Street. Matt had told him the most private section of the river was west of the newly made Flower Lane built as part of Chinatown. The Modoc River descended rapidly at Premro Island but then snaked around and flowed to the west side of Branson in the unsettled cottonwoods, willows and other leaf-bearing trees and brush that lined it. Matt suggested he might be able to swim in the nude there and not be seen except maybe by some Chinese if he stayed on the main trail down to the waterline. It was not a long walk, but it was becoming too laborious for an unnatural gait. He could not wait to strip out of the leather and feel the cool water on his clammy skin. He was getting rashes where the unfinished rawhide rubbed against his moist skin creating raw spots that were becoming painful. He could not wait for Independence Day to end so he could take the leather suit off for the last time and never put it on again.

On Rose Street, two teenage boys about fifteen or sixteen approached him with large, humored grins. "What did you do, disassemble a saddle?" The teenage boy with black hair chided as he stepped in front of Napoleon to stop him. The other teen with blond hair laughed.

"Excuse me, I must go," Napoleon said. He was too hot and anxious to get the suit off to visit or fool around with the two boys.

"Now, hold on," the black-haired boy said. "Are you dressed as a saddle because you want to be ridden? You must be part of the circus. Are you a clown? You look like a clown." The facial features of the black-haired boy suddenly turned threatening.

The blond-haired boy reached over and clasped his fingers on the arrowhead necklace to look at it closely. "Nick, look at this. Is it real?"

"Yes. Excuse me, fellas. I am in a hurry." He had no ambition to play his role as the sun beat down on him.

"Here," Nick Griffin said, straining to pull the cork from the cheap rot gut whiskey bottle they had

53

bought from Ebenezer's saloon. It was the only saloon that his father did not go to because Ebenezer's didn't have any women working there as dancers or entertainers, just alcohol and gambling tables. The cork pulled loose with a hollow sound. Nick took a quick drink. He scowled as he lowered the clear glass bottle filled with brownish-gold liquid. "Wow! That burns. Do you want a drink?" He held it out for Napoleon.

"No. And you shouldn't either. You're too young to begin a life of drinking. Good day." He stepped forward towards an alley between two buildings to leave town and find a place to set his camp.

"Ollie, try this." Ollie took a small drink and shuttered.

"Hey, Leather Man, can you moo for me?" Nick asked. "If you're going to wear a cow's hide, you might as well moo like one. Come on, give me a mooo," he imitated a cow.

"No," Napoleon said without looking back. He stepped into the narrow alley between two buildings. The ten degrees or so difference of being in the shade felt like a brief moment of heaven.

Nick handed the bottle to Ollie, ran forward, and jumped on Napoleon's back. He locked his arms around the stranger's neck and kicked Napoleon's hips with his heels repeatedly while shouting, "Run sow! Run!"

Napoleon fell forward to the ground. "Get off me!" he shouted angrily.

Nick laughed as the man's ridiculous hat rolled off his bald head. "No wonder you wear that dumb hat. You're bald." He stayed on the man's back, pinning him to the ground while patting the bald man's head like a drum.

"Get off me!" Napoleon shouted forcefully. He swung his arm backward to swat the boy.

Nick was humored but had a better idea. "You do look really hot. Let me help cool you off." Nick stood and unbuttoned his pants to urinate on him.

With effort, Napoleon stood up with the extra forty-six pounds of rawhide on him and turned to face the teen. "Get away from me, you little maggot. I'll bust your teeth out!"

Nick laughed as the vagabond picked up his hat and walked away. Nick urinated and buttoned his pants. He turned to join his friend on the street. "Remember when we met Tad Sperry and found that Indian in the alley? I thought I'd pee on this bum like we did that Indian. But this time, the marshal wouldn't catch us."

"Yeah, I remember. The marshal made Tad yell out that he was a girl."

"Yeah," Nick laughed. "Dang, I wish Tad lived in town. He was fun."

Avery Gaines was beginning to hate playing the role of Napoleon the Great. He continued his path across Chinatown and into the trees and brush near the river. He followed a well-used path used by the Chinese down to the refreshing coolness of the water. He walked upstream until he came to a nice, shaded patch of tall grass surrounded by thick brush and trees. He set his bag down and quickly stripped the uncomfortable suit of clothes off. Nude as the day he was born, Avery waded into the cool water. The sweat of the past few days that had dried to his skin was washed away and he closed his eyes as the cold mountain water refreshed his heated body and soothed the burning chaffing of his skin. Avery returned to the shade, sat on his blanket without dressing, and pulled out his journal. He already had a lot to write about and the night's celebration had not even begun. He wrote in his journal while enjoying the privacy of his newfound camp.

Chapter 7

Matt walked into Bella's Dance Hall and wiped his brow. The building was hot even though the main door was propped open. He had noticed all the upstairs windows were opened as well. He did not envy the ladies that would be dancing in their heavy dresses to the band hour after hour in the heat. The men could remove their jackets and vests or unbutton their shirts, but the ladies did not have that luxury. It was not a surprise to see water pitchers on every table and Christine by the bar drinking a tall glass of water.

"Do you want me to grab an axe and chop a hole in the roof to let some of the heat out of here?" he asked as he entered the ballroom.

Christine nodded. She wore a light-yellow dress with white trim at the wrists, shoulder and neckline. It didn't have any ruffles or extra material to add the elegance that most of her dresses had. It was a relatively simple front buttoning dress with a square cut around the collar that exposed her shoulders and neckline. Her long dark hair was swirled around into a tight bun and despite the simplicity of her attire, she looked amazing.

"The heat wouldn't be so bad if there were a breeze, but this stagnant air is humid and horrible," she said.

"Even sweating, you look dashing as ever," he said and gave her a quick kiss. The dance hall was not open for another forty minutes and most of the ladies were upstairs preparing themselves for the night of dancing.

Christine scowled miserably from the heat. "It's an old dress. But it's lighter than all my others. I'm afraid I'm going to be sweating all night. I bathed earlier today, but I think I'll bathe again when we close. Some of the girls wanted to go down to the river tonight to swim, but Bella won't allow any of us to leave. She's afraid of all the men in town."

"I don't blame her. It will get rowdy out there for the next couple of nights."

"You be careful this weekend," Christine said with concern. Independence Day was always a big celebration, but being on a Friday brought everyone to town and the celebration would last all weekend. Rose Street late at night was exceptionally rowdy on Independence Day as the celebrating mixed with alcohol and tempers. Matt and his deputies were not responsible for keeping the peace within city limits, but he intervened whenever necessary as a lawman.

"I will. I was invited to the Annual Slater's Ball

again. Debra brought me an invitation herself. So, I suppose while you're working, I'll be dancing in the mansion's ballroom."

Christine snorted with laughter. "You do that." She knew he had no intention of going. "I might have to walk down to that Debra's office and tell her to leave you alone. Sherry here, too. I understand she was waiting for you to come here every night while I was gone," she said with a flirtatious nod. "You're a wanted man."

"Well, Debra and Sherry can both want to their heart's desire, but it won't do them any good."

"What are you going to be doing tonight? Are you coming here at closing time? We can go up on the roof and watch the stars. It will be a lot cooler up there."

Matt's eyes lifted with interest. "That sounds wonderful to me. I gave my invitation to Nate for agreeing to work this weekend. Phillip wanted the weekend off. Truet is going to Willow Falls for the weekend, and I will be wandering around looking for troublemakers to help Tim's deputies keep things from getting too far out of hand. I'm sure Tim will be at the Slater's ball."

"It's not even Independence Day yet."

"Nope. But no one works tomorrow, so even though it is a Thursday night, it will be equal to a Friday night, just a bit rowdier with a lot more people."

Christine tapped a finger on his chest. "Tomorrow night, you have to be with me at the community dance. You know how much I love community dances," she emphasized her excitement. "Helen and Sam want to go to the circus with us. They've never been to one either. I hope you don't mind if Helen and Sam spend the day with us?"

"That's fine. How are they doing?"

"They are doing well. They are so happy. Helen is pregnant. So, they are very excited to be expecting their first baby."

"I'll have to congratulate them. Speaking of the circus, I did see the circus setting up a big tent just west of town."

"By Chinatown?" Christine asked with a distasteful frown. Her experience with the former Chinese leader Wu-Pen Tseng had spoiled her view of Chinatown as it had many people.

"No. Across the road not far from the livery stable in that open field. Anyway, I went over and introduced myself and met Horace Chatfield and Ivan Bowry, the two owners. I saw a few elephants. I didn't get to see much, but it looks fun."

"You saw an elephant? I have never seen one before. Matt, I really am looking forward to going."

"Three elephants," Matt said, holding up his fingers. "We'll go tomorrow. Mister Chatfield told me that since they are only here for one day, they are doing four circus shows. The first show starts at 10:00 a.m."

Christine wrinkled her nose. "We might have to cut our stargazing time short and get some sleep if you want to go that early."

"With four showtimes, we'll have plenty of shows to choose from. I don't care what time we go. I just look forward to spending the day with you." He put his arms around her and gave her a small kiss.

"And I with you."

Rose Blanchard, a stunning red-headed dancer, came downstairs from her room in a bright red dress and shouted as she approached them, "No! No! No! Bella said there was to be no affection between us ladies and our beaus. That means you two as well. So, break it up." The wry smile on her face indicated a great deal of sarcasm. "Bella," she shouted, "Christine and Matt are kissing again!" She sounded like a child gleefully tattling on a sibling.

Sherry Stewart, the blonde-haired best friend of Rose, shouted toward Bella's apartment intentionally, "That is inappropriate behavior for a lady! Just ask Bella." Sherry's dislike for the rule was well known. She didn't have a particular man to call her own, but she was very flirtatious with every man she found handsome and a kiss for an extra dollar had made her a crowd favorite until Bella tightened the reins.

Christine ignored them with a kind smile. "Kiss me." Her lips pressed against his in an affectionate embrace.

"Oh, horseradish!" Sherry exclaimed, "I get in trouble for that."

Rose went behind the bar to check the liquor bottles and replenish any less than full for the bartender to get through the night. She responded to her friend, "You'll kiss any man, though. Christine sticks to her one and only. Matt, that reminds me, when are you going to bring your deputy Nate in here so I can meet him before Sherry kisses on him?"

Matt's lips broke from Christine's slowly; he stared into her eyes as they separated. He slowly turned his head towards Rose. "Not tonight. Nate's going to the Slater's ball."

"With who?" Rose asked pointedly.

"Not you," Sherry spouted with a laugh.

"No one. He doesn't have a date," Matt answered.

"I want to go to a ball," Rose lamented. "Tell him I want to go."

"We have to work," Christine reminded her.

Rose blurted out to Bella as she came out of her apartment, adjusting the ruffles of her dress. "Nate doesn't have a date to the ball, Bella."

"What are you talking about?" Bella asked gruffly. She couldn't get one of the ruffles in her dress to set right.

"Matt, tell Bella what you told me," Rose said.

"All I said was Nate is going to the annual Slater's Ball and doesn't have a date."

Bella looked at Matt curiously. "Really? Well, tell him he has a lady to take. Tell him to dress nice and come by here. Angela will be ready to go."

"What?" Rose whined. "I wanted to go."

Sherry laughed.

"Rose, you're needed here, Sweetheart," Bella said compassionately. "Matt, I will speak with Angela, but she will be ready."

"I'll let him know right away."

Chapter 8

Protected from the sun by the foliage of the trees and thick brush around him, Avery Gaines sat cross-legged in the shade in the small alcove along the river. He had spread the canvas tarpaulin over the tall grass and laid down to relax while his nude body dried with the day's heat. The bag that he carried on his back as he played the role of Napoleon had a six-inch-wide thin piece of wood at the bottom that hid his journal and writing implements. The thin board was also used to lay across his crossed knees to rest his journal on as he wrote the day's events. One note he had written almost immediately was the leather suit was not made with hot weather in mind. It had felt like he was being baked from the inside out and the refreshing water of the river was his only saving grace.

Rehydrated and feeling better, he decided to wait a few hours for the temperature to cool down before he dressed in the hellish forty-six-pound leather suit and joined in with the townspeople again. It was simply too hot to stay in the Napoleon character, whether the article he planned on writing depended on it or not. He had two more nights to go and then he could enter the stage stop, collect his other bag, change into regular clothes, check into the monarch Hotel, and write his article in comfort. As for now, the solitude of the river was a blessing that he didn't want to leave.

A pesky fly buzzed around his head, but a sudden wave of his hand finally shooed it away. Avery was focused on what he was writing in his journal and had no patience for a fly. Careful notetaking was essential, especially later on when the small details might be overlooked. His article would be interesting enough, but his notes were critical for a book he planned to write over the winter about his adventures. Every assignment he committed to had its individual leather-bound journal devoted strictly to that investigation. His current assignment was not an investigation that would take weeks of undercover deception but a short three-day experiment that was supposed to be more fun and entertaining than not. It turned into the worst experience he had taken part in yet, and it was his own fault. The idea of remaking the leather suit after the peculiar man in the eastern states and pretending to be a form of him in rural Oregon was imaginative, but the July weather was much too hot for him to wear it. How the Leather Man back in New York could wear his all year round without complaint or removing the heavy clothing, Avery had no idea. The truth was the actual Leather Man's leather suit weighed even more than Avery's.

"David, wait up," Avery heard a female's voice call as the sound of someone quickly approaching along the riverbank startled him. Alarmed by the thought of a child seeing him nude, he reached for the edge of the canvas to pull over him, but it was out of arm's reach. With nothing else quickly available, he pulled the board closer to his stomach to cover himself as best he could. He was just about to warn the people that he was there when a man burst through the brush and lower limbs of a birch tree into the clearing. Avery's mouth dropped open, stunned. He could not believe what he was seeing with his own eyes. The man was unlike any other man Avery had ever seen.

The man was slight in build and of average height, dressed in brown pants and a loosely buttoned tan shirt. What made the man different was his face was covered with six-inch-long brown hair. The hair covered his face in places it usually never grew, such as the forehead, tip of his nose and even his eyelids. The man's face was completely covered with long brown hair except for the eyes, nostrils and mouth giving him the appearance of a monster, such as a werewolf. The man's wrists and hands were also covered with extraordinarily long hair. The only bare skin exposed was on the palm of his hands. The man was clearly part of the circus sideshow. Avery had heard of such sideshow attractions, but he had never seen one. It was a bizarre affliction that left Avery stunned.

The man's eyes widened in alarm to see Avery sitting in the grass naked and immediately stepped back into the water, frightened. His terrified eyes stared at Avery in horror. He shouted, "Nancy! Nancy!"

Avery tried to calm the man's fearful shouting by raising his palms. "Hello," he said awkwardly.

"Nancy!" The man repeated with a nervous glance down the river.

"Oh, for Pete's sake, David, what is it?" A female voice asked from the other side of the bushes. She glided through the leaves into the small alcove and looked where David was pointing.

"Oh!" She gasped. The woman was in her mid-twenties, with long brown hair that fell straight onto her shoulders. She had an attractive triangular face with a narrow nose and plump lips. Her round blue eyes appeared just a bit too big for her facial features, but she was quite an attractive lady. There was nothing strange or different about her appearance. "Excuse us, Sir. We don't mean to interrupt you with...whatever you are doing. David, let's go back to the other spot."

"Wait," Avery said. "You must be with the circus?" His interest was most sincere.

The young lady kept her back to the nude man. "Yes, we are. Come along, David."

"Miss, please, what is your name?" Avery asked.

"My name is Nancy Chatfield. My father and uncle own the circus. Now, if you don't mind, I brought a few of our teenagers from the sideshow to the river to swim. One of the things that people don't think about is despite their appearances and deformities, they are still teenagers and like to swim and have fun. However, they are different, and we hoped we wouldn't run into anyone so they could play in the water without being harassed. We'll go back down the river. I just ask you not to let anyone know we are down here, please. Come along, David."

"Wait," Avery called. "I'll keep my silence if you keep yours. Do you see that pile of rawhide clothing? Those are the only clothes I have. My name is Avery Gaines. I'm a reporter from a New York newspaper. I'm pretending to be an insane vagabond looking for my wife and seeing how people treat me for an article I want to write. It's an experiment. Please, don't leave. I'm very interested in meeting you and the gentleman I frightened. I'd like to talk and write an article about the sideshow."

Nancy's back remained turned to him. "Can you cover yourself in something? I hear the girls coming and they will want to see who I am talking to, so please cover yourself or get dressed so I can look at who I am speaking to. I prefer the girls not seeing you like that as well."

"Of course." Avery leaned over, stretched his arm to grab his bag, and pulled his wool blanket around him. "I was writing in my journal. Forgive me for my appearance, but that outfit weighs forty-six pounds and is hotter than hell. Forgive my language. I'm covered now."

Nancy turned to look at Avery skeptically, now that a blanket had covered him. He looked ridiculous with a balding head and lopsided haircut. She asked suspiciously, "You're a New York reporter here? It seems a mighty long way to come just to wear a leather suit for an article."

Avery chuckled, "I suppose it is. I'm playing a role for a story. You can read my journal if you don't believe me." He shrugged with a friendly smile. "If I could, I'd love to visit with you and your friend," he motioned toward David.

Nancy looked at the hair-covered young man. "David, this is Mister Avery Gaines from New York. He says he is a writer for a newspaper. Maybe if you talk to Mister Gaines, he will write a story about you."

David smiled. It was strange to see white teeth appear on a face of hair. "Hello," he said.

Nancy explained, "David is our Tasmanian Wolf Boy. He acts wild in the cage, but he's perfectly tame."

"How old are you, David?" Avery asked.

"Fifteen."

"Fifteen!" Avery's friendly smile faded with an empathetic sorrow. He had assumed it was a grown man with such an awful affliction. His head moved from side to side unconsciously. "Are your parents part of the circus?"

Nancy answered softly, "David's parents sold him outright to my father when he was three years old for the sideshow. He has been a part of our family since. And here come two of our young ladies. This is Alicia; she's actually twenty-seven, the same age as me, but she acts like a teenager. Don't you,

Alicia?"

Alicia stood about four feet eight inches tall and thin. She wore a cotton dress just below her knees and buckle shoes. She had a bald head except for a patch of hair on top in a tight upright ponytail. Her forehead was sloped backward at a sharp angle, making her head smaller than usual. Commonly such birth defects were referred to as pinheads in the sideshows.

Alicia grinned with childlike innocence in her smile and waved her fingers at Avery. She wrapped her arms around Nancy affectionately.

"I know," Nancy chuckled as she hugged her. "You like him, don't you? David, take Alicia into the water, but not too deep. You know she doesn't like that."

"Nice to meet you, Alicia," Avery said as David took her by the hand into the water like any older brother watching out for a younger sibling.

"And here comes our star attraction, Susie," Nancy said. "Come on out here."

"I got a thorn in my hand," another female voice said from behind the brush.

"Did you get it out?"

"Yeah. But it hurts."

"Come meet Mister Gaines. He's a New York reporter who might be interested in writing a story about our sideshow."

A teenage girl crawled forward under the branches and bushes on her hands and feet. She had been born with both of her knees bending in the opposite direction of the normal human knee, which meant her entire torso and upper body could bend forward at her knees and crawl on her hands and feet instead of her knees with her back perfectly horizontal. Her feet were also backward and pointed behind her as well. It was a bizarre sight to behold as her kneecaps jutted out behind her while on her hands and feet, giving her the appearance of a hunched spider about to spring forward. Aside from the unfortunate birth defects of her knees and feet, Susie was an attractive young lady with long light-brown curly hair, an oblong face with soft blue eyes and a friendly smile on her thin lips.

Avery stood carefully, not to expose himself to the ladies with the blanket that was wrapped around him. He bent over to speak with Susie. "I'm pleased to meet you," he said as he shook her leather-gloved hand. Avery talked to Nancy, "I would love to sit down and interview all of you for an article. Is that a possibility?"

"I'll ask my father. He is the boss."

"Is it your job to watch over these people?"

"No. *These people*," she emphasized, "are my family."

"Of course. I meant no offense. Susie, how old are you?"

Susie remained on her hands and heels. "I am seventeen." Despite her reversed appendages and being forced to crawl like an animal to walk, her voice revealed no self-pity.

"Were you raised in the circus, like David?"

"No, sir. I joined when I was fourteen."

"Did your parents sell you to the circus?" Avery

asked. He found it hard to believe a parent would sell their child to a circus. The idea of it was incomprehensible.

"No. My parents didn't want me to become a freak show act. I joined on my own accord, and I had to argue with my parents to get their permission to do so."

"Really?" Avery was perplexed. He carefully sat down with interest. "Why did you want to do that?"

Susie gave a light scoff with a shake of her head. "Nancy, help me to stand." Nancy held her hand as Susie slowly stood on her feet. From the knees up, her body leaned forward at an awkward angle in a standing position, but her reversed knees angled her lower legs forward as well, instead of being vertical like normal knees would. The way she stood reminded Avery of a deer standing on its hind legs to reach an apple from a tree. Susie's reversed feet made it harder for her to remain balanced in the standing position.

Susie raised her eyebrows questionably. "Look at me. Does it look like I can go to school with normal children? Aren't children mean and cruel to normal kids for reasons much less drastic than mine? What about church or just going to town? I got tired of being stared at and figured if I'm going to be stared at, I might as well earn some money and travel the country doing it. There are some things I cannot do, but I'm smart enough to know there is a lot I still can do and that's what I focus on. This sideshow business is a means to an end."

"That is admirable," Avery answered honestly.

"I'm impressed."

"Are you? Well, the truth is, I cannot help how I was born, nor can Alicia or David or any of the others in our sideshow. Our bodies are our burden to bear, but instead of hiding in the closet at home when company comes over like some shameful secret and forever being dependent upon someone else to care for us, we have the opportunity to earn money for ourselves. Do I love being called the Human Camel Spider? No. I'd rather just be called my name, Susie Durden. But this body is what I was born with, and I can make a good living with it. My family is very poor, and I have younger siblings. The circus pays very well, so I can help my family financially and still put money in the bank for me to retire on. I love the people I work with, and we are treated like family. I love the animals, and honestly, where else can I travel and see the world and get paid for it?"

"You're not mistreated then?"

"No," Susie said with surprise. "I have been asked that question before, so it must happen, but not with this circus."

Nancy added, "My father and uncle know one thing: the happiness of the performers is crucial to the show's success. No one is mistreated or taken advantage of. I hope you'll come to see one of our shows tomorrow."

"I will try. I will talk to Mister Chatfield and try to spend some time with you all. That would be a better article than what I'm doing now."

David left Alicia in knee-deep water and stepped

back towards Avery with interest. "Sir, if it is okay with Nancy, can I come back and talk with you tonight sometime? Usually, I read, but can I come back here and talk to you and perhaps swim some in the moonlight? I ask because tomorrow I won't have time to talk and if you want to do an article or book, you know it would be nice to talk for a while. Besides, as you can see, I can't just go walking around town. I try to stay out of sight; otherwise, people...they can be mean."

Nancy was doubtful. "David, I don't think that's a good idea. I don't think it's worth the risk." She explained to Avery, "We don't keep these kids in a prison, and they are free to roam, but at the same time, we have to protect them. People can be terrible, and David is such a good-hearted soul that it scares me if he is caught by some bad characters and made a fool of or hurt for being different. You'll understand."

"Of course," Avery said. Two teenagers had just harassed him for wearing strange clothing. It was easy to imagine what harm could be done if the two teens that attacked him had gotten a hold of David.

David was adamant. "I wouldn't go through town. I would cut across the meadow and into the trees after dark. No one is going to see me. There should be enough moonlight to find my way here and back to my bunk. I wouldn't be that long, an hour or two. If it's okay with Mister Gaines, I would like to have an article written about me." His brown eyes begged for Nancy's permission.

Avery volunteered, "No one else knows I'm here

and I can walk him back to the circus afterward. I'd like the chance to talk in detail with him about his experiences and how he feels about the circus and how people treat him. The way I see it, just from our short moment here, I would write a human-interest story about David and focus on his personality and being a normal fifteen-year-old boy despite the obvious features that set him apart. I would like that opportunity."

Nancy took a deep breath while considering it. "Okay. What time, Mister Gaines?"

"Yes!" David exclaimed quietly.

Avery grinned at the boy. "Well, I understand there is a community dance in the city park that ends around eleven. I plan to go to that in my leather suit and play the role I'm playing. Let's say midnight. That way, I can fill in my journal about what happens at the dance and then focus on you. Does that sound fair enough or is that too late?"

"Sounds good to me," David said quickly.

"Okay," Nancy agreed hesitantly. "Just don't tell father that I let you go out so late. Agreed?"

David grinned. "Agreed. Thank you, Nancy."

Chapter 9

William and Marie Slater had always enjoyed hosting guests in their home, so it was no surprise for them to have a ballroom included on the third floor when they had their mansion built on top of King's Point. The ballroom was a large dance floor with a stage for the band to play on. A grand piano was a permanent fixture. The windows opened to allow fresh cool air into the room as needed and the double doors leading to the large third-floor balcony overlooking the city below also helped regulate the heat of the summer's night. The Slater Balls were by invitation only and to be invited to a Slater Ball showed one's importance in the community. There was no grander upper society event than the Annual Slater's Independence Day Ball.

There was a table of delicious food, wine and champagne of the highest quality. A seven-piece orchestra brought in from Portland played the finest music for the evening. William and Marie

Slater spared no expense to entertain their guests and there would be a fireworks show for his guests at the stroke of midnight. The music and dancing would continue until 2:00 a.m.

Debra Slater was used to the elegance of the ball and was always the most asked lady to dance by numerous men. She was young, intelligent, and stunning in a formal burgundy gown with black ruffled lace around the neckline and down the front bodice. Her blonde hair was braided and weaved into a decorative bun with a burgundy and black lace hair piece holding the bun in place. She had expected Matt Bannister to arrive and hoped that he would come alone. Unfortunately, and to her significant irritation, Nate Robertson arrived with Matt's invitation with an attractive young blonde named Angela at his side.

Debra had hand-delivered the invitation to Matt, but he frankly spat in her face by giving it to Nate. She was angered by the insult and went straight to her older brother Josh and his best friend, Travis McKnight, who were outside on the third-floor balcony enjoying a drink and a cigar.

"Little sis, you look perturbed. What's the matter? Did Pa tell you he offered that idiot Uriah Davidson his job back and permission to court you to get him here?"

"What?" Debra asked irritably. "Please tell me you are joking." Her expression turned coarse.

"Oh. He didn't tell you." Josh laughed.

"He didn't do that? Did he? Yes or no!" Debra's impatience showed in her hardened blue eyes.

Josh grinned as he shrugged his shoulder innocently, not wanting to get the brunt of Debra's wrath. "Pa did send a letter to Uriah asking him to come back to work for us at a higher rate of pay and with some reconsideration, he gave Uriah his permission to court you."

Debra was sickened by the obvious ploy to get even with the ex-employee for trying to sabotage the Slater Mining Company by changing the claim borders and recommending drilling onto the neighbor's claim. She squeezed her lips together tightly before inhaling. She spoke curtly, "It turned out great for us, so why not leave it alone? He should have sent Uriah a thank you card. It would be just as cruel."

"Retribution, Sis. Pa sees what Uriah did as an act of aggression, and he won't let it go until he wins the battle. Uriah's coming here just to be fired again. He did seem pleased to have Pa's permission to court you, though. He's coming clear from some mountain town in Colorado. That's where Pa had him tracked to."

Debra rolled her eyes with frustration. "I should ask Uriah to marry me when he gets here and teach our father a lesson. I am so irritated!"

Travis McKnight spoke, "Don't be irritated, Debra. It's a wonderful night and you look beautiful."

"Thank you," she said kindly. "Do you want to know why I'm irritated, Josh? I invited Matt Bannister here personally and he gave his invitation to Nate Robertson. Nate brought one of the dancers from the dance hall."

"Which one? What is her name?" Travis asked. He tilted his head with interest.

"I don't know. Angela, I think. She's pretty but far below our stature. They shouldn't be here, but what else could I say? I don't want to be rude. I've known Nate forever."

"I'll take care of it," Josh said. "Go enjoy the guests, Sis."

Travis asked, "Why did you invite Matt? He doesn't fit in here any more than his deputy." His tone reflected his resentment towards Matt.

"I like Matt," Debra stated simply. "My father doesn't like him, and I know you two don't, but I do. I just wanted to get him away from that Christine girl for a while so I could talk to him. But he gave his invitation to Nate! How am I supposed to take that? Does that mean he is not interested in me? And if not, then what do I have to do to get him interested? I'm not giving up."

Josh raised his eyebrows and laughed. "That sounds like a question to ponder at one of Mother's Friday night tea parties with the women. Ask them." He spoke to his friend, "Travis, let's remove a deputy marshal and maybe steal his lady for a while."

***

Nate and Angela were seated at a table with their plates from the buffet table. Angela looked as wonderful as she ever had and certainly dressed appropriately for the ball in a flowing pink dress with all the ruffles and embroidered flower design that might be expected at such a high-end event. Her blonde hair was braided into a long ponytail that flowed to her mid-back. Nate was the only gentleman not wearing a black suit, but he did wear black pants and a red button-up shirt. His silver deputy marshal badge was on his left lapel.

Travis McKnight approached with a leering grin that could rival a starving hyena's. "My, oh, my, you are stunning, Angela. I've forgotten how pretty you are. You're more beautiful than Christine ever was. Tell me, how is she?"

Angela was a shy lady and nervous about being in unfamiliar territory with the most influential people in the community with a gentleman she did not know. However, she did know who Travis was and what he had done to Christine. "She is fine."

"Very good. What a year for her, huh? Being shot, kidnapped, I mean Matt has just been bad luck for her all the way around." Travis leaned over the table and lowered his voice so no one else could hear, "She should have stuck with me. I would have married her by now."

Nate swallowed his bite of food and took a drink of his glass of champagne before stating, "You should let your wife know that. If you'll excuse us, we're trying to eat."

Travis stood upright, irritated with the young deputy marshal's words. "Well, you let Matt know I said hello."

"I will."

Josh Slater reached down and intentionally tipped the glass of champagne over into Nate's plate of food. "You were not invited here. You can leave the lady for our pleasure, but you need to leave."

Nate's eyes hardened as he looked up under his brow at Josh. His impulse was to grab the man and pound his face into the table four or five times before hitting him with a solid right to the jaw, but it was only a fleeting thought. Nate set his fork down calmly and wiped his hands on the napkin. "Well, I do have an invitation. It's not made out to anyone in particular, so it must be my invitation. If you two men will excuse us, I believe we'll go enjoy the party."

"No, you won't," Josh said with more authority. "I'm asking you to leave. You were not invited here, and you know it. My sister is quite hurt by Matt giving his invite to you. So, please, I'm asking politely, please leave our home."

Nate stood slowly. "I'll meet you halfway on that. Let us stay long enough to have one dance and then we will leave. How does that sound, Josh?"

Josh was hesitant. "If it avoids causing a scene and embarrassing my parents, I'll accept that."

"Thank you."

Travis McKnight tapped Josh on the stomach. "I believe the entertainment is here." He pointed to the stairway where four men belonging to the Chatfield & Bowry Amazing Circus carried a large wooden box with air holes into the ballroom. An older gentleman wearing a black suit with a jacket with a long tail walked into the ballroom with a young lady in her mid-twenties. She was dressed in a silver evening gown that sparkled in the light with a high slit up the side, exposing her leg above the knee.

The older man spoke into a megaphone that he carried to get everyone's attention, "Hello, one and all. My name is Horace Chatfield, the owner of the amazing circus that has come into your beautiful town. Beside me is my beautiful daughter, Nancy. Together we have brought you some of the world's most peculiar and amazing sights your eyes will ever behold! I kid you not! Only here in the Slater mansion on this night will you get to see and hear and touch some of nature's most profound and mysterious freaks of nature and dangerous wild-life. A twenty-foot Boa Constrictor, a snake so vast it can kill and eat a full-grown man. A four-foot American alligator, a creature so fierce and deadly it can snap a full-grown man's arm clean off with one bite! A spider so large and unbelievable that you will praise the heavens above that these monstrosities only exist across the world in the Arabian sands, yes, a camel spider. A beast with mandibles so large one bite can make a grown man wish he was dead from the pain. A spider so frightening that we dare not take it out of its glass cage or risk it escaping and terrorizing your community forever because these spiders lay thousands of eggs at once. Please, Russel, bring up Gertie the Camel Spider."

A man in a red suit with a long coat tail and a matching red top hat carried a glass case covered by a black cloth to the center of the ballroom where

Horace and Nancy stood. The guests gathered around in a circle to watch with anticipation. Circus employees carried other wooden boxes up the three flights of stairs and set up portable tables for their private showing.

Nancy squeezed her shoulders inward tightly and moved her fingernails to her mouth to nervously chew her nails with a frightened shake of her body.

"Ohh, ladies and gentlemen, my daughter Nancy is deathly afraid of this spider. She has played with tarantulas since she was a little girl. Black widows, she flicks away like flies with her fingernail and Nancy has pulled the legs off the dreaded banana spiders of south America for fun!" he shouted and paused dramatically. "But I cannot get her to pull the cover off the securely locked case of a camel spider. Behold!" he shouted and yanked the black cover off the glass case. Nancy cried out in alarm and turned away from the glass case.

Inside was a large eight-inch camel spider. The eight-legged arachnid did not look like your average spider, and in the deserts of America's southwest, it went by another name, the wind scorpion. However, it was not poisonous. It did not have a stinger but did have large, powerful mandibles. Horace wanted to point out that the hind legs were long and bent backward. His camel spider did not come from Arabia but southern Arizona after hiring several men to find him the largest example of the creature they could find. The insect's life span was about a year, so he had younger specimens being raised to replace this one when it died. The audience was captivated by the size of the camel spider and believed every word Horace spoke to them about this terrifying creature. If he were in the desert states, he would not be showing the insect, but it played for a good show in northern states where the insects were not native.

"Who wants to hold Gertie?" he asked.

"No!" Nancy shouted with a loud stomp as she stepped away. "Don't open the case. Please, Father," Nancy pleaded. She played her part of a terrified girl begging her father to keep the monster inside the case.

Horace sighed compassionately. "Ohh, sometimes it is hard being a loving father. Okay, Sweetheart, I will not release it tonight." He hugged his daughter with a fatherly hug. He explained, "The last time I opened the case in a private showing like this, the menacing creature jumped right out of the case and onto my daughter. These creatures can jump ten feet before you can spit two feet, I kid you not. Five people were bitten that night before we finally caught Gertie. It was terrible and as you can see, Nancy still has nightmares."

He paused as he pointed at a four-foot square box with air holes. "But terror comes in levels and true terror is in that box! She was born in Arabia. A white child, born with a curse. Her father was an archaeologist named Sir Charles Burbank. Do you know the name? Maybe you've read about the story? If not, I'll tell you. Sir Charles Burbank had discovered the ancient city of Kobnerstee in the outer regions of the Arabian desert. It was once a grand city, and to the Hotitiudie tribesmen, it is very sacred. Sir Charles was warned not to open the tomb of the great prophet. Sensing gold, Sir Charles broke that sealed tomb and discovered a lot more than just the gold, jewels and treasure. He gained fame, sure enough, but it cost him. It cost him dearly. The Hotitiudie tribesmen were furious. They could have massacred all of the white-skinned foreigners, but there are things crueler than death. The Hotitiudie witch doctor put a wretched curse on Sir Charles's beautiful wife. Every heir Sir Charles would ever have would not be human. They would be human camel spiders! Tonight, I give you that baby. I give you the world's eighth wonder, the Human Camel Spider!"

A midget dressed in a black suit stood on the box and pulled a rope handle, opening the drop-down door.

There was a short pause of anticipation, and nothing happened.

Horace groaned. "Well, that is a lackluster start to our show. Russel, can you do something?"

Russel, the man in a red suit, walked over to another circus employee and took the man's wooden club. He stood behind the four-foot-long box and hit the back end of the box with a loud bang.

An unexpected high-pitched scream startled the crowd and then, quicker than anyone could expect, Susie Durden sped out of the box on her hands and backward feet toward the guests. She wore a light tan dress and tights of the same color as the camel spider. A leather collar was around her neck with a chain connecting her to the box. Her backward knees allowed her feet to swing under her belly as she ran to the chain's length. In her mouth was a white rabbit skin with stuffing inside to give the body some form and red dye on its neck and around her mouth to give the illusion of blood. Her attractive face was snarling with a growl as she lunged at nearby people.

A few ladies screamed as a loud collective gasp sounded from the horrified guests. It pleased Horace.

Horace jumped quickly out of the Human Camel Spider's reach as she tried to attack him. He spoke into the megaphone, "Ladies and gentlemen, please, do not panic! The chain contains the human insect securely. The Human Camel Spider is a predator of the most carnivorous kind. She would be wandering the streets eating your pets, small animals and maybe even small children if she had not come into our care as a child. After thirteen years of caring for her, as you can plainly see, she is now almost all human, except for that diet. Get a good look! Tomorrow come see our show and see more amazing wonders of nature..." Horace paused with concern.

Susie was at the chain's end, growling at Nate Robertson viciously. Horace sputtered to his megaphone, "Sir, please, for your safety, step back. When she sees red, she craves blood and raw meat." He spoke to his employees, "Gentlemen, please, need I remind you of what happened the last time she got a hold of a young man wearing red. Put her away carefully. Very...carefully. Pull her back into the box. Easy... Very good!" he exclaimed as she went back into the box and the door closed. He exhaled with relief. "Now, where did my daughter go?"

"Father, help!" Nancy yelled from behind the crowd. While the guests were staring at Susie, Nancy slipped behind them and was now wrapped in the clutches of a twenty-foot python.

"Good heavens!" Horace yelled over the gasps and screams of the guests.

***

Angela was disturbed after seeing Susie Durden's act. She clutched Nate's arm with tears in her eyes. "Can we go now?"

"Yes, we can." He did not say goodbye or a single word to anyone as they walked past the four-foot square box. He could see through an air hole the eye of the unfortunate young lady with a birth defect watching them leave. She looked to be wiping the fake blood off her lips.

Angela squeezed her lips together and held onto Nate's arm tightly as they descended the three flights of stairs wordlessly. They stepped out into the night's warm air and Angela stopped and began to weep.

"Are you okay?" Nate asked with concern.

She wiped her tears only to be replaced by others. "I've never seen anything like that in my life. That poor girl. She's younger than me."

"Do you want me to take you home?" Nate asked.

He didn't want to end the night to come to an end.

She wiped her eyes emotionally. "I'm sorry, Nate. You've been so kind. No. Maybe we can find something else to do." She sniffled.

Nate could feel his spirit rising. "Absolutely. I'd give you my handkerchief if I had one handy."

Angela appreciated the thought. "That was horrible. I can't imagine people find her misfortune entertaining. How can anyone force that poor child to act like that? It isn't right."

Chapter 10

Nick Griffin pulled the bottle of bourbon that Elizabeth Chalkalski had taken from her father's private bar to his lips. He was intoxicated and his eyelids were growing heavy as the night wore on. However, girls were present and drunk girls made for an entertaining night; he hoped. Nick planned to snake his way next to Elizabeth Chalkalski and sneak in a kiss or two while she was intoxicated and end her engagement once her fiancé found out. Nick wouldn't have a chance if she were sober, but as long as she was drinking and her inhibitions lowered, he had a good opportunity to be her worst mistake. He could live with that.

Elizabeth was seventeen, out of school and attending college in the Willamette Valley in the Fall. She was the prettiest girl in school and had never said a word to him. He discovered it was her idea to have a party while all their parents were at the Slater's Ball. Elizabeth could have gone to the ball, but she had been to several and had no desire to attend another. She was with her friends, Linda Fowler, Paulina Sorenson, Bernie Townsend and Levi Jensen. Linda's fourteen-year-old sister, Rose Fowler and her best friend, Hannie Longo, had followed along.

Linda and Paulina were cuddled up with their beaus Bernie and Levi as they all sat around the fire. They were on a small island of basalt rock in the middle of the river that had a nice patch of grass to sit on. The island was around the river's bend and out of sight from the town. The island was named Cabbage Island for reasons they didn't know. There wasn't a lot of vegetation on it, but the water was only knee-deep to get to it.

Fifteen-year-old Ollie Hoffman sat between Rose Fowler and Hannie Longo. He was already holding the hand of fourteen-year-old Rose. Hannie sat awkwardly quiet, occasionally glancing at their handholding and appeared to be not having much fun.

Nick had higher aspirations than a fourteen-year-old and had maneuvered closer to Elizabeth. "I like that," he said as he handed the bottle back to Elizabeth. "Have another drink."

She took a quick swig. "My father will rattle my spine when he finds out I took this," she said with a laugh. Elizabeth had not eaten any supper before drinking and was beginning to feel sick to her stomach. She was intoxicated but hadn't yet started to feel the full effects of what she had already drunk.

Nick flicked a small rock at her flirtatiously. It landed on her leg softly. "Blame it on me. Tell the old man you left the door unlocked and I robbed his bar." Nick slid across the grass closer to her and casually moved his right arm over Elizabeth's shoulder. "I'll take the blame for you any time."

"Get your arm off me!" She quickly rejected the action and forced his arm off her. "I am engaged. Go put your arm around someone your own age, like Rose or her friend."

Nick scoffed with repulsion. "I'm sixteen, Sweetheart, not fourteen. We are the same age."

Elizabeth was not impressed. "You said you just turned sixteen; I'll be eighteen in October. And married by nineteen. I'm sure you'll still be delivering groceries to my parents' house by then."

Nick was embarrassed by the remark. It angered him. "Maybe. But your fiancé is at college right now and probably courting another girl that's prettier than you! I know I would be if I was him."

She gasped. "Hardly. I wouldn't court you if you were the last man on earth."

"Oh yeah?" he asked, glaring at her in the fire light. "Well, I wouldn't court you either. You might think you are gorgeous, but let me tell you something, you have a tiny pimple right at the corner of your nose and it's really white. Do you want me to pop it for you? Do you think I'm servant enough to do that?"

Her nose wrinkled, twisting her upper lip into a disgusted scowl. "Not with your grubby fingers, no thanks. Get away from me!" She grabbed the bottle from his hands and scooted a few inches closer to Paulina and Levi. She spoke irritably, "You know, Nick, I didn't even want you here. Linda invited you and Ollie, not me. At least Ollie is respectful. You are plain annoying."

Nick stood slowly and wavered a bit as he stood. His dark eyes roamed over the others and settled on Elizabeth. "I'm annoying?"

"Very."

He raised his voice, "You know, I've tried to be nice to you and what do I get? Ignored, insulted and not even a kiss for bringing you some whiskey!"

"A kiss?" Elizabeth gasped, repulsed. "Are you kidding me?"

Levi Jensen spoke kindly, "Nick, sit down and relax. We're having a good time."

"I'm not!" Elizabeth exclaimed. "How can we have a good time with him? You haven't bathed in how long, Nick? And it's very ironic to mention my one little pimple when your whole face looks like a horned toad's back!"

Nick kicked the fire and sprayed Elizabeth with burning wood, coals and ash. He leaned over her and began cursing at her with every foul name he could think of while she frantically wiped the embers off her clothing.

Levi Jensen stood quickly and drove a clenched right fist into Nick's cheek, sending him to the ground in a hurry. "Leave her alone! She didn't do anything to you."

Nick stood and quickly pulled his hunting knife with a five-inch blade from the sheath on his belt.

He held it firmly in his grasp with a wild look possessing his eyes. He pointed the blade at Levi. "I'll kill you if you hit me again!" His chest rose and fell with deep breaths.

"Hey!" Ollie shouted, standing quickly. "What are you doing? Put that away!"

Levi was surprised. "I don't want to fight, Nick. Just leave her alone or go home."

Nick exhaled to calm himself and returned the knife to the sheath with a stern glare at Elizabeth. He warned Levi, "Don't ever hit me again."

Elizabeth stood as she wiped yet another red ember off her sleeve. "You ruined my dress! You are a creep! I'm leaving. Come on, let's leave him here."

"Where are we going to go?" Paulina asked. She had been having a lovely evening with her newest beau, Levi. Levi Jensen was not a wealthy young man, but he was genuinely friendly and nice. His father, Lloyd Jensen, was killed a few months back in a mine explosion. Their family had run into hard times and Levi had to quit school to go to work with his older brothers at the mine where his father once worked to make do and support their mother. Paulina had always liked Levi, but his dedication and sense of responsibility impressed her more. It wasn't a relationship Paulina's father would approve of, but she had no intention of marrying Levi.

"Anywhere but here, Paulina!" Elizabeth stammered. She kicked a piece of burning wood that was now out of the fire towards Nick's feet in spite. She cried out in fright and jumped back as Nick lunged forward threatening to hit her.

Levi pushed Nick backward. "Calm down! If you can't control your temper, then you need to leave. I'll tell the sheriff or the marshal if you pull that knife on me again. I'm not kidding. You are ruining tonight for everyone. Calm down or go home!"

"Nick, sit down and relax," Ollie said softly.

Nick held up his hands in a surrendering fashion. "Okay. Okay. I'll sit down." He plopped on the ground where he once was. He glared at Elizabeth across the remains of the fire. "You're going to get it," he warned.

"Get what?" Linda Fowler asked for her friend. "Nick, I thought you would be fun. But you're a jerk. Why don't you just go home and get some sleep? We don't want you here anymore."

"You go home!" Nick shouted at Linda. "I told Ollie you rich tramps wouldn't want anything to do with us. Didn't I?" he asked Ollie.

"Yeah, but you're the one being a jerk. Not them," Ollie answered.

"You see?" Linda offered, "Ollie is fine. I'm glad he is here. But no one wants you here, Nick."

"No? Fine, I'll go!" Nick exclaimed. He yanked the bottle of bourbon from Elizabeth's hand and stormed into the water to cross the river.

"Good riddance, Jackass!" Elizabeth hollered.

"Ollie, let's go!" Nick yelled from the darkness. The moon was out, and he could be seen on the bank waiting.

"Don't go," Rose Fowler said softly. She had been drinking and had a sudden crush on the boy who held her hand in the fire light, "I don't want you to

93

go."

"Ollie!" Nick shouted.

"Please stay," Rose pleaded. Her brown eyes stared into Ollie's. "I don't want you to leave."

Elizabeth chuckled. She shouted to Nick, "I think Rose has stolen your man." The comment brought some laughter from the others.

Nick called her a few choice names. "Are you coming or not, Ollie?" he demanded.

Ollie could not break free from the spell Rose had on him. "No. I'm staying," he answered.

"I thought you were my friend!" With several loud curses directed at Elizabeth, Nick stormed along the bank until he was out of sight.

Linda Fowler turned her attention to her little sister. "Ohh... Little Rosie has a sweetheart! Rosie and Ollie sitting in a tree K-I-S-S-I-N-G. First comes love, then comes marriage, and then a little Ollie or Rosie in a baby carriage! I'm telling father. Ohh!" she teased.

Rosie's face reddened. "No, you're not or I'll tell him you let me drink."

Elizabeth gave a slight smile as she directed her attention to Rose. "Okay, kiddo, let's see you kiss him."

Rose grinned hesitantly. She had never been kissed by a boy and was horrified by the suggestion, although not dead set against it either.

Linda pressured them. "Come on, Ollie. Give my sister a kiss!"

Ollie's face reddened. He had no desire to leave Rose's side to follow Nick, but he had never kissed a girl before either. His heart pounded and his ears felt hot with all the others' eyes on him and Rose. Did she want to kiss him? He had no idea. They had been holding hands.

"Come on, you two chickens. Bauwk, bauwk, bauwk," Linda teased. The chicken bauwking was joined by Levi and Elizabeth.

Ollie looked into Rosie's eyes and with the pressure of the others cheering them on, their lips moved closer until the two pairs of soft lips met, puckered into a quick kiss and departed quickly to the cheer of the older group of friends.

"It's official!" Bernie yelled into the night. "Rose has got her first sweetheart and kiss!"

Elizabeth laughed, "Ollie too. How cute!"

"Your turn, Linda," Rose said to her older sister.

"What?"

"You have to kiss Bernie."

Linda didn't hesitate and gave Bernie a deep, meaningful kiss that he wasn't quite expecting. They would have dared Levi and Paulina, but they were already a couple and kissing.

Linda teased her friend, "Elizabeth, you missed your chance to kiss Nick." She hollered, "Oh Nick, Elizabeth has to kiss you!"

Elizabeth found no humor in it. She yelled loudly, so Nick didn't come back, "I'd rather French kiss a slug!" She pointed at Rose. "But I will show you how to kiss a man. And then I want to see you do it. Hannie, toss me your pillow. I'll demonstrate on it."

Hannie, finally being noticed, gladly tossed her small square pillow with gold tassels on the corners and a white horse embroidered on the material to Elizabeth. It was a gift made by her grandmother and her favorite pillow. She had difficulty falling asleep without it and brought it and a blanket to spend the night with Rose. She did not know they would be on Cabbage Island drinking with boys when she left her home.

Elizabeth put the pillow to her open mouth and mimicked a long and passionate kiss with the pillow for the enjoyment of the others. They laughed as she set the pillow down on the grass beside her and wiped her mouth with her sleeve. "And that's how I would kiss my man if he was here. Real kisses don't peck like chickens," she said to Rose and Ollie. "Now, let's see you two do it right."

The teens cheered, clapped and encouraged the young newly formed couple to kiss correctly. Without Nick, the friends could sit around the fire, have a few more drinks and enjoy their youth on a splendid night together that they would never regret or forget. It was a nice feeling to be away from their protective parents and laugh freely together.

Chapter 11

The hour was getting late, and the fire was burning down now that they had burned all the wood they had collected. Ollie Hoffman sat by the fading fire with his arm around Rose Fowler's shoulders as she snuggled against him. Ollie had high hopes that maybe Linda would be interested in him when she invited him unexpectedly to join her and her friends. It was a desperate hope of the slightest chance, but even a tiny glimmer of hope was enough to take a chance. It was soon apparent that Linda's romantic interest was in Bernie Townsend.

Ollie never had a romantic interest in Rose, but she was a distant friend from school who often said hello to him. Rose was pretty but not as cute as her older sister. Rose had a round face with chubby cheeks and was heavy set for a fourteen-year-old girl. Her brown hair was a shade or two darker than her sister's and was in a tight bun earlier, but now her hair fell loose onto her shoulders. What had started as a group of friends drinking had become a circle of three couples cuddling and kissing around a dying fire. Pauline and Levi were established sweethearts, but her parents didn't know about him. Linda and Bernie had been attracted to one another for some time, but no sparks had lit up their world until late this afternoon when Bernie found the spine to ask her to be his sweetheart.

Encouraged by a challenge to kiss, Ollie and Rose had become a couple. The first kiss was as Elizabeth pointed out a chicken's peck, but with some instructions from the older kids and some figuring out of their own, the two of them had kissed numerous times. Ollie had never felt more like a grown man with Rose in his arms while sitting in the firelight. It was the best night of his life, and he did not want it to end, not ever. His crush on Linda was replaced with a growing love for her little sister, Rose.

"Did you hear that?" Bernie asked the others. A twig snapped from someone stepping on it came from the dark forest across the river. "I think someone is watching us."

Elizabeth tossed a sliver of wood into the coals. She yawned as the exhaustion of waking up early and alcohol combined with the late hour mixed in her expression. She had quit drinking when her stomach began to bother her. "It's obviously Nick. He's the only creep creepy enough to hide in the dark to watch us. I know we had different plans, but I have an idea. Why don't we all go back to my place and sleep in the hayloft of our carriage house? There is plenty of room up there for everyone to sleep. My parents will be walking home from the ball, so they won't enter the carriage house. No-body will know we're in there and best of all, Nick, that creep, won't be able to spy on us."

Linda stood and grabbed the blanket that she was sitting on. "I think it's a great idea." She looked at her friend. "Can the boys come?"

Elizabeth was tired. "I don't care. I'm going to sleep."

"Rose, Hannie, let's go," Linda said.

Rose rested her head comfortably on Ollie's shoulder and held his hand. She sighed, "I don't want Ollie to leave. Can't I stay here with Ollie?"

Linda laughed at her sister. "No. Ollie's coming with us. Aren't you, Ollie?"

Ollie had never been invited to anyone's house before, especially to a home on King's Point. "Sure."

Ollie had never had a sweetheart. The unex-pected romance starting with Rose was an exciting moment in his life. He had his first kiss, first time holding a girl's hand and now the night only prom-ised to get better as he would have all night to be with Rose. And maybe, he would be able to hold and kiss her longer.

Elizabeth grabbed her blanket, stepped around the fire, and held out a hand to help Hannie Longo stand. "I suppose it's just us two girls on our own tonight since everyone else seems to have found some romance."

Hannie was tired. She said, "I'm going home. I'm tired."

"Me too," Elizabeth said.

Hannie had just turned fourteen and had long blonde curly hair that fell over her shoulders. She was a pretty girl, but she wasn't as interested in boys as her friend Rose was. Hannie knew all too well that there was no way on earth that her parents would allow her to have a sweetheart at her age. She was the daughter of Jim and Karen Longo. Her father was a supervisor at the Slater Silver Mine and her Uncle Ron Dalton was the mine manager. She was a Fasana, the granddaughter of Joel and niece of William and a cousin to the Bannisters. Her family's standing in the community put her in a more popular group of friends, even if her parents weren't as wealthy as her friends were.

If not startled, Hannie was surprised to witness her best friend hold hands with Ollie Hoffman and then shocked to see them kiss upon a challenge and then kiss on their own accord. Rose had always thought Ollie was handsome, but Hannie had no idea how much Rose liked him, to ignore her and continuously kiss Ollie. Hannie wasn't having any fun and felt left out of the group. She didn't like the taste of alcohol and had already decided that she was going home if everyone was going to Elizabeth's house.

There was a bad feeling stirring in her stomach and Hannie felt like they were being watched. She had whispered it to Rose before the twig snapped, but Rose pushed her away and went back to kissing Ollie. Hannie thought she was spending the night with her friend, and being an obedient child, she was not comfortable being on the island with boys and liquor. She was going home.

Hannie carried her blanket in her arms while wading across the river to reach the bank. It was a short walk around the bend and onto the open beach area beside the falls of Premro Island. The music from the dance could still be heard and drew the group of teenagers quicker, like moths to light, to reach the dance before walking to Elizabeth's house.

"Wait!" Hannie exclaimed when they reached the beach at Premro Island. "Elizabeth, do you have my pillow?"

"Why would I have your pillow?" Elizabeth sounded irritated.

"Because you borrowed it to show everyone how you kiss."

Elizabeth laughed lightly. "Oh yeah. No, I don't have it. I set it on the ground."

"I have to go back," Hannie said tiredly. "Rose, come with me."

Rose had lost all interest in her friend. "I can't. Ollie and I want to dance before the dance is over."

"We do?" Ollie asked more to himself. It surprised him.

Elizabeth offered, "I have pillows you can use."

"My grandmother made that pillow for me. I have to go back and get it. Rose, come with me, please?"

Linda was annoyed at her sister's friend. "Hannie, get it tomorrow. The dance is going to end pretty soon. We don't have time to go back and get it."

Hannie was insistent. "I have to get it. My Grandma Longo made it for me. Rose, come with me," she pleaded with a glance towards the dark woods. She still had the sensation of being watched from the dark forest and it scared her. "Rose, aren't you going to go back with me?"

Rose kept walking away from her with Ollie's arm around her shoulder. She kissed him quickly. "I'll see you tomorrow if you're not coming with us."

"Rose…" Hannie begged.

"I want to dance with Ollie. Just run. I'll see you tomorrow."

Bernie Townsend was growing impatient with Linda's little sister's friend. The girl was a bore anyway. "Quit being a baby and go get your stupid pillow! You'll be fine. Let's just leave her."

She stood alone on the beach and watched her friend leave her behind. It wasn't a creepy foggy night with a full moon, but it felt like one for some reason. Maybe it was because she knew she'd get in trouble if her parents knew where she was or perhaps it was because she was beside the river and she didn't know how to swim if she fell in where the water was over her head. Whatever it was, it didn't feel right. Hannie looked into the dark woods where she suspected Nick was watching them. On the count of three, she ran as fast she could go along the bank around the bend and, lifting the hem of her dress, waded into the shallow water to the island. Hannie located her pillow with gold tassels on the corners and an embroidered white horse running free where Elizabeth had set it down. Hannie could not escape the sensation of being watched as she held up her dress and waded back across the water.

A large moon filled in the sky and the sound of the rippling water and the distant band playing were the only sounds until she reached the bank next to the woods when she heard rustling in the brush. She glanced into the trees and saw a were-wolf's thick hair-covered face watching her in the moonlight.

Petrified, she screamed and stumbled backward a few steps while staring with terrified eyes at the monster in the trees. She fell into the water and splashed in a panic while trying to get to her feet. Hannie got to her feet but slipped on the rocks and fell into the water again in her frantic state. Blubbering, sobbing and screaming involuntarily, she got to her feet and ran as fast as possible with her heart pounding within her chest so hard it would have broken out of the skin if not contained by her sternum bone. She ran around the bend and onto the river's beach near the falls. The tall and lanky figure of Nick Griffin had crept out from under the island's first bridge holding the bottle of bourbon to see what she was screaming about. Recognizing Nick, Hannie ran to him for protection.

"A monster!" she wept as she let the pillow fall and wrapped her arms around Nick, terrified. "It was a werewolf! I saw a werewolf!" she cried in terror.

Nick's angry eyes narrowed as he felt her arms around him. "You're wet!" he complained as he tried to push her away. She refused to let him go as she hugged him, sobbing. He put his arms around her wet dress and could feel her warm body against his. "Hannie, little Hannie," he mumbled into her ear, "you're so pretty." He kissed her neck while he ran his hands down her back.

She stepped back, not liking the sudden uneasiness in her stomach. It was a sickly feeling that she had never felt before. Hannie couldn't define the sensation of dread, but she knew she needed to get away from him. "There's a werewolf! We have to go." She took a step to run away, but Nick grabbed her wrist and yanked her into his arms. Dizzy from the sudden change of direction, she turned her head away from him as he tried to force a kiss on her.

"Stop it! We have to go! Nick, stop!" she demanded while pushing against him to try to escape his clenched arms around her.

Nick grabbed a handful of blonde curly hair that fell down her back and jerked her closer to him. "Knock it off! I saw you looking at me. No one will see, don't worry," he said.

"You're hurting me, stop! Let me go, Nick! Let me go!" she shouted.

Nick covered her mouth with his right hand. "Shh! I told you, be quiet!" He forced her to the ground with a slight turn of his body and lay on top of her. Nick switched hands to cover her mouth and tore at her dress to rip it open with his right hand. Seeking a kiss, he tried to replace his left hand with his lips, but Hannie turned her face away and cried out for help in resistance. Nick grabbed her chin firmly with his left hand and pressed her cheeks against her teeth to open her mouth.

"Stop fighting me!" he demanded in a rage-filled guttural low voice that was just as terrifying as the wild and fierce eyes that glared down at her. He pressed his mouth against hers while holding her mouth open. His right hand pawed at her dress to remove the material as fast as possible.

Hannie dug her fingernails into his cheek and ripped downward to free her mouth of his tongue and release the pressure of her cheeks being cut against her teeth. Nick pulled away from the kiss painfully and touched the burning on his cheek. He knew the scratches were deep. Furious, he slapped the side of her face as hard as he could to stop her screaming. It was ineffective as her response was to drive a thumb nail into his chin and continue to cry out for help. He was older, bigger and stronger, but she refused to be intimidated into submission. Maybe it was the Fasana blood in her veins or simply the will to live, but she would do everything she could to fight him.

Nick uttered a curse from the sharp pain in his chin. "Shut up!" he demanded. Nick clenched his fist and hit her face. Though stunned for a moment by the blow, she wailed louder and cried out with more desperation between her sobs. "Get off me! Help!" she cried out loudly, followed by high-pitched wailing.

He sneered, "Shut up!" His jaw clenched as his hands went to her throat and clenched tightly as he repositioned his body to sit across her chest and put his weight on her throat. Her nails dug into his forearms and wrists to break the stranglehold. Every sensation of her fingernails tearing into his skin increased his rage. He lowered his center of gravity onto his waist and began pulling her head up and slamming it down against the ground by her throat to make her stop scratching him.

Nick squeezed her throat until she was no longer fighting him. Satisfied that she was beaten into submission, he released her throat, but to his horror, she was not moving. Her eyes remained open and unfocused as her head turned lifelessly to the right. A wave of terror went down his spine.

"Hannie? Oh no! Oh no," he said as he realized she was dead. He stood up quickly and turned around to look around him. He didn't see anyone, and the only sound was the waterfall and the band playing a happy jig in the park. "Oh no… Oh my…" he repeated as the seriousness of his actions settled onto him. "Damn it, Hannie, why did you have to scream? Look what you made me do!" he exclaimed quietly while running his hand through his hair.

Breathing hard and afraid, Nick had an idea. He tried to pick up the young girl but picking up her limp body was more challenging than he expected. Fixated on his plan to escape guilt, he had no choice but to pick her up by the shoulders and drag her up the grassy knoll. Carefully looking around to make sure no one would see him, Nick drug her body onto the first bridge over the flowing twenty-foot-wide narrow passage of deeper water and stood her against the short railing.

"What are you doing?" he heard a man yell as Nick pushed the body off the bridge into the water. He watched her fall into the river as the current rushed her body towards the deep pool of water. He hoped Hannie's body would sink to the bottom, but it didn't.

"What are you doing?" Nick heard a man ask urgently. He watched as the stranger clad in thick leather ran down to the water's edge and began to strip off his leather clothes.

Avery Gaines urgently pulled off his knee-high boots, dropped his coat to the ground, pulled the leather suspenders off his shoulders and allowed his heavy pants to fall. He stepped towards the river as he pulled his leather shirt over his head and tossed it aside.

The water felt good on his overheated body, but his attention was on the lady who had fallen into the river. It was clear that the man was drunk, and she appeared to be passed out by her limp body. The drunken fellow had tried to rest her on the bridge rail, and she fell in. She floated face down, but he hoped to get to her before she drowned. He grabbed her and began to swim backward to bring her to safety. "Hang on, young lady," he said as he pulled her to the river's bank.

***

Nick watched with alarm as the leather man swam out to Hannie's body, pulled the girl back to shore, and dragged her out of the water. The stranger kneeled beside Hannie to check her breathing. He yelled at Nick, "Go get the doctor! Go now!"

Nick looked around Premro Island and the road and could see three men walking towards the bridge to leave town, but they were still a ways away. He hurried off the bridge and down the knoll, pulling his hunting knife out of its sheath on his belt as he approached the crazy stranger. He yelled furiously, "Get off my friend! Are you trying to rape her!"

"What?" Avery stood in surprise. "Go get a doctor as I said!" He pointed up the hill as Nick approached him.

Nick drew near quickly and faked a left jab to the face to trick the leather man into lifting his arms to protect himself.

"What are you doing? Hey, I'm trying to help her..." Avery said, not understanding why he was being attacked.

Nick swung the knife around in a wide arch and drove the blade into Napoleon's side just below his rib cage to the knife's handguard. He withdrew the blade and plunged it into the leather man's abdomen as the man leaned towards him from the previous blow. Over and over, Nick plunged the knife into the man's belly and then the side of the neck just before the man fell. Knowing the three men were coming closer and the leather man was not dead yet, Nick drove the knife into the soft tissue of Avery Gaines's throat and sliced it open.

Nick's chest heaved from breathing hard as he watched the man bleed and struggle for a breath. Nick pulled the arrowhead necklace off the man's neck as he struggled to grasp for a breath of air. "Hurry up and die," he said coldly.

The sound of someone fleeing through the brush in the woods caught Nick's attention and he ran towards the woods with a wild expression on his face. If there was someone there, they too had to be killed to stop them from identifying him. He could hear someone run through the brush, but Nick could also hear the laughter of the three men nearing the bridge. He cursed silently and ran towards the road frantically. "Help! Help! He was trying to rape my friend and I had to kill him! I think she's dead too. Help! Someone, help me!" He dropped to his knees on the grass and began wailing. Blood saturated his hands and shirt. "I think he murdered my friend," he sobbed convincingly.

Chapter 12

Matt Bannister held his hand over his mouth as he knelt beside the deceased body of his cousin Karen's oldest daughter. It was haunting to see the expression of horror frozen on the young girl's face in the moonlight. He ran his hand over her wet hair and wiped a drop of water from her eyes that glistened in the faint light like a teardrop. Matt had looked upon many bodies over the years, but he had never gazed upon a child's body that was part of his family. The shock of realizing the victim was Hannie hit him with a blunt force of a bullet to the heart. He had always been able to separate his responsibilities as a lawman from the emotional impact of crimes, but the lines had suddenly blurred. The deceased body lying on the grass was no stranger. She was family. Technically speaking, the murder took place within city limits, and it fell under the jurisdiction of the Branson Sheriff's Office. Blurred by the emotional impact or not, there was no way he would leave his young cousin's murder investigation in the incompetent hands of Tim Wright.

The murder of a child was never easy to deal with as a parent, relative or friend, but it was also hard to comprehend as a lawman. A child's death could be explainable if the child had died of natural causes or an accident, but a murdered child could never be reasonably reconciled. A human being intentionally caused Hannie's death and there was no way to comprehend such evil. She was a beautiful and lively young lady with a bright future ahead of her and her life was cut short by a man's hand. The family may never understand why, but it was certain that they would spend the rest of their lives missing her. If there was any crime that deserved a swift death sentence carried out promptly, robbing a family of a child's life was it.

Matt's experienced eye noticed her dress was torn at the collar, to rip it open. She was soaking wet, as was the nude body of the stranger who identified himself as Avery Gaines. His leather clothing was scattered in a progressive line fifteen feet towards the water, indicating he stripped quickly while approaching the river. He was deceased with multiple stab wounds and a slit throat. Hannie's pillow was lying nearby, close to a mostly empty bottle of expensive bourbon several yards away from the bodies. There was no other visual evidence near the bodies that Matt could take note of that helped explain what had happened.

He had not spoken to the only witness, the young teen that killed Avery Gaines. Matt had not

yet grasped his emotions and allowed the first lawman on the scene, Sheriff Deputy Alan Garrison to
talk to the teenager. He did have Alan keep the boy
there so Matt could speak to him. Alan updated
Matt on the story that Nick Griffin told him.

"Alan, take Nate and go question Nick again. Let
me know if his story changes any," Matt said. He
used two fingers to close the eyes of the young lady.
He had no doubt she was strangled. He sniffled as a
wave of emotion came over him. He fought it away.
He had no time to be emotional; he had a crime to
solve and a job to do. He remained kneeling beside
her and ran a hand over his hair.

Sixteen-year-old Nick Griffin told Sheriff's
Deputy Alan Garrison that he and his friends
were drinking on Cabbage Island. He argued with
Elizabeth Chalkalski, who had stolen the bourbon
bottle from her father. Nick admitted taking the
bottle and leaving the group of friends while angry
at Elizabeth. Nick claimed he was drinking alone
in the woods when he heard Hannie screaming
and by the time he got to the edge of the woods, the
screaming had stopped. Nick saw that the leather
man was naked and trying to rip Hannie's dress
open. Enraged, Nick ran forward and confronted
the stranger, who then attacked Nick.

Nick claimed the leather man went crazy with a
wild and bloodthirsty look in his eyes. He grabbed,
scratched, hit, and tried to reach for Nick's throat to
strangle him. The older and more muscular leather
man eventually got the better of Nick. Knowing his
life was in danger, Nick had no choice but to pull his

knife and stab the vagabond in the side, abdomen several times, and throat in a desperate fight to save his own life. "Look at what he did to me! The man was crazy!" Nick had lamented to Deputy Garrison as he exposed the scratches on his face and arms. Nick claimed he thought Hannie was knocked out. He had no idea she was dead when he confronted the leather man.

Matt recognized Nick from a chance meeting when he caught three teens urinating on his passed-out friend, Chusi Yellowbear, in an alley many months before. He only caught one of the boys, a lad named Tad Sperry, but Matt recognized the other hoodlums as Nick Griffin and Ollie Hoffman. He knew Nick wasn't the most behaved kid, but he also knew the boy delivered groceries and was able to keep a job while earning high praise doing so from his employer and the residents he delivered to.

Alan returned and told Matt that Nick's story had not changed.

"Do you believe him?" Matt asked the two young lawmen.

"I do. Nick's pretty shaken up. I think he's telling the truth," Nate said.

Alan nodded in agreement. He added, "He got pretty scratched up in that fight. It's hard to see in the dark, though."

Matt stood and spoke to the deputy, "If you get into a brawl that ends up on the ground quite often, you get scratched. I have. I'll go talk to him and his friends." He glanced at his deputy, Nate

Robertson, "Nate, go get our horses. Get William's too. Alan," he said to Alan Garrison, "go with Nate and get a wagon from the livery stable and haul these bodies to the mortuary. Wait there until my uncle Solomon arrives. He's at the Slater's Ball with her parents and about everyone else." The sheriff's deputy, Mark Theisen, would remain on the scene to keep everyone away from the bodies and protect the area.

"Are you okay?" Nate asked with concern.

Matt nodded sadly. "Hurry up with the horses. I'll go notify William. I'll meet you at the Monarch Hotel."

Matt's heart was heavy. It wasn't just his cousin on the ground that made his feet feel like lead blocks; it was knowing he was the only reason Hannie's murderer was not in jail. His desire to question Nick and the other teens was delayed because he would have to face Hannie's best friend, Rose. She was with a group of teens standing with Nick. It was hard to question Hannie's friends when he knew Hannie would be alive and well if it wasn't for his decision to free a stranger.

Matt took a deep breath and walked up the short hill towards the group of teenagers who had been drinking with Hannie. They had been at the dance when they heard a girl was killed at the river. Nick stood with them, acting just as stunned as the other kids were to find one of their own murdered. Matt nodded to the others and knelt in front of Rose Fowler, who sat on the grass. She was weeping hysterically with her face covered.

"How are you doing, young lady?"

She lowered her hands and saw Matt's misting eyes. She babbled, "I should never have left her," she sobbed.

Matt set a hand comfortingly on her shoulder and tightened his lips. "It's not your fault, Rose. Do you hear me? It's not your fault."

Linda Fowler offered, "We were going to the dance. Hannie went back for her pillow. We never thought anything could happen, Marshal Bannister," she wept.

Matt stood. "You kids go home and wait for your parents. I'll talk with all of you soon." His eyes went to Nick. "Nick, hold on a minute."

"Marshal, I already told Deputy Garrison everything that happened twice now," Nick said. He seemed anxious to leave.

"I know. How are you doing? The first time taking a man's life can be disturbing, especially doing so in such close quarters."

"Yeah…it is." Nick seemed to be searching for the correct answer. Matt didn't miss it, nor was the change of interest in Matt's eyes missed by Nick.

"I bet. I've been in many brawling fights myself like the one you had. I've gotten scratched up quite a bit. It hurts. I see the ones on your face and neck. Can I see your arms and hands?"

Nick was growing nervous. He had no issue lying to Deputy Garrison or Deputy Nate Robertson because they were young and inexperienced. Matt was a different breed of lawman altogether. He scared Nick.

"Yes, sir. As I said, the man went crazy when I confronted him." He held up his arms for Matt to see the scratches on his forearms and the top of his hands. Even with the moon's light, it was too dark to see them clearly.

Matt's eyes rose to look Nick in the eyes. They were no longer misty and in anguish. They were hard and accusing. He spoke softly, "I need to leave to notify her parents. I'd like to talk to you tomorrow between 10:00 a.m. and noon, let's say. I know it will be a busy day, and I hate interfering with your fun, but two lives ended tonight. You are the only witness I have. Hannie is my family, and I have a few questions that need to be answered and perhaps you can help, maybe not. There's no reason for you to be afraid, so relax." He offered a barely noticeable smile. "I'll come by your place. It won't take long, and then you can have fun. Go get some rest. Oh…and thank you for trying to protect Hannie."

"I'm sorry I didn't get there faster, Marshal. She'd be alive if I did."

***

Joshua Bannister was a large and husky boy at sixteen. He was physically built like his father, Albert; broad-shouldered and muscular. Josh had a square-shaped face with short dark hair combed neatly to the side. Joshua had kind brown eyes and a friendly smile that he wore most of the time. He worked the evening hours at the front desk of the Monarch

Hotel. Dressed in tan checkered suit pants and a white button-up shirt with a bowtie, he dusted the fine woodwork inside the lobby for something to do. The hotel had very little business happening after the restaurant closed. With the Slater's Ball and community dance in the park, even the Monarch Lounge was empty of customers. Joshua watched William Fasana leave the bathhouse and walk towards the lobby after finishing a routine check of the facility to ensure the back doors were secured for the evening. William appeared to be as bored as Joshua was.

Being a student of fisticuffs, Joshua gave William a playful shove as he walked by. "Do you want to fight?"

William raised his eyebrows with interest. He was about forty years old with a rugged, weathered oblong face with sky blue eyes. His long wavy blond hair was pulled into a ponytail neatly. A crooked smile appeared on his lips as he answered in his deep voice, "Sure. Let's see your stance, boy."

Joshua set the feather duster down and put one foot in front of the other about a shoulder's width apart at a slight angle and raised his fists.

William did not take a posed stance. Instead, he quickly fired an open-handed left jab that was blocked successfully by Joshua. As promptly as William drew his left arm back, he kicked Joshua in the lower leg, pulling the boy's hands downward. William's quick hands slapped Joshua's cheeks with a right, left and another right forcing Joshua to take an off-balance step back as he raised his guard.

Taking advantage of Joshua being off-balance, William shoved him against the wall forcefully. Joshua hit the wall and turned his profile to William to escape being trapped, and William kicked the back of Joshua's knee with enough force to collapse his leg. Joshua fell to one knee, and William drove a knee forward and stopped it short of Joshua's face.

"You would have lost, Josh," William said simply enough. "In that position, I could knee your head all day long and leave you a vegetable by the time I was done."

Josh stood back up, rubbing his leg. "You can't kick in boxing!" he complained.

William grinned at his young cousin appreciatively. "You didn't say we were boxing. You asked if I wanted to fight. There's a big difference between the two, Josh. There are no rules in a fight, and you need to remember that if you ever get into one. But if you ever do get into a fight, learn to finish it quickly using the weapons you always have: hands, forearms, elbows, knees, shins, feet and your head. Use them all and use them effectively. Boxing is a great sport and skill to know, but outside of the ring, you have other weapons you can use."

"Yeah, but that wasn't fair."

William drove his clenched fist into Joshua's bicep without mercy in the power of the punch.

"Ouch!" Joshua shouted as he rubbed his sore arm with a sour expression.

"What did I just say?" William asked with a chuckle. "I said there are no rules in a fight. Therefore, the word *fair* does not apply in a fight. Boxing, yes, fight no. Winning the fight is the only thing that matters. Understand me? Joshua, honestly, if you get in a fight with the wrong person, winning could be the difference between life and death. Learn to end it quickly."

"Yeah. I get it. I'm going to have a bruise."

"Good! It will make you tough. Now let's try it again. This time, expect the unexpected and attack," William said. He raised his open hands and moved his head and shoulders to the left and right. "Come on, tough guy, let's see what you got."

The front door opened, and Matt Bannister walked into the hotel's lobby.

"Uncle Matt, William's hitting on me," Joshua tattled.

"Good," he said halfheartedly. "William, I..." he hesitated. "I have some terrible news."

William frowned. He could see the sorrow on Matt's face. "What?"

The words wouldn't come out easily as Matt's eyes watered. He pointed with his thumb towards Premro Island. He took a deep breath to speak, but no words came. He had notified families in the past that their loved one was gone, but it was never an easy thing to do. "William, Hannie was murdered down by the river."

"What?" William shouted. "My niece, Hannie?"

Matt nodded sadly. "Yes."

"Hannie?" Joshua asked. He had grown up with her and was much closer to her than Matt was.

"Who did it and how?" William's light blue eyes were growing fiercely dangerous.

"It appears she was strangled by the man that came to town wearing all that leather. Nick Griffin says he tried to stop the stranger in time to save her and the man attacked him. Nick stabbed the man to death in self-defense. Unfortunately, he was too late for Hannie. I'm sorry."

William's voice had become as cold and dangerous as it could be. "Who is *that* man? I don't know a man that wears all *that* leather!" His chest rose and fell heavily.

Matt answered softly, "William, I'm not sure who he is. He showed up in town today dressed in rawhide, claiming to be from the middle earth. He called himself Napoleon Pickle, otherwise known as Napoleon the Great. Later, he told me in confidence that he was a reporter from New York playing a role of a crazy man for an article he intended to write. I don't know if he was telling me the truth or if he's a lunatic who told me a story. All I know is he and Hannie are both dead. The only witness is Nick, who admits to killing the man that called himself Napoleon Pickle, the middle earth king and Avery Gaines, the reporter from New York. I will find out who he is soon enough. Right now, my concern is letting Jim and Karen know their daughter is..." He paused. "Nate is getting your horse and will be here momentarily. I thought you might want to go with me."

William nodded. "Where is Hannie Bear?" William asked, using the nickname he had given her since her birth. His blue eyes clouded with rare tears and his lips twitched with emotion.

"She's by the river. Alan Garrison is bringing a wagon to take her to the mortuary. Uncle Solomon is at the Slater's Ball. I'm sure."

"I want to see her."

"You can see her in the privacy of the mortuary. Not now in front of all the people down there."

"And the guy who did it is dead?"

Matt nodded.

"Too bad. I'd like to kill him myself. If you'll excuse me for a minute," he said with a cracking voice and went into his room and closed the door.

"Why would someone kill Hannie, Uncle Matt?" Joshua asked. His bottom lip was trembling.

Matt was overwhelmed and shook his head before answering. "I don't know, Josh. When I get more answers, maybe I can answer that, but right now, I don't know."

"Nick Griffin killed that man?" Josh asked.

Matt leaned against the curved front desk. "That he did. Do you know Nick very well?"

"I know he doesn't have many friends. I'm not his friend."

Matt exhaled to calm the nerves that rattled inside of him. He loathed having to tell his cousin that her firstborn was murdered. "Nick was drinking on Cabbage Island with the two Fowler girls, Elizabeth Chalkalski, Paulina Sorensen, Bernie Townsend, Levi Jensen, Ollie Hoffman and Hannie. I think that's it."

"Those are my friends, Uncle Matt, not his. I don't know why they would be drinking on that island to begin with, especially with Ollie and Nick.

That makes no sense to me."

"Nick got into an argument with Elizabeth and left them," Matt explained. "Do me a favor and talk to your friends and if anything interesting comes up, let me know. They might tell you more than they'll tell me. It may not make sense, Josh, but I can also guarantee you that Hannie's death will never make sense for the rest of your life, even if we find the reason why. And that is infuriating."

After a few minutes, William came out of his room carrying a bottle of whiskey. His eyes were red and watery. He took a deep breath and exhaled. "Let's go tell my sister."

Chapter 13

Matt, William, and Nate rode their horses up to the Slater mansion, tethered them out front and climbed the three flights of stairs to the grand ballroom. It was a large open room, square in shape, not as big as Bella's Dance Hall's ballroom, but far grander. The mansion walls were elaborate Cherrywood paneling throughout the first and second floors, but the ballroom was bright with light oak flooring and bright white walls broken up by decorative inlaid arches painted pink that encircled the room. The double doors entering the ballroom and the double doors leading to the third-story balcony had decorative pink drapes to match the room's design. Large crystal chandeliers lit up the large room wonderfully. On one end, a stage was set back into the wall with large pink drapes hung like banners for the orchestra to play comfortably without interfering with the dancers. A full bar at the other end provided drinks and a table was catered to provide enough food for the guests. The ballroom's design, colors, and flow created a magnificent ambiance that lifted one's spirits upon entering. The double-opened doors to the large balcony allowed a nice breeze to blow into the open room and cool the bodies of those dancing.

The dress code for the ball was a black suit and bowtie for the gentlemen and the women were always elegant. The orchestra played expertly, and the music was superb. At first entrance, Matt was surprised by the size and beauty of the ballroom. He didn't expect it to be such an elegant and sizable room. Under different circumstances, he would have been impressed. Matt regretted not taking advantage of the past balls he had been invited to; Christine would love the Slater's ballroom.

The three men stood at the entrance in their casual clothes with their gun belts on. Nate had taken Angela back to the dance hall when he retrieved the horses. It was a sour ending to their evening, but there was very little he could do about that. He had already been asked to leave once, and he knew Josh Slater and Travis McKnight would comment on his returning uninvited when he saw the arrogance on Josh's smirking lips.

Josh met them at the door. "Is there a law against kicking out an uninvited deputy marshal, Matt? Nate wasn't invited, nor was he wearing a black suit. I hope that's not why you're here," Josh said with a cocky grin.

"I couldn't care less about your ball," Matt replied dryly. He spoke to Nate, "Go find Tim Wright. William and I will lead Jim and Karen downstairs to notify them. Let's not make a scene and ruin the ball for everyone else."

William crossed the dancefloor and interrupted the dance between his sister Karen and her husband, Jim Longo. He asked them to follow him. Taking notice of something being wrong, William's other sister, Olivia, grabbed her husband, Ron Dalton's hand, interrupting his conversation with Wally Gettman at a table, and led him towards the stairs. Observant of William's expression and his cousins leaving the ballroom, Albert Bannister tapped Lee's arm and the two brothers left their table to follow as well.

Matt had been standing alone and was quickly approached by Debra Slater, who looked stunning in her dress. She'd had a few drinks and her artificial smile did not contain her disappointment in Matt. "So, you made it. You know it was supposed to be a black bowtie and suit. I suppose you didn't read your invitation before giving it to Nate. I don't believe he read it either because he came in a red shirt with no jacket."

Matt was in no mood for idle chitchat. "I'm not here for your ball. So, if you'll excuse me, I have work to do."

"I invited you here to dance with me," she persisted. "When are you going to realize that I have my eyes on you and you're not going to get away from me?" Debra asked boldly.

"I'm engaged, Debra. And that is not going to change. Now, if you'll excuse me," he said in a rougher tone. His eyes revealed his irritation as he looked at her.

Debra scowled. "Don't look at me like I'm one of your criminals. I'm your friend and the best friend you'll ever have. I can do more for you on any given day than that dancer can. The only thing she can do for you is cook and clean because she will not be beautiful forever. I heard she can't even have children anymore. She'll just become a burden to you, Matt. She'll always want more than you can provide."

Matt's attention was on William as he led his sister Karen and Jim towards the door. "Take them downstairs. Karen, Jim, Olivia, Ron," he greeted them as they walked past him. Albert and Lee approached quickly.

"What's going on, Matt?" Albert asked with concern. He was dressed in a rare black suit, white shirt and black bowtie around his thick neck. Lee was dressed the same.

Matt rolled his head back towards the stairs. "Come with me." He left Debra standing in the entrance and led his brothers down the stairs to the first floor, where William had just told Karen and Jim about Hannie. William wanted to tell them outside for more privacy, but Jim Longo demanded to know what was wrong then and there. Karen's mournful cry echoed up from the bottom foyer. Olivia and Ron tried to comfort the two grieving parents as Matt and his brothers reached the bottom floor. Matt had already notified them on the stairs.

Karen collapsed in grief as her wails continued to echo in the mansion. Jim Longo and Ron helped her stand and began to walk her slowly towards the main door to exit the mansion and go home.

"Where is he? Where is Matt?" they heard the angry voice of Sheriff Tim Wright from the third floor. Tim came down the stairs in a hurry and pointed at Matt accusingly. He yelled loudly to be heard by everyone, "I told you that man was crazy and dangerous! Now that little girl is dead and it's your fault! He would have been in jail if it wasn't for you. Bob was arresting him for the weekend, but you had to interfere. You let that crazy man go free, knowing good and well that he was a crazy vagabond. Now their daughter is dead and that's on you! I told you he was dangerous. And don't say I didn't. I warned you this could happen!"

"Not now, Tim!" Matt shouted viciously at the sheriff. His eyes burned with fury as he took a single step toward the sheriff.

Tim raised a hand submissively and retreated quickly back upstairs. "It's his fault!" he exclaimed under his breath to Debra as he passed by her. She had followed downstairs.

"Who hurt my daughter?" Jim Longo asked emotionally with a quivering voice. "Who is he talking about, Matt? Tell me who did it!" he shouted.

Ron Dalton urged his brother-in-law towards

the mansion's front door. "Jim, we have time for that in a bit. Right now, let's get you and Karen home." Ron questioned Matt, "We need answers. Are you coming?"

"I'll be there shortly."

William stopped at the door and watched his mourning sister and brother-in-law walk down the mansion stairs towards Ron's carriage. He turned back towards Matt with watering, bloodshot eyes that were reddened and appeared an inch thick. "Did you know that man was dangerous?"

Matt sighed. "I don't know that he was. I got two stories, one of a crazy man living in a fantasy and one in private of a perfectly sane reporter playing a part for an article. I believe he was a reporter playing the part of an insane man. But that doesn't mean he didn't attack Hannie."

William's fury came through his voice, "What does that mean? Did he kill her or not?"

"I don't know, William."

"You didn't arrest the boy. So, you must believe the stranger did it, right?" William demanded to know.

Matt lowered his head, not knowing what to say.

"Right?" William demanded.

"I'm not sure, William. He may have, but I don't know yet."

"Did you let that man go free, as Tim said?"

"I did."

William's shoulders sank like the life went out of him. He rotated his head slowly. "Tim was right. It is your fault."

Matt ran his hand over his hair in frustration. "William, you can't arrest someone for no reason."

William stepped towards Matt with a fierce shout, "If he was in jail, Hannie would still be alive! You and your damn righteousness. I'm going to Karen's. You should stay away from me for a while."

"William..." Matt called.

William's eyes were vicious as he pointed at Matt. "Stay away from me! Don't come near me again."

"William," Solomon Fasana called as he came down the stairs in a hurry, "I just heard about Hannie. I am so sorry. She was such a beautiful girl. I hoped to catch Karen and Jim. Please give them my condolences and ask them to come by the mortuary tomorrow afternoon."

William slowly grimaced. "Uncle Solomon...I hope you get a good look at Hannie because it will be the longest amount of time you've ever been involved in her life. Don't pretend to mourn for her, Uncle Solomon; you have no idea who she is. I don't even know if we should call you uncle anymore. You sure as hell have no part of our family. Does he, Matt?" He walked quickly out the front door.

Solomon turned to Matt with a hurt expression. "Allow me to take Delores home and I'll hurry to meet your deputy at the mortuary." He went back upstairs, passing Debra Slater on the way. Debra stood six stairs up, watching Matt compassionately.

Matt stood alone in the foyer, feeling more alone

than he appeared. His brothers had gone up to get their wives and a heavy layer of guilt was forming in his chest as he wondered if doing what seemed right had led to Hannie's death.

Debra spoke compassionately, "Matt, I'm sorry. I didn't realize why you were here. Please, give Karen and Jim my love. If there is anything I can do, please, let me know. I want to help."

***

Delores Fasana held a glass of wine in her hand as she laughed. She was outside on the ballroom deck talking to Josh Slater, Travis McKnight and Tim Wright. Tim had just returned and told them what he had said to Matt. Travis had made a joke.

"I don't know why you're laughing. That little girl is related to you," Travis chuckled.

"She's not related to me, dear boy, my husband," Delores said.

"Shhh!" Travis hushed her with an urgent finger to his mouth. "We don't talk about husbands and wives out here." He peeked around her shoulder to cast a view inside the ballroom. "My wife might hear and come out here and we don't want that!"

"Eek, no, we don't! I don't want my husband coming out here either," Delores said. "I already know what he'll say, 'Delores, is that your fifth or sixth stiff drink?' and I'll say, 'I'm just trying to save on the future cost of embalming fluid, dear.'" She bent over, laughing at her own joke while resting her hand on Travis's chest. She kept it there. "I'll be as good as pickled by the time this night's over!"

"Delores, you're a kick in the pants. I sure do like your fine company," Travis said with a grin.

"Well, don't say I don't drink too much; I'm just having too much to drink!" she laughed.

Solomon Fasana stepped out onto the deck and approached his wife. "Delores, we need to go."

"Huh?" she asked with a sour expression. "I'm having fun."

Solomon was in poor spirits. "Yes. You certainly are, I can see that and hear you over the music, but we must leave. My niece was murdered, and I must go open the mortuary."

"That's Matt's fault," Tim offered. "I wanted that man locked up from the moment I first saw him."

Solomon shrugged. "That's something I don't know anything about. Come along, Sweetheart. Say goodnight."

She leaned against the rail between Travis and Josh and crossed her arms. "Goodnight, Sweetheart. One of these fine gentlemen will give me a ride home when the ball is finished."

Solomon narrowed his eyes. "Delores, it's my niece."

She stretched out her arms and widened her eyes, unconcerned. "I don't know her! Why should I stop my fun on account of your family? They're riff-raff. Every one of them, except Lee and Albert, of course."

Josh Slater spoke sincerely, "I didn't know that little girl, but that is heartbreaking for Jim. He works for us at the mine."

"Good!" Delores exclaimed. "Maybe he has the money to pay for the funeral bill. Charge them extra, Solomon, because the cost of building the new furniture store and mortuary is outlandish! I thought the Chinese laborers were cheap, but no! Leave it to Solomon to go cheap and end up paying twice what we would've if we hired the most expensive builders."

"I'm not charging my family extra. Let's go, Delores," Solomon said with more authority. He was already troubled by what William had said to him but hearing how his wife talked about his family struck a nerve that made him realize William was right. He did not spend time with his side of the family. He used to be part of the family when he was younger, but it all stopped after marrying Delores.

Delores locked her arm around Travis's. "You go home, Solomon. I'm having fun. These handsome young men will drive me home later. Just go, Solomon. We don't really want our husbands or wives out with us anyway, do we?" she asked Travis.

"No, Ma'am," Travis agreed.

"I know," Delores said. She walked to the double doors and yelled, "Rhonda! Hey, Rhonda!"

"Don't! What are you doing?" Travis questioned. "She's calling for my wife," he complained to Tim.

Rhonda McKnight was a lady in her mid-thirties, with wavy dark brown hair that fell to her shoulders and wore the same silver dress she wore to the last ball. It had already been a conversation among the social group that Delores mingled in.

"Oh, I didn't realize you all were out here," Rhonda said. "I've just been sitting at our table waiting." Her discontent with being abandoned by her husband was noticeable in her expression.

Delores answered her comment, "And you're sitting there very good like the well-trained dog you are."

"Excuse me?" Rhonda asked bitterly.

Solomon heard enough. "Delores! You've had too much to drink and you're being rude. It's time to go home."

"Hush it, Solomon! I don't want to go home because I'm having fun. Travis is having fun and Rhonda is bored to death. You can see it right on her prissy face; she looks as dead as your niece. We all know she doesn't like being here, so take her home. Not our home, but her home and I'll be home later."

Rhonda was furious. "I'm not listening to this pig stuffed in a dress any longer. Travis, I'm going home."

"I'll gladly take you," Solomon said with a harsh glare at his wife. He stopped and turned back to Delores. "Sometimes, I despise you."

She laughed. "You'll get over it. You always do." She turned to the three younger men. "Do I look like a pig stuffed in a dress? Travis, your wife, is riff-raff like my husband's relatives. I married him before I ever met them. How can you stand your wife anyway?" Delores questioned, ignoring her husband completely.

Solomon and Rhonda both walked away.

Travis leaned into the door to peek out. "I can't stand her! But I'm married."

Delores laughed. "So am I, but who cares? Solomon is as boring as a mile-long slug race."

"Ah! Well, he and Rhonda should have a good time then. She's as exciting as a two-mile snail race."

"Shall we get this party started? I imagine you'll be taking me home, Mister McKnight?"

"Of course."

Chapter 14

David Chatfield laid on his thin mattress pad, too troubled to sleep. He was in shock, afraid and too stunned to say a word. He had seen people with abnormal birth defects that horrified spectators to the point of screaming and running away in tears. But he had never seen anything more horrific than a young man with no birth defects murder another human being. How a man can be so angry in life while having everything to be grateful for from all appearances made no sense to David. The young man he witnessed was brutal and callously evil.

David left the circus after eleven and went to the river to meet with Avery but found the place where he camped empty. His bedding and bag were there, but Avery was not. David didn't mind waiting while letting his feet soak in the river. Solitude could be hard to find in the circus world where so many lived and traveled together. He savored the time alone and the quiet while listening to the distant band play in the park. A reasonable sum of his fellow circus friends went to the dance or the saloons for the night. It was a night to celebrate, and circus people were no different than anyone else; they enjoyed celebrating too. Unfortunately, the sideshow individuals who were not so publicly welcomed.

David was lucky enough not to be dragged to the Slater mansion as a sideshow attraction to a private party like Susie was. David was being saved for tomorrow's sideshow attraction. Most people in the world had never seen a real werewolf and he was the real-life Tasmanian Wolf Boy! They would have to start calling him the Tasmanian Wolf Man at some point because he was sixteen now, not that anyone could see his age behind the hair that covered his face.

The sound of female laughter piqued his interest and David moved through the dark woods to spy on a group of teenagers sitting around a fire on a small island a short way from town. They were drinking alcohol, laughing and having what sounded like fun.

To sit hidden within the dark trees and brush alone while watching kids his age enjoying each other's friendship was about as close as David would ever be to joining them. He could not walk out and introduce himself and hope they would allow him to join in their fun. The girls would scream at first sight of him and run away while the boys either told him to get lost or beat him up for merely being different. He had experienced both reactions in the past and one reaction didn't necessarily hurt worse than the other. One just hurt a lot longer.

Names, he amused himself by listening to the conversations and trying to memorize the teenagers' names. The more he listened, the more he yearned to be a part of the group or have a group of friends of his own. To sit in the open and share a time of youth and laughter while flirting with romance and the opposite sex was one thing David never had the opportunity to do. Of all the things he may have desired, the one constant was the desire that all sixteen-year-old boys have, a beautiful girl to call his own.

He was most attracted to Elizabeth of all the girls he watched around the fire. He could fantasize about meeting her and her falling in love with him, but the truth was she was just a pretty face, and he would never meet her. He would move on with the circus and would never see her again. Romance and love, even though both were as natural as any human desire, they were two things that circus freaks like him discovered were not easily attained. David had hoped the article written by Avery Gaines would show him as a person with a good heart and more human than a monster. He hoped Elizabeth and many other pretty girls like her would read the article and perhaps say hello to him rather than offering looks of horror, disgust and walking away afraid. Elizabeth's fiancé was a lucky man. That was all David knew.

He watched the argument develop between Nick and Elizabeth. Nick stopped and looked right at

David as he stormed off the island, but David's dark hair and black clothing made him hard to see in the forest's dark shadows. Nick called for his friend Ollie and stormed off on his own when Ollie chose to stay with the romance of a female over his friend.

David's heart sank when Elizabeth and the others decided to leave the island. He did not know them, but David felt a kinship with them. A desire to be their friend and the longing to have such friends. He watched them leave and was going to go back to see if Avery had returned, but he noticed they had forgotten a small pillow. It wasn't just any pillow; it was the pillow that Elizabeth had pressed against her mouth to mimic her fiancé. If she was going to leave it behind, David figured he would take it for his bed. It was the closest he would ever get to touching Elizabeth's lips with his own.

He waited until they left, and David slipped to the forest's edge where the moonlight touched the ground with a gentle kiss and then he froze. He could hear the running steps of one of the other girls as she approached and ran across the shallow water to get the pillow. As she turned back towards the woods, her eyes connected with his. The girl whose name he never did hear screamed in terror. The girl with the prettiest blonde curls ran like she had seen a real-life monster. If only she had taken a moment to say hello, she might have realized he was not a monster but a caring young man with a heart and soul just as gentle as her own. He would never want to hurt her or anyone else, but he would almost do anything to make a new friend. Not surprisingly, she screamed and ran.

Disheartened, David turned and began walking back towards Avery's camp. He could not stay put for long as her friends might return to search for a so-called monster. He didn't walk too far when he heard the same girl screaming. It wasn't the same startled scream she had done with him; it was a scream of awful intent and terror, absolute terror and not fright.

David could not believe what he was witnessing. Nick sat on the young girl's chest and strangled her. Her hands clawed for her survival, but slowly her hands faded to the ground. Too shocked and afraid to move or make a sound, David watched as Nick struggled to pick up the girl and drag her onto the bridge and toss her over the edge.

The voice of Avery Gaines quickly approaching was like a cavalry call to a poor helpless family surrounded by Indians. It was a comfort to hear in the frightening situation. The following five minutes were absolute horror as Avery tried to save a lady heroically and was stabbed like a meaningless melon repeatedly until there was no life left in his new friend. It was a sight David could not get out of his mind as it played constantly. Even in the safety of his bed surrounded by family and friends, he could not escape the horror of what he had seen nor the fear that Nick had seen him in the moonlight. David knew the only reason Nick did not chase after him was because of the men approaching the bridge.

David wasn't hard to recognize and if Nick came

to the sideshow, he was bound to realize it was David in the woods and a threat to his freedom. A small bruise and knot were on David's forehead from running into a tree limb when he glanced back to see if Nick was chasing him. A moment later, he heard Nick call out to the men. What he had told them, David didn't know. He had run.

Fearing Avery's camp would be discovered by Nick and his journal found, David realized if Avery had written about meeting him and their scheduled late-night interview, Nick would know who witnessed the murders and where to find him. It may have been an unreasonable fear, but it was a fear just the same and David wasn't going to take any chances of his life being snuffed out early. He grabbed Avery's large bag and opened it. It was full of leather scraps and very little else. There was no wonder why Avery didn't fear it being stolen; it was a large ugly bag full of garbage. A thin board was under the leather strips and scraps, and pulling the board up was a hidden compartment where the journal and pens were held. It would not have been noticed to anyone casually searching the bag, but knowing it was under the board already, David found it quickly enough. He didn't take the whole bag, but he took the leather-bound journal, a fine pen, and the writing board and carried them home to the circus.

David had not spoken a word since climbing into bed. He was afraid, in shock and feeling a great deal of guilt for not helping the girl and not helping his friend. His emotions were like trying to catch fleas;

they were jumping everywhere. Shock, disbelief, shame, guilt, fear, doubt, surprise, shame, and guilt returned to take a broader base and began settling in as he should have done something to save them both. He was a coward, a yellow-spined dog-faced coward.

He prayed in a barely audible whisper, "Jesus, I should have tried to save them. He killed that girl and Avery, and I could have tried to save them. Please forgive me." His eyes closed tightly, and he clenched his pillow slip in his fist. His shoulders quivered as he wept silently. "Lord, please, forgive me. I was there and I could have tried..."

Chapter 15

Nick Griffin had explained his story to the men who had first come by the river. Then, he explained again and again to various people to practice his facial expressions and eye contact to convince the one person he had to convince, the Marshal, Matt Bannister. He knew Hannie was related to Matt and that would involve him more than it would the sheriff. A false story had to be foolproof and the scratches on his cheeks, neck and arms were not going to be unnoticed. And they certainly were not. Matt had taken great interest in the scratches and looked at Nick suspiciously. Nick had walked away, not so sure he had convinced the marshal of the vagabond's guilt. It concerned him. He could not think of a way to reasonably explain the scratches beyond the vagabond doing it while they fought. Most men did not fight by scratching like a girl desperately trying to save her life with her fingernails. The thought had plagued Nick since he had been home. Luckily, Nick had tonight to remain free, but he knew Matt would be more aggressively investigating tomorrow. The fact that he pulled a knife on Levi Jensen was going to come up and it wasn't going to help prove his innocence. Nick needed a way to verify, unequivocally, that the vagabond gave him the scratches to get away with his crimes.

Nick could not sleep knowing his freedom; his life depended on the story he told the marshal. Little by little, he picked his story apart in his mind and the questions he asked himself were getting harder to answer. Nick had done his best to spin the story, but it wasn't enough. An idea came to mind that would prove without a doubt that his story was true, but he couldn't do it alone. He didn't have much time to think it over; it was already after 3:30 a.m. Nick needed to move quickly.

His apartment was dark, and his father snored loudly in his room. Leonard Griffin had come stumbling through the door around one-thirty and said a few sentences that didn't make much sense. He stumbled into his room, fell onto his bed, and passed out with his boots and hat still on.

Nick slipped on his boots, grabbed his father's leather work gloves, and stepped out the back door to walk around the apartments to Ollie's apartment. The rear doors of the Dogwood Shacks didn't have a door lock; instead, they had a piece of wood on a nail that could be twisted in front of the door to stop it from opening. Nick had been locked out of his apartment by his father enough times to know he could wedge his penknife blade between the door jamb and slide it upwards to twist the piece of wood out of the way and enter. He entered Ollie's apartment the same way and woke Ollie with a soft shake and a low voice, "Ollie. Hey, buddy, wake up. I need your help."

"Hmm?" Ollie grunted as he awoke from a deep sleep. The alcohol had put him to sleep immediately upon laying on his bed. "What?"

"Shh, be quiet, Ollie. Don't wake up your mother. I need your help. Hurry and get dressed."

"No, I'm tired." Ollie turned his back to Nick as he shifted to go back to sleep.

"Ollie, get up. You're my friend and I need your help. Come on, buddy, you owe me. Remember, I took that man's necklace for you? Come on, buddy, you owe me, and I need your help right now." He had given Ollie the arrowhead necklace that the leather man had worn.

Ollie sat up on the edge of his bed and rubbed his face tiredly. He wore the necklace proudly around his neck. "It's still dark out."

"Shhh, come on." An idea occurred to Nick. He whispered, "The girls snuck out and Rose and Linda are waiting for us outside. Rose wants to see you. She is hooked on you, bud."

Ollie's head rose. "Really?"

"Oh, yeah. Rose said something about kissing under the moonlight. Hurry up, let's go."

It only took a moment for Ollie to dress and his attitude changed from exhaustion to excitement. They went out through the back door and walked across town under the pretense of meeting the girls.

At the newly constructed two-story brick building of the Fasana Furniture & Undertaker's Parlor, Nick put on his father's leather gloves and went to the back door with small square paned windows. He broke out a pane with a fist and reached in and unlocked the door.

"What are you doing?" Ollie asked, confused. He was expecting to meet his new sweetheart up on King's Point.

Nick grinned in the moonlight as he opened the door. "Come inside."

"I don't want to go in. Let's go meet the girls."

"Get in here before someone sees us," Nick urged. He closed the door after Ollie came inside. "Ollie, I need your help. I can't do this alone."

"What?"

"Well, we're going to steal a table, but before we do, I need to find the man that killed Hannie." He pulled a box of matches and a candle out of his front pocket. He lit the candle.

"Why?" Ollie was horrified by the thought.

"Because he scratched me up. The marshal will think Hannie did it if I can't find a way to prove the leather man did. Ollie, I'll be hung or sent to prison for the rest of my life if I can't prove I'm telling the truth. Look at me. I'm all scratched up. I pulled a knife on Levi, remember?"

"I don't know…" Ollie was hesitant.

Nick continued pointedly, "Ollie, I didn't kill Hannie, but I didn't scratch up the leather man and nor did Hannie when he strangled her. I'm the only one scratched up and it makes me look guilty. Hannie is related to Matt Bannister, and I could see it in his eyes, he is suspicious of the scratches. I need your help, Ollie. My life depends upon it and you're my friend and the only person I trust. So please, help me."

"Help you do what?"

Nick slowly grinned. "You'll see."

They found the stairway down into the basement and discovered a large room with various items and tables holding three bodies on them. Two bodies were covered with sheets, but the third was an old lady in a dress with her hands professionally placed on her abdomen. A lovely brooch necklace was set on her breast and her diamond wedding ring was on her finger. Her face and hair were done neatly and if the boys were not in the mortuary's basement, they might think she was sleeping peacefully and could wake up at any time. A wooden casket set on a cart with wheels was placed next to the table she was on. Neither of the boys recognized the lady.

Nick pulled a sheet back and exposed the face of Hannie Longo. He pulled the sheet back over her face without comment and moved to the following table and pulled the sheet back to reveal the face of the strange man that he had killed. He looked at Ollie, who had not walked too far into the room. "Over here is where I need your help."

Ollie was horrified. A strange, unpleasant scent added to the knowledge that he was in a cold and dark room filled with death. He was surrounded by dead bodies and the fear of being caught in such a forbidden realm of the macabre paralyzed him. His imagination was getting the better of him and he was afraid of Hannie sitting up and talking to him or the murderer coming off the table to kill them. His heart quickened and his clammy hands brought a cold chill. He wanted to leave immediately. "We got to go," he said with a high-pitched voice. His emotions were beginning to weaken.

Nick shrugged his shoulders nonchalantly. "Buddy, it's fine. No one is here and we'll leave in a minute. Come over here." He looked at the strange man's unkempt face in the candle's light. At the river, the leather man's mouth was open, but now it was closed. He tried to open the man's mouth using the leather gloves and found it more difficult to open than he thought it would be. Unlike the living, pressing on the sides of the jaw did nothing to open the mouth. He had to use both hands and strain to pry the mouth open. He looked at Ollie, who remained by the door.

Nick chuckled at his friend. "They're dead. They aren't going to jump up and bite you on their own, but I need your help for the leather man to bite me. I need you to force his jaw shut really hard. That means you're going to have to pull on his jaw."

"I'm not touching him!" The horror turning to an unspoken panic showed in Ollie's nerve-struck expression.

"I'm the one being bit. Here wear my Pa's gloves." He removed them and tossed them to Ollie. "My life depends on your help, Ollie. Do you want me to go to prison for the rest of my life if I'm that lucky? I could be hung like those Chinese men, but I didn't do anything except try to save her!" He pointed at Hannie's sheet-covered body. "Just toughen up and come help me. The sooner we finish, the sooner we can leave. In a few days, life will be normal again and you can forget all about this and have all the time you want with Rose. Just think of her and let's get this done. Trust me; I'm the one that is going to feel the pain. Not you."

Nick put his left forearm in the man's mouth while Ollie stood at the top of the leather man's head and cupped his jaw with both hands. On the count of three, Ollie leaned his weight backward and pulled the jaw towards him with all the might he could until Nick could no longer stand the pain of the man's teeth cutting into his skin. Ollie releasing the force of his pulling, did not release the bite's pressure as it remained like a vise.

"Get it off my arm! Open his mouth, Ollie!" Nick exclaimed when the pain was more than he could bear. "Hurry up!"

Ollie strained with all he had to push the jaw open just enough to release Nick's arm. The teeth had penetrated the skin and drops of blood slowly flowed. Nick grinned when he saw the teeth marks. "Oh yeah, that will work."

"Can we go now?" Ollie asked anxiously.

"Not yet. One more." Nick put the flesh between his right thumb and index finger into the man's mouth. He took a deep breath and exhaled. "One last time. Make it good."

Again, Ollie grabbed the chin, leaned back, pulled until Nick could not stand the pain, and cried out for Ollie to stop and then forced the mouth open. Happy with the results, which would undoubtedly remain for a day or two, Nick pushed the leather man's mouth closed as it was and covered him with the sheet. Upstairs to the furniture store, Nick removed a lamp and set it in the middle of the aisle to verify it would be noticed. He grabbed the small bedside table it had set on and handed it to Ollie as they left out the back door. Nick reached back in through the broken windowpane to lock the door.

"I got you a table for your help. Thank you, Ollie."

Ollie shook his head, disturbed by what they had done. "Where am I supposed to tell my mother I got it from when she hears someone broke into the furniture store and stole a table? That's a nice table. We can't afford it. She'd whip my hide."

"I don't know. I can't keep it. I'm sure Matt Bannister will be coming to my house tomorrow and I can't have him seeing it."

"Leave it here then," Ollie snapped.

"We can't leave it here. The whole idea of taking it is, so they'll think someone broke in to steal it." Nick paused. "I know, we'll leave it outside the Lucky Man's Bunkhouse and they'll think some drunk did it."

"Fine."

"Ollie, we can't tell anyone about this ever. Okay? My life depends on it, right?"

Ollie nodded.

"Now, I owe you, my friend. The next man that treats your mother wrong, I'll take care of him for you. You have my word. Let's just get this table to the Lucky Man's Bunkhouse and get home before the sun rises."

Chapter 16

Matt sat at the table in the marshal's office, drinking a cup of coffee. He was tired as it had been a long and emotional night. He had gone to his cousin Karen's home but was not warmly received. He went to offer his condolences and offer what information he could, but answering questions turned into angry accusations as William's anger at Matt had spread like an infectious disease to the rest of the family. Answers were not sought; blame and accusations were. In the act of decency, Matt refused to have the crazy man dressed in leather arrested for vagrancy over the holiday weekend. It seemed the right thing to do, but if he were the one that murdered Hannie, it would be a hard burden to carry.

The facts were unclear. It was certainly possible that the Leather Man, as the public was calling him, had killed her. Matt did not know a thing about him. Still, the marks on the boy were consistent with the defensive wounds of a girl being attacked. It made him suspicious, and his gut told him something wasn't adding up. Matt trusted his instincts and he could not say the leather man had committed the crime. The fact that he was naked and soaking wet and Hannie was soaking wet as well, yet, the boy was bone dry, made no sense. The initial observation put the leather man and Hannie together, which matched the story given by the boy who intervened just a bit too late. There were questions Matt needed to be answered and Doctor Ryland was doing the autopsy on Hannie that morning, but Matt chose not to be there while he did it. A man could separate himself from most victims, but he could not separate himself from family.

Matt did not know Hannie all that well, but he had gotten to know her over the past year and a half that he had been home. She had an adorable cuteness, and beyond the shyness, she was a goofy girl that could bring a smile on a cloudy day. Matt regretted not getting to know her better, but he had known her well enough to move beyond the shy stage. He smiled just a touch as he thought of her. A wave of moisture filled his eyes like an ocean wave rolling over the beach and then fading away as the remains evaporated into the sand.

The office door opened, ringing the cowbell, and Reverend Eli Painter and his wife, Beatrice, walked into the office. "Matt, I want you to know we are praying for you and the Longo family. We have the congregation making meals for them for the next week or two. Is there anything we can do for you or any other family members?" Beatrice asked.

Matt shook his head slowly to answer. "Just prayer and what you're doing." He remained seated at the table.

Phillip Forrester left his desk to go into the jail and bring out their son, John Painter.

Eli asked, "Do you want to come by this evening or tomorrow just to talk? You must get heavily burdened with all the wickedness and evil you deal with as often as you do. I just want to remind you that I'm always available to talk with."

Matt offered a small half-hearted smile. "Thank you. One of these days, I'll take you up on that." He wasn't in the mood for conversation. He was waiting, somewhat impatiently, for 10:00 a.m. to come around to meet the doctor at the mortuary. Once he had more information, he could talk to Nick Griffin and the others with more of an idea of what happened.

John Painter walked out of the jail cell and hugged his parents with a large grin. John's transformation was like night and day. He had been working at the granite quarry and doing his part to keep his deal with Matt to keep him out of prison. He had recommitted his life to Jesus and his appearance had changed significantly. His long and ratty hair was now cut short and combed over respectfully. His beard was shaved off and he had gained weight and muscle tone. In new clothes, he was utterly unrecognizable than just a month before. And to his mother's relief, his teeth were clean, and his smile no longer disgusted her. Her face beamed with pride to see the change in her son since the Lord's return to his life. John was a new man with a future blooming ahead of him.

John turned to Matt appreciatively. "Thank you, Matt, for letting me enjoy the day with my parents."

Matt nodded. "You're welcome. John, there will be a lot of alcohol out and about today. I don't need to tell you that if you disappear to get a drink, I will find you and our deal is off. Don't mistake my favor for weakness. Have fun but be here promptly after the fireworks. You'll wake up in the city jail and face trial if we have to find you." His countenance was subdued yet severe.

John was surprised by the tone in Matt's voice. He had not heard that tone since Matt confronted him in the city jail a month before. "I know. Trust me, Matt, I have no desire to wrong you, my parents or the Lord. I'll be here and very grateful for the opportunity you're giving me."

When the Painter family left, Matt spoke, "Nate, go walk along the river west of town and see if you can find Napoleon's camp. Look for a large leather bag and bring it back here if you find it. Bring everything you find back." He wanted to read the man's leather-bound journal and learn what he could about the stranger. Was he a journalist playing a part of a crazy man or a crazy man telling him a story to stay out of jail? He hoped the journal would answer that question.

***

Matt entered the Fasana Furniture & Mortuary feeling an uneasiness that he was not accustomed to feeling. He went downstairs and looked at his young cousin on the table sadly. A clean sheet covered her with only her face exposed. Doctor Ryland had a scalpel in his hand and was doing an autopsy on the leather man's body.

"Matt, let me cover her face," Doctor Ryland said. He washed his bloody hands in a large bowl of water.

"I can do it," Matt said dryly and pulled the sheet over her face. "What did you learn? Was she molested?"

"No. She was not," Doctor Ryland answered promptly. He leaned against the counter while he dried his hands. "Hannie has a scratch caused by a fingernail on her sternum. Most likely caused by her dress being ripped. There is also a jagged cut on the crown of her head from being hit by some blunt force, but that's not what killed her. Her cause of death is not drowning either, but strangulation. The bruising on her throat indicates it was done with a pair of hands. Those are the only marks I noticed on her. I did not do a full autopsy, so I don't know her stomach's contents. According to what you told me, her friends said she had a drink or two. I have no reason not to believe them; there is no smell of any elevated alcohol in her system. I cleaned under her fingernails and found an abundance of skin particles."

"So she did scratch up her attacker?" Matt asked while lifting his head with interest. It would prove Nick was the one that attacked her.

"Not exactly. Hannie has severe eczema on the inside of her elbows and knees that has been scratched to the point of bleeding. I can see that she has been scratching at her eczema a lot. I can't say any of it comes from another person because as much she has been scratching herself, the skin under her nails very well could be her own."

"What about him?" he pointed at the leather man.

"He was stabbed near his kidney, a right-handed thrust by a knife approximately five inches deep. I don't know the order, but he was stabbed several times in the abdomen and the side of the neck just behind the artery. I could give you all of the medical terms and my written report will, but obviously, his cause of death was having his throat cut, to keep it simple. Other than the stab wounds, there is not a mark on him. There is no alcohol in his stomach and oddly enough, despite his long and filthy fingernails, his hands are not calloused, except for a small one on the edge of his right index finger and thumb. Most likely caused by holding a writing pen or pencil."

"Any skin under his fingernails?"

"Some. But again, wearing all that leather in the heat chaffed his skin in the upper thighs. He had quite a nasty heat rash in his nether region, which was scratched aggressively. Another heat rash is under his arms."

Matt chuckled sardonically. "In your evaluation, who scratched up Nick Griffin? He has scratches on his cheek, neck and upper wrists and hands. They look like defensive wounds to me. Nick says it was him when they fought. You'd be amazed how many people say it was a dog or cat that scratched them."

Doctor Ryland waved a hand towards the table. "Hannie had more skin under her nails. I would normally say it was consistent with scratching a male attacker. But again, having significant eczema scratched to the point of bleeding in four areas of her body, it could easily be her skin. With the heat and sweat, she scratched herself raw."

Matt closed his eyes and rubbed his forehead. "What you're saying is I can't prove it's his skin."

"In my experience, between the two people lying here, she would have enough skin material under her nails to say she was the one that scratched him. His nails were embedded with dirt. Almost like he was digging a tunnel with his fingernails, there was so much dirt."

"He told me he was a reporter for a newspaper and doing an article based upon how he was treated over this weekend dressed like he was and telling a story about living in the middle earth. Do you think he intentionally filled his nails with dirt to play that part?"

Doctor Mitchell Ryland shrugged his shoulders. "It would fit. What skin he had under his nails was probably from scratching himself. His nails are longer than Hannie's, so if he did cause the scratches on the person he was fighting with, the dirt was packed deeper into the nails and some of the skin may have been washed away by the river. This is just one of those times I can't say for sure because they both have skin irritations that have been itching."

"That's it?" Matt asked, more frustrated than not.

Doctor Ryland nodded. "Basically. She was strangled, probably because she was screaming in an attempted rape. I have no idea why she and he were in the water, but she didn't drown. I think she might've been dead before she went into the water. I compressed her stomach and lungs to see if any water came up, but not a drop. I think I can safely say her lungs and stomach are not full of water without opening her up."

Matt's brow narrowed and his head tilted as a thought occurred to him. "Napoleon or Avery, whatever his name was, his leather clothing would sink, would they not? How much do you think his clothes weighed?" Matt walked over to a table where the leather clothes were piled. He lifted the shirt, which happened to be on top. "If she was already in the water, he may have stripped to go and get her. Thank you, Doctor Ryland. I'm going to see Nick. Have you seen my Uncle Solomon?"

"Yeah, someone broke in last night. He's fixing a broken window on the back door."

*****

Solomon was irritated. "Yeah, someone broke the window and stole a seven-dollar nightstand. It was just a small one but made of cherry wood. Interestingly, the lamp on the bed stand was worth much more, but whoever did it set the lamp down in the aisle. It was worth three times as much. Whoever it was doesn't know the value of an imported French lamp."

Matt leaned against the wall while watching his uncle removing the glass from a broken pane on the back door. "I'm sorry to hear that. If we catch a thief, we'll look for a nice bedstand."

Solomon appeared tired and worn down. "I'm lucky they didn't go downstairs. Missus Garvin's wedding ring and brooch are in plain view. If those were taken, the Garvin family would be furious beyond measure. It scared me enough that I am putting locks on the basement door and elevator to make sure no one goes down there." He paused. "By the way, I want to apologize for my wife last night. She was very drunk."

Matt wasn't sure what he was referring to. "What about her?"

Solomon sighed. "She was just rude. We had a family emergency, and she wasn't willing to understand that. What William said to me last night kind of hit home. I haven't been around the family too much, have I? I haven't seen Mary and Charlie in a long time. We were close growing up, you know, Mary and I."

"Uncle Solomon, it's rather sad that we refer to your wife as well, *your wife* and not Aunt Delores. She's rude all the time and wants nothing to do with our family. We're all okay with that. None of us care to see her either. But it would be nice to have you around the family again. We have a funeral coming up. It would be good if you were part of the family and not the mortician."

"You don't like Delores much, do you?"

"What am I to like about her?" Matt shrugged. "She has no interest in anyone who isn't a socialite and wealthy. It's all fake nonsense. I have no desire to try to get to know her. As I said, no one says her name, Uncle Solomon. It's just Uncle Solomon's wife."

"I'm going to try to change that. I hope you and the family will give her a chance once we start showing up at family functions. I know I'm missing holidays with my sister and brothers."

"If you can get her to show up, that might be a good starting point."

Chapter 17

The Independence Day festivities were already taking place. Main Street was full of stores having sales, vendors with booths set up on the street, and various people selling anything from garden beets, sour dough starters, to puppies. The horse races, foot races and family games, and a large barbeque of a roasted steer or two were happening just east of town. Nick Griffin knew a parade would be starting soon and of course, there was the circus that many people, including Nick, were excited to see.

However, he knew Matt Bannister wanted to talk with him today and with the fresh bite marks that he painstakingly had done, he did not want to miss talking to Matt to clear any suspicion of the crime on his part. He stayed home even though Ollie and his mother knocked on the door to see if he wanted to join them in the day's festivities. Ollie was going to enter the fifty-yard dash foot race and wanted Nick to join him for the three-legged race. Nick would have loved spending the day with them, but he had a larger goal on his mind and Ollie knew it, so he didn't press the issue. Ollie's mother, however, did try to pressure Nick to join them and Nick hated to tell her no.

Now he waited at his apartment and hoped the marshal would come by soon. He didn't want to waste the day of celebrating staying at home. He wanted to show the bite marks while they were still fresh.

His father came out of his room dressed in the same clothes as the night before. "Why didn't you wake me up?" It was noon and he was irritated about missing the morning events.

"I figured you were sleeping," Nick replied.

"Well, no crap!" Leonard snapped at his son. "The horse races are happening this morning and you know I like to bet on those. You should have woken me up!" he went back into his room to change his clothes. "What time did you wake up?" he hollered from his room.

Nick knew if he said he awoke early, his father would just be angrier. "An hour ago. There is nothing to eat here, just so you know," he added.

Leonard stepped into his bedroom doorway and glared at Nick as he buttoned his shirt. "You work at a grocery store. Bring some food home if you want it. The way I see it, you're sixteen and a man. You quit school, so what responsibility do I have for you? If you want something, earn it. And it's time for you to find your own way in the world. I'll be expecting you to find your own place soon. My time as your father is done."

Nick nodded shortly. "Nice. That means I can move in with Ollie and his mother, huh?"

"Nick, I couldn't care less what you do," he answered simply and turned to go back into his room.

"Good," Nick said for something to say.

A knock on the door took Nick's attention off his father.

"If that's Jake, tell him I'll be right there," Leonard hollered from his room.

Nick opened the door; Matt Bannister stood at the door alone. "Marshal Bannister, come in," he said. He was relieved to see the marshal so he could free himself and enjoy most of the day.

"Nick," Matt greeted him. "I'm a little surprised to find you at home. I thought you might be out enjoying the festivities."

"No, sir. You said you were coming by today." He couldn't help but glance down at the Colt .45 on Matt's hip that had killed enough people to make the man famous.

"I appreciate that. Are your parents home?"

"I don't have any parents," Nick answered loud enough for his father to hear.

"Who is here?" Leonard asked as he came out of his room. He paused, surprised to see Matt standing in his apartment. "Marshal Bannister...I'm Nick's father, Leonard Griffin. Is my son in trouble? What did the dumbass do now?"

Nick responded with a callous glare, "You just said you're not my parent anymore. So, it's none of your business what I did. Go to the horse races or saloon or wherever you're going."

Matt raised a hand to quiet the hostility that was growing. "Let's get back to why I'm here. Mister Griffin, your son was involved in an altercation last night at the river…"

"What did you do? What are those scratches on you? Who did you hurt?" Leonard asked accusing-ly. He had not noticed the scratches until now.

"I didn't hurt anyone!" Nick exclaimed. The re-sentment of his father showed in his eyes.

"Obviously, something happened or the marshal wouldn't be here!" Leonard snapped impatiently.

"Excuse me," Matt spoke loudly to end the argu-ment. "Mister Griffin, if you want to listen in, then please have a seat. I need to question your son, and I'd appreciate you not antagonizing him. To answer your question, my cousin's young daughter was murdered last night, and Nick admitted to killing the man he claims killed her. Now please shut up and let me ask my questions."

"What?" Leonard asked quietly. He was shocked by Matt's words and looked at his son with genuine concern. "You didn't tell me about that?"

Nick glared at his father with a cold expression. "Why would I?"

"Because I'm your father," Leonard said lightly.

Nick gave a soft disgusted scoff. "That ended when Mother died. You've reminded me of that ever since."

Matt leaned against the wall and carefully watched Nick's eyes and body language. The more he watched the boy interact with his father, the more it became clear that he lacked control of his anger by the glare and clenched fist at his side near a sheathed knife.

Leonard sighed. "Do you think I don't have a reason to? You cursed her!"

"I didn't have a voodoo doll or a crystal ball, now, did I?"

Leonard glanced at Matt and waved a hand like shooing away a fly. "Talk to the marshal."

Matt spoke, "Doctor Ryland did an autopsy on Hannie this morning. Is there anything you would like to change about the story you told me last night?"

Nick's eyes widened just a bit. "No, I don't think so. I saw him on Hannie. I ran and dove on him to try to save her. We fought and I could tell he wanted to kill me, so I stabbed him. That's all I know. Unfortunately, I didn't get there soon enough to save her."

"How good of friends were you with her?" Matt asked.

He rotated his head. "Not very. She was friends with Rose Fowler. That's why she was there."

"Why was she going back to the island alone?"

He shrugged. "I don't know. I wasn't with them. I got into an argument with Elizabeth and a fight with Levi. I was drunk and stupid. I kicked the fire towards Elizabeth and Levi hit me for it. I pulled my knife on him, Marshal, but I put it away. That ruined the night and they wanted me to leave. I got mad and went into the woods to drink alone."

Matt had watched him talk carefully. "I will be honest. I am having trouble understanding why you have the scratches that are common defense wounds of a female trying to save herself from being strangled, but the man who apparently did strangle Hannie doesn't have a single scratch. Can you explain that?"

"No. What I can tell you is if you don't believe me, I have bite marks where he bit me as we fought. Look," he pulled up his sleeve to show a bite mark penetrating his left arm and right hand's skin. "They're his teeth marks. If you want, you can double-check that, but Hannie didn't bite me and I didn't bite myself. The man scratched and bit, Marshal. I told you, he was crazy."

Matt looked at the bite marks curiously. He had knocked on the door convinced Nick had committed the crime a moment before, but the bite marks, if they matched the leather man's teeth, would add some credence that they fought, but it did not vindicate Nick from murder.

Nick continued nervously, "I'm not a great fighter, but I don't bite and scratch. He did. I got my scratches from him."

"I want to have those bite marks examined by Doctor Ryland at the Mortuary. Would you mind coming with me?"

"I'm fine with that. I don't have anything to hide."

"He's there right now finishing up. Let's go. Mister Griffin, you're welcome to come along if you wish."

Leonard nodded. "Is my son a suspect?"

Matt answered honestly, "I'm investigating that very question."

***

Doctor Ryland carefully studied the bite marks on Nick's arm and verified that they were indeed from the leather man's teeth. Satisfied, Matt sent Nick and his father home. Nick stared at the wedding ring on the deceased lady's finger as he departed the mortuary.

Matt stayed in the preparation room with Doctor Ryland and his uncle Solomon. Matt was troubled. "Fellas, there was a burglary here last night. What are the chances he came in here to fake those bite marks? I ask because I spoke to Nick last night at the river, and he didn't say anything about being bit nor do I recall seeing a bite mark on his hand. It was dark, but I saw his scratches."

Doctor Ryland shook his head undoubtedly. "There is no way he could have done that. Depending on the time the burglary took place, the body would be entering rigor mortise and the jaw is one of the first joints to stiffen and difficult to open and close. To apply that much pressure to penetrate the skin would be...dare I say, impossible to do alone. Matt, I'm not a lawman, but as a medical doctor, if that man bit me that hard while we were fighting, I would stab him with a scalpel. As much as that had to hurt, anyone would draw a knife and stab him to end it."

Solomon offered, "I closed both of their mouths when I brought them down here last night. His mouth was still closed this morning. Did you notice how that young man stared at Missus Garvin's wedding ring when he left? If he was here last night, he would have taken it. I have no doubt."

Matt was perplexed. Every time he thought he had solid evidence to arrest Nick, there was a reasonable doubt that followed it. He had seen too many defensive wounds from women being attacked not to recognize Nick's injuries for what they were. It made no sense for someone to strangle her with bare hands and not have a single scratch, puncture, or defensive wound from a girl fighting for her life. The leather man had no such injury, but Nick had several on his lower arms, wrists, top of his hands and face. It was all the evidence Matt needed to arrest him, except there was no proof that his testimony was false. It was possible the leather man did scratch Nick; Matt had highly doubted it until now. The bite marks could not be disputed, and a man that bites may just as well scratch. The leather man's fingernails were undoubtedly long enough to do so.

"Matt, you look deep in thought. You should go enjoy the festivities with your lovely fiancée," Doctor Ryland said as he covered the leather man's face with the sheet. "I'm going home to do just that myself."

Matt spoke slowly, "I will shortly. I was almost convinced…no. I was convinced that Nick had killed Hannie. But now I'm not so sure. Those bite marks may just prove he's telling the truth. I didn't believe Avery Gaines was responsible, but that cut on Hannie's head you mentioned earlier, Doctor Ryland, if he used a rock to knock her out, he wouldn't have any scratches while he killed her…" He didn't finish his sentence because he did not want to admit that he let a killer roam free in his community, and Hannie paid the price. He'd be living with it for the rest of his life.

Solomon asked, "By Avery Gaines, you are referring to this John Doe? Is that his name?"

Matt was troubled. "I don't know. That is one name he gave me. But he also said his name was Napoleon Pickle, so I don't know. I need to go back to my office and see if Nate found his camp and brought his bag to the office. If he was telling the truth while being Avery Gaines, he should have a leather-bound journal that he was keeping notes in. If not, then bury him as John Doe."

"Well, I think we are done in here. I'm going to join my family and enjoy the festivities. Matt, go see your fiancée and have some fun," Doctor Ryland said.

Matt looked at a clock on the wall. "I'm meeting her and her friends at one."

Chapter 18

The Chatfield & Bowry Amazing Circus & Side-show was set up just west of the livery stable in a large expansive red and white striped tent. The game booths were off to the side in smaller tents set up in rows. A black curtain seven feet tall encircled the sideshow so no one could see what was inside without paying. A ticket booth at the entrance invited the public to enter the world of the bizarre and unbelievable acts of nature. The macabre drew folks like yellow jackets to a family picnic.

Matt had too much on his mind to want to go to the circus with Christine and her friends, Helen and her husband, Sam Troyer. However, Christine had been looking forward to enjoying the day's festivities with him all week. He had missed the entire morning but promised to meet her at one to enjoy the circus.

It was good to see Helen and Sam again. Helen's days of being a ballroom dancer were behind her and her life had taken a new exciting turn since her wedding. She had recently discovered she was pregnant. Helen no longer wore expensive dresses or worried too much about her hair. She wore a typical tan dress with a flower pattern and her dark hair fell casually onto her shoulders. She was a sawmill laborer's wife, but she was happily married and wouldn't change it for the carefree life she left in the dance hall.

Rose Blanchard and Sherry Stewart joined with fellow dancers Jenny, Loretta and Bonnie at the circus and sat behind the foursome in the bleachers as they decided to tag along with Christine and Helen. Sherry had taken Helen's place at the dance hall when Helen left and for reasons that no one could understand, Sherry took an immediate dislike to Helen. Casual insults were covered with the sweetest chocolate, but the underline tone was not unnoticed. To Helen's credit, she took it in stride and counted it as jealously of her apparent happiness in her marriage. Christine had told Helen about Sherry and her adulteress affair that left her stranded in Branson when her husband went back to Ohio without her.

Matt ignored the female antics and watched the action taking place in the forty-two-foot center ring as a woman in a long ankle-length dress stood on the bare back of a beautiful white horse and ran around the circle at full gallop. She jumped, kicking her legs out parallel and landed faultlessly on the back of the running horse. She did a front summersault to stand on one foot. The skill and art of such equestrian trick riding were simply astounding. Whether it was the man standing on two parallel horses galloping full speed around the ring and jumping over two three-foot-rails while keeping perfect balance or the clown trying to get one of the same horses to jump over a six-inch-tall rail in a comedy routine, the horsemanship and training were phenomenal.

Clowns juggled and acted out skits that had the audience roaring with laughter. One act was a knife thrower who threw knives at a woman, apparently his wife, as she was twirled around on a spinning vertical platform. His aim and precise throws drew many gasps but were safely placed around his wife. A clown assisted by stopping the rotating wheel, and when asked by the knife thrower to return the knives to him, the clown began juggling the blades while the man tried to grab them. The man's constant angry yelling to get his knives back and failed attempts to snatch a knife out of the air had Christine laughing so hard that tears were running down her cheeks while she stomped her feet. The joyful sound of her laughter always made Matt smile. He was laughing more at her than the comedy routine.

In awe, they watched as three elephants loped into the center ring and did a selection of tricks, including a lady lying under one as it stretched out over her and later placing a giant foot on her head. For most everyone in the audience, it was the first time they had witnessed an elephant's massive size and uniqueness.

The ringmaster, dressed in a red and white

striped suit to match the massive big top tent, took to the center of the ring as the three elephants were led back outside. He held a megaphone to be heard clearly.

"Ladies and Gentlemen, elephants are amazing creatures, are they not? God certainly had an extraordinary imagination to create the creatures he did. Elephants are not only massive creatures; they are also incredibly smart, social and interactive with each other as a strong family unit—elephants are truly amazing creatures. And for a small fee after the show, you can have the opportunity to ride one of our elephants out behind the circus grounds. We can put two adults on at a time for a dollar per person or three children for a single dollar. You may never have the opportunity to ride an elephant again."

He pointed towards the back of the tent. "Ladies and Gentlemen, from the outbacks of Australia, I give you our strongman, the great Ozzy Meldrum!"

A short but barrel-chested man ran to the center ring as the circus employees rolled out a table holding various items with cloth drapes over the sides. Ozzy had long black hair and a six-inch beard on his square-shaped face. He was dressed in leotard pants to expose his muscular upper body. He held one finger to the audience as he grabbed a black iron bar.

The ringmaster narrated, "Ozzy will attempt to bend a steel bar with a one-inch circumference. Solid steel, ladies and gentlemen. He has bent half and three-quarter-inch steel bars in the past, but this is the first time he has tried one full-inch circumference. Quiet please…"

Ozzy grabbed the three-foot-long bar and took an exaggerated breath. He grunted and flexed his muscles as he agonized to bend the bar. Slowly it began to curve while his face reddened as he strained with all the power he had. After a minute of pure exerted force, the bar bent. He held it up to show the audience his success while he tried to catch his breath. He set it on the table and grinned with satisfaction. He shouted with exuberance and flexed his muscles victoriously.

The crowd laughed as a six-foot-tall muscle-bound kangaroo slowly hopped into the ring.

The ringmaster groaned into the megaphone. "Ozzy, Darren followed you out again."

"What?" Ozzy was annoyed. He turned around just as the kangaroo hopped to the table and picked up the steel bar Ozzy had just bent. The kangaroo straightened the bar and tossed it at Ozzy's feet with no effort at all.

"I just bent that!" Ozzy shouted in his Australian accent. He picked up the bar and tried to bend it again. The kangaroo snatched it from Ozzy and bent it quickly to the crowd's amusement.

Ozzy pointed towards the exit of the tent. "Go home! I told you it's my show, not yours."

The kangaroo huffed at him and leaped past Ozzy to look at the audience and waved while Ozzy raised his hands helplessly, not knowing what to do.

"No! Go home. I'm the star, not you!" Ozzy

yelled, irate.

The ringmaster sighed. "Ozzy, please. Darren cannot be our strongman. Can you control your pet, please? Darren is Ozzy's pet kangaroo, but Darren is becoming a pest week by week. We can't have him interrupting the show, Ozzy."

"Fine!" Ozzy shouted and tried to grab Darren from behind. The kangaroo's tail rose into his groin and Ozzy collapsed to a knee. It brought a roar of laughter as the kangaroo waved to the audience.

"Ouch! Are you okay?" the ringmaster asked into the megaphone.

Ozzy nodded and stood. "Darren! I'm not playing. Now go!" He pointed at the tent's exit. The kangaroo turned to square up to him and pointed its arm to indicate Ozzy should leave.

Ozzy pushed Darren, and the kangaroo rolled back on his tail, then quickly moved forward and pushed Ozzy. To the audience's delight, the Australian strongman fell to his back and rolled backward twice before coming to his feet.

"There's only one way to settle this!" Ozzy shouted.

The kangaroo held up its hands in a fisticuffs position.

"You want to fight?" Ozzy asked, perplexed.

The kangaroo nodded.

"Fine! Don't cry if you get hurt." He raised his hands to box Darren.

Ozzy threw a left jab at Darren, but the taller animal blocked it. The kangaroo immediately threw a right hand that hit Ozzy square in the face. He fell flat on his hind end, stunned.

"That is it!" He yelled and stood and tried to grab Darren, but Darren wrapped his arms around Ozzy and began to hop in place while shaking Ozzy back and forth like a rag doll before throwing him down. Ozzy rolled across the ground and got back to his feet. He glared at Darren with a furious expression, stuck out his tongue, and then ran out of the ring as Darren chased him, stopping short of leaving the ring. Ozzy ran out of the tent.

Darren, the kangaroo, hopped back to the front of the ring and raised his hands victoriously to the crowd's delight.

The ringmaster was angry. "I swear, for a strongman, Ozzy is losing control of his pet. Get this creature out of here. He is ruining our show!"

Three clowns came forward to remove the kangaroo. A series of hits, falls and chasing the cowardly clowns around the ring continued until Ozzy returned to the ring carrying a rifle. He aimed the long arm at Darren. He shouted, "I'm tired of you pushing me around, Darren!" He pulled the trigger. There was a loud bang, but a flag came out of the barrel that unfolded with the word: *Bang*.

"Dang!" Ozzy yelled. "Wrong gun."

Darren held out his arms for a hug and tilted his head. To the crowd's amusement, the two best friends hugged.

The ringmaster shouted in his megaphone, "The great Ozzy and Darren from Melbourne, Australia, folks."

Ozzy and Darren both bowed to a loud and well-earned cheer.

The ringmaster added, "Ladies and Gentlemen, I was told that we have a celebrity in our audience. One of the most famous lawmen in America. A gunman with a reputation for being as good with his hands as he is with his gun. Where is the U.S. Marshal Matt Bannister? Stand up, Marshal."

"Stand up," Christine urged. She was still laughing from the antics of the kangaroo.

Matt stood awkwardly and waved.

"Marshal Bannister, I wondered if you would like to spar a round with Darren?"

Matt laughed. "No, thank you."

"Awe, come on. We always give a local tough man a chance to spar with Darren."

"No, thank you. He's too tough for me," Matt declined and sat down to the disappointed urging of the ladies around him and calls of coward from some of the people in the audience.

"I'll do it," Saul Wolf shouted as he stood and stepped down the bleachers carefully. His massive size and brute strength could be seen through his long sleeve shirt. "I know Matt well, and I've seen him fight. I'm telling you all right now that he is no coward. I'm Saul Wolf. I was a professional fighter known as the Unbeatable Goliath. Matt is the only man I will never want to fight, if that tells you anything. Let me fight Darren. I promise I won't hit him too hard."

The ringmaster's mouth dropped open. "I've heard of you. You were a world heavyweight contender. I don't think our gloves will fit your hands.

Secondly, it's all in fun. Not hitting hard to you might knock out a normal man. We don't want Darren hurt, so I must decline."

"Alright," Saul sighed and turned back to his seat. The ringmaster watched him go back to his seat. "Ozzy and Darren!" He announced ending their part of the show.

The circus continued with various acts combining the daring with humor making it a joyful hour and a half of pure entertainment. The final acts were a high wire balancing act and the fantastic flying trapeze.

At the end of the circus, the ringmaster said, "From the bottom of our hearts, thank you for coming and we hope you enjoyed our show. Laughter is a good thing, folks. We hope you had a wonderful time and had a few laughs. We have another show later today and tonight if you want to come back. Do not forget the elephant ride and our small zoo. Where else can you shake a kangaroo's hand or pet a twenty-foot python for fifty cents? Pet a bear cub, perhaps? There is good food and fun games in the fun center and for those daring enough, there are some of the world's most bizarre and unbelievable twists of human nature behind the black curtain of our sideshow. Please, enjoy your day and, most of all, have fun. May the Lord bless you all."

Chapter 19

"I want to ride an elephant. Matt, will you ride with me?" Christine asked as they exited the circus tent.

He chuckled. "If you want to, I will. That's something I've never done before."

"Oh, look, popcorn bars. We have to try one of those," Christine said, pointing at a vendor with a large red sign with a painted popcorn bar. The carnival atmosphere was alive and well and the scent of popcorn and roasted peanuts hung heavily in the air as the people lined up for the quick snacks outside the main circus tent. A row of booths was nearby, with men calling out invitations to throw a ball or toss a coin into a dish and win a prize echoed through the air. It was common to see a parent being led by the hand by their children towards the snacks, the family games or the zoological exhibit behind the large tent.

Helen said, "We will go find the elephant ride and get in line. If you buy me a popcorn bar, I'll save you a spot in line."

THE LEATHER MAN'S JOURNAL

"Okay. Do you want one, Sam?" Christine asked.

"No thanks. I have my eyes on some raw oysters."

"Ick," Christine said with a distasteful grimace. "We'll meet you two in line."

"No," Matt said softly. "It wouldn't be fair to the people behind us if we cut in. We'll get you a popcorn bar, Helen, but we need to go to the back of the line."

Helen scoffed lightly. "Take a chance on having some fun, Matt. We'll save you a spot in line."

There were no weapons allowed in the circus and the only people allowed to carry a gun were the town's lawmen. It was a fun and carefree atmosphere that did not tolerate any kind of aggression. The Chatfield & Bowry Circus knew well that people worked hard for their money, and a day of celebration and excitement often brought out the criminal element in every town. The circus was an easy place for pickpockets to work their wicked schemes and snatch innocent people's hard-earned money. There were circus employees with a well-trained eye to look for pickpockets to protect their customers. There was a tall white post in the center of circus grounds to shackle pickpockets and other criminals to until they were arrested by local law officers. A large sign pointed at the post reserved for pickpockets and thieves so everyone would know who they were and why they were shackled. At the moment, no one was there. Matt appreciated the effort.

The excitement of the children and adults alike was plain to see, except for the parents who could not afford to pay for the snacks, games, an elephant

179

ride or any other fun that their children longed to do. It was a playground, but it took paying the fees to play.

That was particularly true of a young boy and girl around six or seven who wanted a popcorn bar. The mother and two children had sat two rows down from where Matt and Christine were seated in the bleachers with Helen and Sam. Matt noticed how well the children behaved and found the sound of their laughter bringing a smile to his face, despite the heavy burdens on his mind. A popcorn bar was a mixture of caramel and popcorn that was allowed to dry and then cut into small bars. They were twenty-five cents apiece and the two children wanted one but were quite downcast with a pouting lower lip when their mother declined their request for lack of money after paying the fee to see the circus.

"Please," the little boy begged.

"Your father has the money, not me. He gave just enough for us to see the circus," the young mother explained. The sadness of not being able to partake in any more of the attractions was evident in her voice.

Matt tapped the mother's shoulder politely. "Excuse me, Miss, but I'd be happy to buy your children a popcorn bar if you don't mind. May I?" Matt asked.

"Please, Mom?"

She smiled at her son. "Okay."

Matt handed a quarter to the boy and one to the little girl. "Happy Fourth of July. Get your mother one too," he said with a wink as he handed another quarter to the boy.

"Thank you, Marshal," the mother said appreciatively. "I haven't met you yet. My name is Holli Richards. This is my son Dickie Jr. and Luetta, my daughter. My husband is Dick Richards. I don't know if you know him. He works for the timber company as a lumberjack."

"I don't think I have met him. I'm Matt, and this is my fiancée, Christine."

Christine shook Holli's hand. "Your children are adorable. Matt and I couldn't help noticing their gleefulness during the circus." She opened a small money purse and handed Holli a five-dollar bill. "Please accept this. I would like to pay for a ride on an elephant for you and your children."

"It's too much," Holli protested.

Christine shunned her protest. "No, it's not. Please. Your children deserve a special day and memory with you. And the Lord put your family in front of us in that large tent and out here too. I believe I am just doing my part to make today a special one for you."

"I thank you both. My husband paid our way inside the circus and left to watch the horse races. I'm sure he's betting and probably losing, but we are here and enjoyed a fantastic circus. And now this. Thank you so much."

"You are welcome. Does your family have a church you go to?"

She grimaced slightly. "No. My husband says there is no need."

Christine wrinkled her nose. "I would disagree with that. But if you and your children want to go, Matt and I invite you to come to the Christian Church on Sunday or anytime, if not this week."

"Thank you. But I don't know if my husband will let us go. I'll ask him."

"You can't decide that?" Christine asked skeptically. "I'm sorry. It's none of my business."

"It's okay," Holli said, relieved to be finished with the conversation. "It's been nice talking to you and thank you both so much."

Morton Sperry was standing behind Matt and Christine, waiting to be recognized, but so far hadn't been. He watched and listened and their conversation with a crooked twist of a smile.

"Matt," Morton said, "you're making me think you're a softie." He was standing with his brother Henry and Henry's wife and children.

Matt grinned, surprised to see him. "Only when it comes to children. How are you? Did you enjoy the circus?"

Morton gave a rare chuckle. "Yeah, we did. You remember my brother Henry and his wife, Bernice."

"Of course." He shook Henry's hand and Bernice's as well. The scar on Henry's neck from being shot by Elias Renner a few months before at the Sperry farm was thick and ugly, but he had survived. His wife, Bernice, was an attractive red-haired lady who had always seemed kind. She had their two young children at her side.

"This is my fiancée, Christine. This is Morton, Henry and Bernice Sperry."

Christine shook their hands. She was a little anxious as the Sperry-Helms Gang had a terrible reputation and Morton appeared too rough and frightening to be a nice man. She put her attention on Bernice and their children. "Did you love the circus as much as I did?" she asked the two young kids.

"Matt," Morton said, "can I borrow you for a moment to introduce you to my older brother Alan. He just got out of prison. He's with the rest of the family over yonder."

"Sure." He walked with Morton a short distance, where he immediately recognized the matriarch of the family, Mattie Sperry. "Hello, Missus Sperry," Matt greeted her with a kind smile.

Her weathered face nodded a simple greeting. "You're not here to threaten my son, are you? He just got home from five years in prison, and I have a very special present arriving for him next week. He needs to be here when it arrives. I know you lawmen want him back in prison as soon as possible, but could you have the decency to give him a few days to unwind before you start to harass him?"

Matt narrowed his eyes questionably and chuckled. "I didn't come over to harass him."

"Ma, stop it," Morton scolded. "Matt, this is my brother Alan. This is Matt Bannister," Morton introduced them.

Alan reluctantly shook Matt's hand. "Marshal." He was a tall and lanky man about forty years old. He had short brown hair and a clean-shaven face. He was thin and dressed in newly purchased clothes. There was absolutely nothing intimidating about Alan except for the coldness and emptiness of his light green eyes. They displayed a man who cared nothing about many things, including life. There was no emotion on his face as he stared at Matt with his cold eyes.

Matt remained pleasant. "Nice to meet you, Alan. To answer your mother's question, I was notified that you were being released and coming home. The prison warden and the state think you're a high-risk felon and bound to be back in prison or dead before long. But all I have to say to you is welcome home. As far as I'm concerned, you did your time and paid your debt. Your slate is clean. What you do with your life from this point on is completely up to you. If there is anything I can do to help you, let me know. Now, if you'll excuse me, I must get back to my fiancée. She wants to ride an elephant before the line gets too long."

"Thank you," Alan said.

"You bet. You folks have a great time today."

"Marshal," Mattie called as he stepped away. He turned towards her. "Thank you," she said sincerely.

"I'm a fair man, Missus Sperry. Enjoy the circus."

***

Behind the red and white big top tent was a small petting zoo with animals such as the python, a black bear cub, opossum, skunk, and other small animals that could be petted or gazed upon if they were too dangerous such as the four-foot alligator in a shallow tub of water. There were not a lot of animals, but the main attraction was shaking hands with Darren, the kangaroo and the elephant rides.

A good-sized three-acre parcel was fenced off with thin metal posts and a red ribbon around the poles to create a large ring. The large and heavy wagons that carried the elephants were lined closely together. Each had a detachable steel staircase on the side of the wagons for easy access to the roof, where a detachable metal guardrail protected people from falling off the oversized wagons. The elephant handlers guided the massive beasts beside the wagon, where a gate was opened to allow people to step in or out of the sturdy wicker basket set on the elephant's shoulders. The wicker baskets had a bench seat wide enough for two adults or three children to sit comfortably. One elephant, the largest one, had a larger wicker basket securely fastened to it that held two rows of bench seats for larger families or groups. There were three elephants giving rides once around the three-acre circle.

Matt and Christine reached the top of a wagon and watched the elephants slowly stroll around the three-acre parcel to give a dollar's worth of adventure to all who paid the fee to ride an elephant.

Matt allowed a circus employee to help Christine into the wicker basket and then Matt stepped down onto the basket and took a seat beside his lady. The elephant stood twelve feet, putting Matt and Christine about fifteen feet above the ground. It was unsettling to be sitting so high in a basket, but it was made more uncomfortable when the massive creature took its first step. The wicker basket rocked from side to side while they looked over the elephant's huge gray head and wide flopping ears that shooed away the flies buzzing around its eyes, making the experience far more surreal.

Christine grabbed Matt's arm and snuggled her head against his shoulder. "I don't know if I like this after all. It reminds me of sitting behind the cantle of your saddle that one day we rode up the hill and I struggled to stay on."

"Oh, hogwash," he laughed. "We're not going to fall off. This basket is just a bit different than my saddle but just as safe, I'm sure. At least I hope so because it would be a long fall if it breaks loose, huh?"

Christine leaned her head over the side and looked down while holding onto his arm tightly, fearing her weight shift might tilt the basket too much her way. "We're so high."

Matt grinned at her uneasiness. "You must admit this is amazing. Can you believe people in India ride these things as commonly as we do a horse? That's what the man back there was telling me anyway. Are you having as much fun as you expected?"

"I am. I thought the circus was fantastic. That kangaroo made me laugh. I'm glad you didn't fight that kangaroo. It would ruin your reputation if he made a fool of you."

Matt smiled slightly. "That it would."

She looked at him with the sincerity that had won his heart. "I know it can't be easy to have what happened to Hannie on your mind and be here with me too. We haven't had the chance to talk, but I am so sorry, Matt. How are you doing?"

He grimaced with a shake of his head, perplexed. "I can't figure it out, Christine. I tend to want to believe Nick did it because of the scratches on him, but I don't know anymore. The boy Nick has bite marks that broke through the skin, which Doctor Ryland confirmed were from Avery if that's his real name. A man who bites in a fight might as well scratch in a fight. Nick may be telling the truth. But yet, I still get the feeling that Nick's guilty. It's the same feeling I had before I hung Izu and Wang Chee. I thought they were innocent and came to find out I was right." He exhaled. "I have the same gut feeling about Nick being guilty, but the evidence is leaning more towards proving he may be innocent. I can't put the pieces together in a manner that makes sense, except believing his story."

"That is bothering you a great deal, isn't it?"

"Far more so today after talking to Doctor Ryland. Nick has scratches on him. Both Hannie and Avery had skin under their fingernails, but both had skin conditions that were scratched raw. If Nick said it was a dog that scratched him, I have no proof it wasn't. Even if I arrested Nick on speculation of the scratches and the skin under Hannie's nails, a lawyer could get the case dropped for reasonable doubt on the evidence alone." Matt was hesitant. "Avery didn't have a single scratch on him, but Hannie was hit over the head, which means she could have been unconscious when she was strangled. I am tempted to say Avery did it and close the book on it, but I can't. The truth is, I still think Nick did it."

"Is there a particular reason why?"

Matt took a deep breath and bit his bottom lip tensely. "Yeah. One, I don't want to be wrong." His eyes filled with moisture. "If Avery did it, my family will always hold it against me. I let him go, Christine. He would have been in Tim's jail if it wasn't for me. Karen, Jim and William and the rest don't want anything to do with me now. They blame me. And perhaps they should."

Christine could see the agony in his eyes and the anxiousness caused by the upheaval within his close-knit family. Christine knew that Matt wasn't that close to Karen and Jim Longo, but he and William were. "I'm sorry, Matt." She didn't know what else to say. She knew from experience that losing a child was the worst thing she had ever experienced, and her baby was a toddler that died of sickness. Jim and Karen had raised their baby for fourteen beautiful years and now she was gone by the hand of an evil man. She could not possibly say she knew what Karen and Jim were going through or how angry they were.

"I'm afraid I'm…" He paused emotionally.

"Afraid it was him?" she asked knowingly.

Matt nodded. "Yeah," he spoke softly. "I don't know how to feel about that. If Avery is the one who killed her, I may never forgive myself."

"But you don't think he did it?"

Matt's head turned back and forth slowly, thoughtfully. "I don't. But again, I don't know. I keep going back and forth like the basket we're riding in every time the elephant takes a step. When I think I'm making progress in the investigation, I'm taken right back to the beginning. Either a sixteen-year-old kid is outwitting me or I'm missing something." He grinned with a slight laugh of frustration. "Or maybe I'm just not willing to see what's clear to everyone else."

"Matt," she said, taking hold of his hand, "let's pray that the Lord will expose the fiend responsible and that your family will be reconciled no matter who did it. I know you usually pray, but I want to pray this time:

"Lord Jesus, there is so much to pray for today. There are so many broken hearts and no answers for those suffering. Jesus, I pray for your peace and comfort for Karen and Jim and their family. I know they are hurting and angry, but I ask that you'll give them a sense of peace in their broken hearts that only you can provide. I ask that you will be with Matt as well. I know his heart is hurting more than he is saying and that weight of the unknown is heavy upon his soul. Jesus, help Matt to find the man responsible and bring justice to the Longo family. Let the lies be found and the truth become as bright as the noonday sun. Lord, be with Matt as he goes through this time of agony with determination to solve this terrible crime. Thank you, Jesus, for this day and the blessings you give us each day and for your great love for us. In your Name, we ask. Amen."

***

Their elephant ride had almost come to its full circle. "Thank you, Christine. I apologize for ruining your elephant ride with my frustrations."

She offered an understanding, sad smile. "Not

everyone has such a serious conversation while riding an elephant, but I'll bet even fewer take the time to kiss their fiancée on an elephant. I'd rather have the kiss than an apology."

Matt moved his head to kiss her just as the elephant took another step and jolted the basket his way and Christine slammed her face into his unexpectedly. Their lips came together in a painful collision.

Christine grimaced and covered her mouth with her hand.

Matt rubbed his nose. "Are you okay?" he asked with concern.

She nodded with a furrowed brow. Her top lip had been jarred against her teeth. Her lip was not bleeding, but she could taste a faint hint of blood.

Matt added, "That's just my luck today, Hon. How about we try it again when we get off this creature?"

"That might be safest," she agreed. Her top lip was swelling.

Chapter 20

> *Dare to Enter the World of the Obscure Curiosities and Wonders of Chatfield & Bowry's Amazing Sideshow. See the Unbelievable Tasmanian Wolf Boy, Human Camel Spider, Ugliest Woman in the World, 500 Pound Balloon Man, The Human Clam, Arnie the Grumpy Dwarf, Bigfoot Alice, Twin Pin Heads Alicia and Bart, Theodore the Giant and more. Or are you afraid to enter?*

Christine was hesitant as she read the sign. "I don't know that I want to go inside."

Helen rolled her eyes with a huff. "Don't be a coward. It's part of the circus, so it has to be fun. Sam and I are going in. What about you, Matt? You're not afraid to go in, are you?"

"No, but I am here with Christine and if she doesn't want to, then we'll do something else."

Helen turned her head to look around the circus grounds. "Like what? We've done everything else. Christine has been avoiding this area the whole day and it's the most popular attraction! They're just freaks, Christine. They can't hurt you."

"I know. But they are people."

"So? Rose!" Helen called as Rose Blanchard and Sherry Stewart walked from the popcorn vendor toward the games area. "Rose! Didn't you and Sherry go into the freak show?"

Rose walked casually toward them, holding a bag of popcorn. She popped a kernel into her mouth. "Twice. It's well worth the money." She looked at Sherry, "Do you want to go in again with them?"

Sherry grinned. "Sure. That dog boy is kind of cute."

Helen gave a disappointed glance towards her best friend. "Christine's scared to go in."

"Why?" Rose asked with a shrug. "It's no big deal. There is nothing horrible in there or sad. Trust me, if nothing else, you'll come out thinking it was silly to feel hesitant to go in. Come on; I'll give you the tour. Heck, we've done it twice already."

"Please come with us," Helen begged. "Please."

Christine looked at Matt. "What do you think?"

"I'm a little curious what they have in there. I've already seen the worst of humanity. I don't know if anything else can shock me."

"Okay. We'll go in."

"Yes!" Helen exclaimed. "I don't know what a camel spider or a human clam is, but I want to find out."

A seven-foot wall of black drapes surrounded the sideshow to keep its secrets hidden from the public without paying the entrance fee. The drapes were connected to lightweight metal posts and the bottom of the drapes were staked down to keep anyone from crawling underneath. To make the sideshow all the more eerie, there was a five-foot tunnel of black cloth to walk through at the entrance before it opened to the exhibits. To keep the flow of traffic moving from left to right, a seven-foot black curtain continued straight down the middle, ending at a stand with three shelves on each side containing large jars of deceased animals and a stuffed two-headed calf at the end.

"Arnie, we're *back*," Rose flirtatiously emphasized as they stopped in front of a wooden platform covered by a red tent. Arnie, the Grumpy Dwarf, was showcased inside a securely locked cage with a padlocked door. Arnie was a three-foot dwarf with a long gray beard, wearing a green stocking cap with a pair of green pajamas. He smoked a pipe while casually sitting on a small stool shaped like a mushroom. Behind him, there was a tiny bed and dresser in the corner used as props to reflect his home. Arnie wore a bitter scowl on his face as he kept his eyes on the side of the tent except when conversing with customers.

Sherry threw a piece of popcorn at him to get his attention. "Arnie, it's too bad there are bars between us; that bed looks comfortable. Look what you could have if you just handed me the key to the door." She raised the hem of her dress above her left knee flirtatiously. "Tsk, tsk, tsk."

Arnie turned his head and scanned her leg with his permanent scowl. "I've seen less prickly legs on a cactus! Now go away and leave me alone." His high-pitched voice was bitter and rough, which added to the humor. Despite his angry act, it was easy to tell he enjoyed his interactions with the customers.

Matt laughed, as did the others.

"Oh, don't be so grumpy," Sherry replied mockingly. She was an attractive blonde-haired girl in her mid-twenties. Her thin oblong face could draw a man's attention, but her expressive sultry blue eyes tended to lean towards the naughty side. "Don't you want to be my sweet little man, Arnie?"

"Take your red-headed mongoloid friend and move on. I've seen better-looking carp than you two," Arnie grumbled.

"Now, now," Sherry chided, "haven't you ever heard if you have nothing nice to say, then say nothing at all?"

"Pssh!" he exclaimed. He crossed his arms and turned away.

Rose's mouth had dropped open. "Mongoloid?" she gasped.

Off to their side, Mattie Sperry was with her sons Vince and Jack and her grandson, Tad. Mattie had been listening and was irritated that the little man had insulted such an attractive young lady. She approached the iron bars and scolded Arnie with a pointed finger, "If those bars weren't there, I'd grab you up and whip your hind end before washing your mouth out with soap for insulting her. That young lady said nothing to you to invite such a horrible insult!"

Arnie turned towards the small crowd to see who had spoken to him. "Oh! Excuse me. If carp had hair, they'd look like these two." He puckered his lips and opened and closed his mouth silently to imitate a fish out of water. "But even though they are ugly, I'd drown myself diving in the deep end to kiss a carp if I were *your* husband, Ma'am."

"Watch it!" Jack Sperry warned. He did not appreciate his mother being insulted.

Arnie's eyebrows rose with interest. "I can't stand to look at her any longer! Listen, young man, I'll give you some free advice. Put your mother on a box out front and start your own sideshow."

Vince Sperry rushed the iron bars and tried reaching in to grab Arnie. He shouted with a fierce sneer, "Come here, you little freak! I'll cut your tongue out! You son of a..."

Arnie leaped off his seat, turned his back to Vince, bent over, and rotated his butt back and forth. "You can't touch me! You can't touch me!" he sang.

"Vince!" Matt shouted coarsely. "Back off! He's the grumpy Dwarf. It says so right there. Walk away if you can't take a joke."

Vince cast a ferocious glance at Matt and pulled his arm from between the bars. "It's not funny! He insulted my mother."

Matt couldn't help but grin. "Vince, it's an act. That's what he does. It also explains why the door is padlocked. Undoubtedly, it's for his own protection."

Mattie was offended. "Vince, leave the freak alone and let's go."

"Please, don't go," Arnie the Dwarf pleaded, "I never get to see freaks."

Vince spoke coldly, "Little fellow, if you only knew who I am. You're lucky the marshal's here."

Arnie put his hands on his hips and rotated them. "Ohh...I love threats, fat boy."

Vince walked past Matt. "That freak needs put in his place."

"Have a good day, Vince," Matt said with a chuckle.

"Lawman," Arnie started with his eyes on Matt, "thank you for saving me. It's not every day a Sioux want-to-be saves a white man. Shave half of that beard off and you could be our half man, half woman and have your own spot in our show."

Christine and the others laughed. Including Jack Sperry. Who had stayed when his mother and Vince moved to the next tent. Fifteen-year-old Tad Sperry laughed as well.

Matt's grin faded to a humored smile. "That's funny. Listen, Arnie, my name is Matt Bannister, the U.S. Marshal. I have my gun," he said with a wink and a pat on his sidearm.

Arnie raised his hands in a surrendering fashion and bowed as he took a step backward. "A small joke among friends harms no one."

"No harm done at all."

Jack Sperry held out a hand to shake Rose's. He

had been fixated on Rose since he first danced with her months ago. He had danced with her a few times but had never spoken to her outside of the loud and busy dance hall. "My name is Jack Sperry. I've danced with you at the dance hall a few times."

"Yes, we've met." She knew who he was as he had introduced himself to her every time they danced. The Sperry name was rather hard to forget within Jessup County.

"I know, but never in a place where I could talk."

Arnie saw an opportunity. He mimicked a sheep as he cried out in a high-pitched voice, "J-a-a-a-c-k - J-a-a-a-c-k." When he had Jack's attention, he explained, "I hear your wife calling."

Matt laughed heartedly.

Jack narrowed his eyes as he glanced at Arnie. A slow grin formed on his face. "What is your problem, pal?" He asked Rose, "Can we get away from this jackass? Do you mind if I join you and your friend?"

"Please," Rose said. "And, yes, let's leave the rude midget."

"Don't leave me, J-a-a-a-c-k. Déjà vu, right?" Arnie called as they left him behind. He put his attention on the following folks that stood before him.

Christine held Matt's bicep as they slowly moved past the 500 Pound Balloon Man, which was no more than an obese fellow in his thirties sitting on a circus stool used for the elephants to stand on while eating a turkey leg. His mouth and chin were coated in the juices and bits of flavoring and meat.

The Ugliest Woman Alive was a sad exhibit of a woman in her forties with a deformed elongated face and bulging eyes. Her left eye wandered sharply to the left. She sat in a rocking chair, knitting a bright multi-colored scarf. Quite frequently, she would look up and let the people gaze upon her. Deeper than the appearance, her eyes showed a gentle and genuine soul that seemed unaffected by the comments and insults cast by Tad Sperry and others who found their fun in insulting those less fortunate than themselves. She was an easy target and appeared to accept it with grace. She knitted peacefully.

Christine rested her head on Matt's shoulder, heartbroken for the lady. Her attention wasn't on the woman's face but the scarf's design and color choices. The woman's skill was top-notch. Christine found it was something she could honestly admire about the lady while others insulted and laughed at her. Christine spoke loud enough to be heard, "I love your scarf. Your talent is wonderful."

The lady smiled warmly. "Thank you." She went back to knitting.

The Twin Pinheads, Alicia and Bart played paddy cake with childish glee. Theodore the Giant was a young man who stood well over seven feet tall and didn't do much other than stand and let people gaze up at him. Bigfoot Alice was a lady in her twenties with deformed feet three times that of an average man's size at twenty-nine inches long and swollen to eight inches wide. She sat in a rocking chair and read a book with her bare feet exposed to the audience. She answered questions about her custom-made boots set along the cage so people could get a good look at them. There was no fear of them being stolen because it was impossible to squeeze the shoes between the iron bars.

They reached the midway point of the sideshow, where the center drapes ended at a booth with shelves of pickled oddities in large jars and two-headed calf taxidermy. Many sideshows touring America had a collection of jarred oddities on exhibit, including human stillborn babies and fetuses. The Chatfield & Bowry Circus had none of those in their collection.

The Human Clam was a man in his thirties with deformed hands. Both hands were like a seal's flipper, and he would put them together and open and close them like a clamshell. The Human Clam seemed to relish the attention as he made a show of his hands.

The last two exhibits had drawn a lot of attention from the crowd; wolf calls, gasps and tears were occasionally seen as people left the sideshow. The final two exhibits were both contained in wagons with iron bars; The Tasmanian Wolf Boy and the Human Camel Spider.

"Oh, lord," Christine gasped quietly as they approached the Tasmanian Wolf Boy. There was no way of knowing the man's age by all the long hair covering his face and upper body. He wore brown pants cut off at the knees to show his hairy legs and feet and a shirt for modesty reasons, but it was ripped and torn to reveal his wild nature and long body hair. The wolf boy bounced around in his cage, growling and sneering his teeth at the crowd. Occasionally, he howled like a wolf and tore at the piece of raw steak and fat trimmings that were in his dinner bowl. He held a long trimming of beef fat between his snarling teeth and bounced from one side of the cage to the other. A billboard beside his cage told how the wild wolf boy was caught in a Tasmanian jungle living with a pack of wolves.

The wolf boy lunged forward against the bars and reached through the bars to grab someone while he growled hideously. A lady surprised by the sudden leap upon the bars screamed in fright.

The wolf boy's eyes turned towards Matt and Christine, and the piece of beef fat dropped from his mouth. His hands held the iron bars while his snarl faded, but his eyes remained unmoving from Matt and Christine.

A lady holding a tablet and pencil a few feet away spoke to Matt, "Marshal, you can even calm the beasts. I haven't seen him do that once today. I'm trying to draw him, so I've been here for a while," the lady explained as she showed him her pencil drawing.

"That's good," Matt studied the likeness.

"Thank you. I'm Betty Brown. I like to think I'm an artist and have been sketching all the exhibits here. I'm going to paint them and see if I can't sell them at the pottery shop or somewhere. This is the first circus to come here. I think people would be interested in purchasing a painting to remind them of it."

Christine could not take her eyes off the so-called wolf boy. She didn't know what it was, but something in his brown eyes drew her to him. She was overwhelmed with empathy as she watched him. He touched her heart. Slowly, the wolf boy began his routine but frequently glanced back at the two of them.

Matt and Christine moved on to the Human Camel Spider and Christine began to weep. The young lady with the deformed knees and feet was such a beautiful young lady that she would have taken young Tad Sperry's breath away on any given day. Instead, Tad Sperry stood with his family making rude and insulting comments about her deformities. His crude comments sickened Christine's stomach while her heart broke for the beautiful young lady. The life she was given with backward knees and feet was bizarre and sad, but it was not near as tragic as how others treated her.

Christine was emotional. "Young lady," she called to Susie Durden, "I think you are absolutely beautiful."

"Thank you," Susie replied with a soft smile.

Tad Sperry had already been scolded by his grandmother, but the temptation was too much. "I think you're beautiful too," he shouted. "In fact..." he made such a crude comment that it should have degraded everyone who heard it.

Matt spoke to Tad harshly, "Knock it off! I've been listening to your grandmother telling you that since we came in here. Now I'm telling you to knock it off! No one wants to hear your foul mouth, especially me."

Christine added irritably, "You have a horrible, filthy mouth! I have been listening to you degrade these people all through here and you are heartless!"

Tad stared at her for a moment and then laughed. "And?" he asked carelessly with a grin. He didn't like being scolded by a woman.

Matt answered roughly, "*And* if it doesn't stop, I'll make our own little sideshow right here with you screaming you have menstrual cramps. If you want to humiliate these folks, I can quickly turn that around! Not another word, Tad, or you'll be the newest attraction." He glanced toward Mattie Sperry and his uncle Vince. Vince looked away, but Mattie gave an approving nod.

Matt and Christine walked out of the sideshow knowing if either of them had been born with such birth defects, they might be right beside those they had just witnessed. Sometimes it was too easy for people to mock others for conditions they have no control over or neglect to realize the so-called freaks were real human beings with all the emotions and desires that everyone has. As the fifteenth-century English preacher and martyr John Bradford said, "*There, but for the grace of God, am I.*"

Chapter 21

David Chatfield had not slept well the night before. It was hard to get any sleep at all after witnessing the murders of a girl who was not a whole lot younger than himself and his new friend Avery Gaines. David could not get the memory out of his mind, and he could not shake the fear that seemed to take refuge within him. He was safe, and he knew it within the confines of the circus, but even still, the horror of what he had seen left him shaken to the core. He wanted to take the day off, but he couldn't without having a fever or vomiting.

The Tasmanian Wolf Boy was an act where he got to play a wild man. Perhaps it was why he connected with Avery the way he did because they were both playing roles in public but could be themselves in private. The ripped pants and shirt were no more than a costume and the raw meat, growling, barking and howling were all for the audience's entertainment. It was a job well done if he could alarm someone and bring out a frightful scream. The circus was a business, and the sideshow was the honeypot that brought in as much money as the circus big top did. All of the sideshow attractions were acts to entertain and shock the paying customers, some more than others.

Some people criticized freakshows as exploiting the unfortunate for a profit, but the truth was if it weren't for the sideshow David and his friends would have no future. They would be at the mercy of family to provide and care for them or sent to a sanitarium to keep them out of public view. David had heard the critics and activists trying to save him and the others from being taken advantage of by profiteers using their deformities for gain.

Those who protested and wanted to see the sideshows ended for the so-called freaks' sake had no consideration for the so-called freaks beyond their own viewpoint. They never asked the very freaks they wanted to run out of business what they thought of having no other way to survive with their strange abnormalities and conditions that isolated them from society.

David was not offended by rude comments, gasps of horror or laughter at his appearance. What he was perceived to be by the public and who he truly was were quite different. It was a career that paid him good money. His money went into a bank, and he never spent a dime on anything because the circus already paid for everything he needed. Eventually, that savings account would become his survival in later years. For now, it was fun to try to make people scream and play the part. He only wished those who complained of the circus owners exploiting the disadvantaged would understand that to the people like him, the freak show was a financial blessing.

Of course, they all wished they had been born normal people, but they were not. For whatever the reason, they were born abnormally and given their abnormalities to function and survive within society. David could be angry about having the disease that caused his hairy condition if he wanted to, but it would do no good to be angry. He was what he was, and nothing could change his appearance.

"He could shave his face and get a normal job," a lady once stated as she stared at him in horror.

He could. David could use a straight razor and shave his forehead, around his eyes, eyelids, nose, and on top of his hands and feet every day. That's what it would take to appear normal. Not excluding using scissors to trim the rest of his body hair once a week to appear extraordinarily hairy, but at least at an average length. That is what it would take just to be *normal* to someone else. The straight razor would scar his face and probably blind him trying to shave the hair on his eyelids, but to please others, at least he could have a regular job.

It was easy for some to speak their minds as they watched him, but they fell short of what they really knew about his condition.

The crowd in Branson had been quite good as David chomped like a cow on a long chunk of dangling beef fat from his mouth while staring at a chubby lady and her husband. He didn't like the taste of cold beef fat, but it was part of the act. He backed up against the back wall and ran forward, jumping into the bars while grasping out to grab the lady. She screamed.

He then recognized the U.S. Deputy Marshal Matt Bannister at first sight. He had never laid eyes on the man before, but the description he had read of Matt in Avery's journal was detailed and accurate.

Walking into the U.S. Marshal's Office, I expected to find an older man in his fifties, bowlegged and gray-haired. A man with cold eyes and a weathered face from his years of traveling and gunplay. A man that has seen more violence and killed more men in his lifetime than most outlaws ever will. I expected to meet a gnarled old man with a bitter view of life.

My expectations could not have been more disappointed. You can imagine my surprise to find that the man behind the legend is only in his mid-thirties, young, handsome, and friendly, to my great relief. Tall, broad shoulders and muscular. Matt Bannister has long dark hair that he keeps in a ponytail and a finely trimmed beard and mustache. I can not avoid the fact that his brown eyes, ever observant, were also kind and joyful. His voice was soft and a well-spoken man.

After meeting with Matt twice, once as Napoleon Pickle and then to reveal my identity and purpose. I felt that my secret was secure and that he truly is a fair and good man who treats even such odd ducks as Napoleon Pickle with respect. He was not at all what I expected to find, and respectively so. My impression of Matt is strength under grace. I believe Jessup County and the city of Branson are blessed beyond measure to have such an honorable lawman in their midst and he loves this community. It is plain to see.

David could not take his eyes off the lawman or the beautiful lady that clung to his arm. He was sixteen and like every other sixteen-year-old boy in America, heroes were far and between. The dime novels about Matt Bannister increased his reputation far beyond the west and he was a name that many boys looked up to. David had no idea Branson was the legend's hometown until he read Avery's journal. And then suddenly, there he was with his silver badge and famous sidearm not fifteen feet in front of David, looking straight at him. David was stunned.

Like any other sixteen-year-old boy in America, David was interested in girls. A harsh reality was they were not interested in him for obvious reasons. He had the privilege to travel across America and had seen many beautiful girls his age and older that came to the sideshow. Very few matched the beauty of the lady holding onto Matt's arm. She was stunning and once David made eye contact with her, he had almost forgotten about Matt.

For a long moment, David stood frozen, staring at them. Slowly he became aware of his staring and started to get back into his performance, though not as heartedly. His eyes kept going back to Matt and his lady until they moved on to The Human Camel Spider.

An hour after Matt left, a cold chill ran down David's spine and paralyzed him in terror, freezing him in place like one of the steel bars of his cage. He no longer ran wildly from side to side with a chunk of steak in his mouth. The chunk of meat fell from his lips as David stared helplessly at the tall, dark-haired young man he had watched murder his new friend the night before. David had hoped the killer was arrested by now, but there he stood at the velvet rope four feet away from the bars with a grotesque expression on his blemished face staring at David. A tsunami of dread poured over him like a rock on the seashore. His heart began to pound, and his breathing quickened to shallow breaths. Pressure in his chest made it hard to breathe. He gasped involuntarily. He wanted to run out the back door screaming for the marshal, but he was too afraid. David noticed the knife on Nick's belt, and a flash of anger rose, guns were not permitted in the circus, but knives were not considered dangerous weapons and permitted past the security check at the entry gate. The panic seizing David was beyond any he had experienced and the fear of being recognized left him feeling sick. There was nowhere for him to run. All he could do was stare and hope he wasn't recognized.

The young man had caused enough trouble among his friends on the island the night before that David knew Nick's name. The blond-haired teenager with Nick was also on the island kissing a girl named Rose. David had heard his name spoken on the island but couldn't remember the blond boy's name.

Ollie laughed. "He must like you, Nick. He hasn't moved since he saw you."

"Is that a walking mutt or a man?" Nick asked. "Gross either way. I'll bet he has fleas. Scratch for us, dog boy!" he ordered. "Go on, scratch!"

"Why isn't he moving?" a lady asked her husband.

The question pulled David out of his momentary shock, and he sidestepped to the other side of the wagon and back again, trying not to look at Nick. He tried to give the crowd a growl, but his throat was too tight and nothing came out. He picked up his piece of raw red meat and ripped at the tissue with his teeth with half the effort he had before. He prayed silently for Nick to leave.

Ollie spoke, "It says he was caught in Tasmania and he raised by wolves. I don't know if he understands English, but you may not want to make him mad. He might break those bars down."

"I have my knife if he does. I killed a big dog that attacked me once with my knife. I can do it again." Nick shouted, "I said, scratch boy!"

The words sent a cold chill down David's spine.

Ollie observed, "He looks like those pictures of a werewolf from the sixteenth century we read about in that book. Remember?"

Ollie's words drew David's attention and he paused when he recognized the arrowhead necklace Avery wore on Ollie's neck. David's chest heaved in and out at a faster rate as a panic attack gripped him like a giant hand of doom. He pulled the meat out of his mouth with shaking hands. He wanted a drink to wet his parched throat, but he was too stiff to get down on his hands and knees and lick it up out of his water bowl.

Nick didn't seem to notice. "He looks like a mongrel mutt to me. Come here, boy." he whistled and patted his thigh.

"Why does he look afraid of you?" Ollie asked as he watched the freak's widened and nervous eyes.

Nick's brow lowered and then his eyes widened as Hannie's words returned to him from the night before, *"I saw a werewolf."* Nick's eyes shifted to the wolf boy with a murderous expression. He answered his friend coldly, "I don't know. Let's move on."

They moved on to gaze at the Human Camel Spider, but Nick's eyes kept glancing back at David. Now that it was pointed out to him, the panic in the wolf boy's eyes was more noticeable than the hair on his face. Nick knew he was looking at the monster in the woods that Hannie had seen. The only witness to his crimes.

"What is wrong with her?" Ollie asked, staring in disbelief at the Human Camel Spider as she scurried across the wagon's floor on her hands and backward feet. "Nick, are you even looking at her?"

"Yeah," Nick answered, removing his eyes from David. "Let's go."

"Look at her," Ollie was captivated by the strange sight of the attractive girl with deformed legs.

"Ollie, I'm suddenly not feeling good. I need to go home. I'll see you later," Nick said with one last glance at David.

"You're leaving?"

"Yeah. I have to go."

***

Nick entered his apartment and sat down on his davenport. He had tried to cover every aspect of guilt, but now he knew there was a witness that he could not get to easily. He had to make choices, flee and hope never to be found or find a way to get the sideshow freak alone to silence him. Gradually an idea came to him.

He left the apartment and went back to the circus. He went to the first circus employee he saw, a guard at the entrance who was verifying no one carried a gun into the circus. "Hi, I'm Nick Griffin. I'm looking for a job and would like to join the circus doing anything you need. Do you know who I should talk to?"

Chapter 22

The sideshow closed for two hours at 5:00 p.m. to have a dinner break. They would open back up at seven for three hours for a last circus performance and sideshow before leaving town.

The cookhouse was in a large tent with a buffet of prepared dishes for the circus employees. The cooks always prepared good meals and there was no hurry to get in line as there was always plenty to eat. However, David had lost his appetite and went to his bunk rather than the cookhouse. He sat on the edge of his bed and covered his face with his hands.

The girl with pretty, blonde curls had run away screaming that she saw a monster, and now Nick had to have known it was him in the woods. There was only one person that looked like a werewolf and it was him. The look in Nick's eyes while he was leaving revealed that he did know and would have no problem murdering again to keep his crimes hidden.

What to do? David could barely breathe. His chest felt caught in a tight crevice between two cliffs. One side urged him to go to Matt Bannister and tell him what he saw, but he could be killed if Nick found out he had spoken to Matt. Even if Nick were arrested, David would be kept in Branson to testify in court. The circus would leave without him, and David would be all alone and vulnerable to any of Nick's family or friends that wanted to silence him. Even if not, he was a freak and would be ostracized and gawked at if not laughed at, harassed and perhaps beat up without the safety of all he knew about life, his family in the circus. Being taken from the circus and left behind scared him as much, if not more than seeing Nick.

The only other option he had was to remain silent and leave town. It would take a day to break everything down and load the wagons, but within forty-eight hours they were leaving Branson behind and when they did, he would be free of the fear that plagued him. To hit the road and leave the memory of Nick behind was what he looked forward to. He had two hours to rest before going back into his wagon for three hours and ending the final show.

He took a deep breath and exhaled in an attempt to relax.

Arnie, the Grumpy Dwarf, walked into the tent, turned towards the door flap, and spoke loudly, "Yeah, Nancy, he's in here. Come on in." He spoke to David, "Nancy's looking for you." He went to his cot and sat down.

Nancy Chatfield entered. "There you are. You better go get some dinner because there won't be anything to eat until breakfast and we have another show to do."

"I'm not hungry," he answered.

"You will be later. You better go eat. Are you feeling okay?"

He nodded quickly. He couldn't admit the fact that he was anxious and troubled.

"What's wrong?" she asked.

"Nothing."

"Did somebody say something hurtful?"

"Nothing I'm not used to. I'm fine. Just tired."

"You look tired. Well, take a little nap if you need to. I'll pick up some fruit for you. Hey, did you see the marshal Matt Bannister come in? I wasn't there, but I heard he went through the sideshow."

"I saw him," David answered.

Arnie the Dwarf laughed. "I told him he could be our half man, half woman." Arnie was not his real name, and he wasn't grumpy either. His name was Paul Harris, a fun-loving and fatherly figure to the younger folks at the circus.

"How'd he like that?" Nancy asked.

"Well, he reminded me he still had his gun," Arnie laughed. "He seems like a nice man."

Nancy sat beside David. "I hoped he would be at the ball last night, but he wasn't. I did see him later on. He came to get some people and let them know their daughter was killed last night. It was really sad. I heard she was related to Matt somehow."

David took a deep breath to calm the rush of anxiety that continued to grow. "He should be trying to find the killer instead of coming here." His mouth was dry.

"I'm sure he is or maybe he already has. Are you sure you're feeling okay?" she asked him.

"Yes. I'm just tired."

She patted his leg. "Take a nap. I'll wake you up in an hour. Tomorrow will be a long day of packing up. I talked to Father and we are all going just north of here to a hill to watch the fireworks tonight. That should be fun."

Chapter 23

Jim and Karen Longo were devastated. They were surrounded, loved and helped by family and friends, but the loss of Hannie was an emptiness in their hearts and home that would never be filled. The anguish of losing their fourteen-year-old daughter was inconsolable and the reason for it incomprehensible. No number of tears or wailing dimmed the heartache and life as they knew it would never be the same. What was supposed to be a fun day for the family turned into the worst day of their lives.

Karen had just woken from a three-hour nap and the Longo home was quiet and somber. She had been up all night grieving until her body shut down. Jim Longo was in no better shape; he just hid it from others better than Karen. Hannie was his firstborn, and their relationship was a good one. He was very proud of his girl, and now she was gone for reasons that made no sense. Exhausted and worn down to nothing more than a flicker of what he was the day before, Jim sat on his comfortable davenport holding his beloved wife.

Lee and Regina Bannister were there, Karen's sister Georgina and Ron Dalton, Robert Fasana and some friends. Many people had come by offering their love and condolences and as much as it was appreciated, it didn't ease the numbing shock and tragedy that had entered their lives.

William Fasana came in through the front door, solemn and without his usual fire in his soul. "Sis, I can't wire Pa today. I'll wire him first thing in the morning. He'll come home as soon as he can, I am sure. The funeral should wait a week for him and Uncle Luther to get home."

Karen sniffled and gave a nod but didn't reply.

William took a seat in an empty dining room chair placed in the family room. He wished there was a fire in the fireplace, kids screaming or some other form of noise because the silence was deafening. William had never experienced the kind of heartache he was experiencing. He had fallen in love once and had his heart broken, but it wasn't nearly the same. He never thought he would ever need anyone for any reason, but he wished his dear lady friend Maggie Farrell was with him now to share in his sorrow. He had recently gone west to Portland and spent some time with his old Uncle Floyd Bannister, Maggie's stepfather. It was a good trip, and he had a wonderful visit with Maggie, Uncle Floyd and Aunt Rhoda. He and Maggie had shared a kiss or two and even talked about making their courtship official, but William couldn't do it. He didn't want to get married, and courtships lead to marriage just like bait leads to a hook and he wouldn't fall into that trap. However, now, in the silence of Karen's home, he would have liked to have had Maggie beside him.

"I guess we'll have it next week when your pa and Uncle Luther come back. I imagine Billy Jo will be coming too," Jim said softly.

Georgina replied softly, "Undoubtedly. She wouldn't miss it. Her heart is going to be broken, too."

"Did you see Matt out there?" Ron asked William.

William spoke through a bitter expression, "No. I imagine he's at the circus."

"He wouldn't be at the circus on a day like this," Ron said. "I'm hoping he finds some answers."

William's anger snapped sharply, "The man was crazy, and Matt knew it, but he let him run free anyway. The answer is just that simple." He continued, "Our sheriff's a weak link and a piece of bad work, but at least he had the notion of locking the man up for vagrancy so he couldn't hurt anyone! Hannie…" William's voice faded as his jaw clenched. "Matt's responsible."

Lee offered, "Matt was doing what he thought was right."

"Vagrancy is a crime here. The man was a crazy vagrant and Matt knew it," William argued.

"Please stop," Jim Longo said softly. "We don't want to hear it. We're just trying to keep ourselves together and it's hard enough without listening to any arguing."

"Fair enough," William said.

Before too long, there was a knock on the door, it opened, and Matt stepped inside with Christine. He said hello and walked over to hug Karen. "I don't have the words to offer how sorry I am."

William couldn't resist, "It's a little late, don't you think?" It aggravated him how anyone could allow a crazy person to run free when Matt should have known better.

"William, please…" Karen pleaded.

William's hot temper got the better of him, "No! Matt should have let Bob arrest him instead of being the good Samaritan hero you always try to be. Hannie is gone, Matt! That is the price we're paying for your stupidity." His ice-cold blue eyes glared at his cousin coldly.

Matt sighed inwardly. There was nothing he could say. Perhaps William was right. The decision to come to Napoleon's rescue had backfired in a way that no one could have foreseen. He could not argue nor accept William's accusation. The best he could do was not respond at all. It felt like a nail had been driven deeper into his chest.

"What have you found out today about that man?" Ron asked.

Matt shrugged with upturned hands. "Nothing. I sent Nate to find his camp and collect his bag. Nate found his camp west of town along the river, but there was nothing worth finding. Like I told you last night, he told me he was a reporter from New York…"

William shouted, "That should have been your first hint that he was crazy! New York's a long way from here. I swear, Matt, there is a part of me that just wants to tear your head off, and I don't even care that you're family. My niece is dead because of you!" William's eyes bore into Matt like an angry bull about to charge.

"Stop it!" Karen shouted. "I can't stand it." She rose quickly and hurried to her bedroom, sobbing.

Jim Longo stood to go after her. He spoke to Matt, "I agree with William. I'm sorry, Matt, but I really don't want to see your face here again. Please leave. And don't come to the funeral."

"Go back to Wyoming, Matt," William added. He turned his head from Matt.

Matt nodded quietly. Another strike of the hammer drove the nail deeper into his heart. He took a breath and was about to speak but hesitated. There was nothing left to say. "Let's go, Christine."

William stood quickly and faced Matt. "I'll bet you went to the circus today, didn't you?"

"We did."

William gave a resentful half-grin. "Figures. While we're all here hurting, you're off having fun. If that doesn't speak louder than a train's whistle, then nothing does. Get out! And you know, to me, we aren't family anymore."

"So be it," Matt said as he and Christine walked out the door. The nail struck deeper.

Christine spoke as they walked away from the house, "I'm sorry. I didn't mean to cause any friction between you and your family. I just thought it would be fun to go to the circus."

"I did all I could do today. William's angry and hurt, rightfully so. I wouldn't have been welcomed even if we skipped the circus and spent the day with them. Setting that man free was the tightening of the noose around my neck as far as they are concerned. To them, I'm to blame, and if Avery or Napoleon did it, then I am, to a certain extent, to blame. I need to figure out who the leather man is, a lunatic or a reporter trying to write a story." He sighed tiredly. "I don't know, Christine, I can track a man for a hundred miles and arrest him or shoot it out and be competent. But I'm not so sure that I'm good at what I'm doing anymore. I have hung two innocent men and now I don't know what to think. One hand says the boy did it, but all the evidence, as strange as it is, points to the vagrant I freed. And yes, if you want to be technical, Tim did have the right to arrest him legally, I guess one could argue, but not morally. I don't know. I'm even questioning that now."

Christine stopped and turned to face him. "Matt, you are the most competent and fair lawman this county has ever known. I think the closeness of Hannie and your family have you flip-flopping more than you would be if she weren't related. Look at the evidence, listen to your soul and lay some mortar between the bricks to firm up your beliefs. If there is a fact, cement it and find the next brick. Build your wall on facts until you are convinced one way or another. The more you flip-flop, the weaker your foundation will be. You're not Tim

Wright; you're Matt Bannister, be that solid wall that I know you are. If the truth is not obvious, then find it. Stop second-guessing yourself and follow your gut instincts. It may be the Holy Spirit leading you the right way. In the meantime, I'll be praying for you and your family."

"Thank you, my lady. I'll try to do that."

"Don't try, Matt. Put your family aside and do it. It's what you do best and so far, your gut instincts haven't been wrong yet. Trust it. It might just be the Lord urging you in the right direction."

Chapter 24

The second show wasn't the great last draw that the circus hoped for. The community dance drew most people to the city park to eat a free meal, listen to the orchestra play and dance. The community dance was always a big event, and many wanted a good seat to watch the fireworks display after the dance. A good practice for getting the best view was placing tablecloths and blankets down to claim their spot for the show later on. Other folks went to the last circus, but the earlier shows saw much greater numbers. The sideshow was busy for the first two hours, but as the third hour drew to a close, the circle of oddities emptied.

David was relieved as the final show wound down. It meant they would have the rest of the night off and start packing everything up in the morning. The circus was a big event with many pieces that had to be carefully packed into their thirty-two wagons and eventually, they could leave for their next show. Getting to Branson was difficult as the terrain was seldom flat and the roads were narrow and more weather-worn than many other places, but thank goodness they were about to close the circus down and leave town. David couldn't wait to reach the next town.

David had less than half an hour to act like a wild wolf boy and then his nightmare would be over. Being a public display, he had no control over who entered to get a look at him nor could he respond when someone talked to him, he was, after all, a boy raised by wolves and not domesticated. It was an art one had to learn not to be affected by the cruel words people would say or comment to others. Unlike Arnie the Grumpy Dwarf, David was not permitted to talk but to play the role he was given. It was showmanship and the show overrode his feelings. He could not show emotion other than the wildness of a wolf boy who could not understand English. He was, for all practical purposes, an animal. It was fun, though. It was fun to play the role.

Usually, he was sad to see the last show end, but he couldn't wait to be finished. He wanted to surround himself with his family and ease the feeling of being a trapped animal in a cage with a predator on the prowl. He could not wait to open in a different town where he would no longer feel anxious and afraid to see Nick walk out of that black entrance tunnel.

Finally, George, one of the guards that stayed within the circle of oddities, announced that it was closing time and ushered the few spectators out of the exit. When the last one walked out, David sighed. It was over.

He walked to the back of the wagon and opened the door to step out. There was a narrow three-foot section for a walking path between his wagon and the black drapes surrounding the sideshow. David stepped out and walked to the end of his wagon. He was quickly grabbed and pulled into the narrow space between the back of the wagon and a tent set up for the Human Clam.

"Shhh!" Nick Griffin held a knife to David's throat. He placed David's back against the wagon's end and waited as the Human Camel Spider, Susie Durden, walked past on her hands and backward feet as she spoke to herself, "Whoof, what a day," She passed by, not noticing the two boys wedged against the wagon.

Nick glared at David with a wicked scowl. David was too scared to speak and had already urinated in his pants. The urine dripping from his pants onto the ground was audible. Nick hissed with a harsh whisper, "I know you saw me last night. I know you saw everything. You're the werewolf Hannie said she saw. I heard you in the brush. I should kill you right now! Who have you told?" The knife blade was pressed tightly against his neck.

"N...N...No one," David sputtered slowly in a shaken voice. "I haven't told no one." His tears rolled down the hair on his face like a sleeping-eyed dog. "P...P...please, I...w...won't tell. P...p...please, d...don't hurt me. We're l...leaving town."

Nick moved the tip of the knife under David's chin. "Yes, we are. I'm an employee now and I'll be seeing you every day. We may even be bunkmates. I'll know if you tell anyone what you saw or about me. If you do, I swear I will cut your throat before I'm arrested. I'm leaving here with you just to make sure you don't say anything because if you do, you'll be the deadest freak there has ever been. Are we clear?"

"Y...Y...yes." He began to whimper.

"Good. Keep your mouth shut. I mean it. We might even become friends."

"David," Nancy called from the circle entrance, "are you in here?"

David's attention went to the sound of Nancy's voice. Terrified, he screamed, "Help! I'm here! Help!"

Nick plunged the knife into David's abdomen. He pulled it out and thrust in again and a third time. "I told you!" Nick sputtered. In a rage, he thrust the knife into David's body again. David slowly slid to the ground.

"David?" Nancy called, getting closer. "Where are you?"

Knowing time was short and desperate to get away without being seen. Nick forced himself to remain calm and not make any noise as the sound of the lady drew closer. He pressed himself against the edge of the tent, waiting for her to step into view.

"David?" she questioned as she walked behind the tent into the small space between it and the wagon. She didn't see Nick before the butt of the knife handle struck a solid blow just behind the temple of her head. She dropped to the ground, unconscious.

Nick had no idea who the young lady was. All he knew was David would soon be dead and she was out cold. He hurried along the black drape wall and stepped out through the slice he had cut in the drape to get into the circle of oddities unnoticed. Rather than walking back across the circus, he darted across the field to enter the town through the livery stable's pasture unnoticed.

***

David could feel the blood flowing between his fingers as he held one of the four stab wounds. He didn't feel a thing at first except for the knife plunging into him. But now that Nick had left, the wounds began to burn, and the pain increased. He was vaguely conscious and could see Nancy lying on the grass with her eyes closed. A gash on her head bled profusely. David knew he was dying, and there wasn't much he could do for himself, but his love and concern for Nancy was worth all he could give to her.

The stab wounds penetrated the abdominal wall and to use those muscles to turn and try to stand was unbearable. He collapsed and groaned as he stretched across the ground to reach for her. Taking a deep breath and expanding his abdomen was excruciating. "Nancy," he said in a strained soft voice. "Nancy," he said and closed his eyes as exhaustion took over.

Slowly, Nancy lifted her head, touched the knot on her head, and looked at the blood on her fingers. A wave of panic swept through her as the dream-like state of shock filled her mind. What had happened? Did a cable snap? An overhead sign come loose? Was she attacked? And then she saw David lying on the ground in a pool of blood, unconscious. "David!" Her concern now on her brother, she forgot about her aching head and the blood on her face. "David!" She crawled to him and turned him to his back. His white torn shirt for the show was saturated with blood. She began to sob. "Help!" she screamed. "Someone help! David's hurt!" She rubbed the hair on his face as she wailed. "Don't die on me, David. Do you hear me?" She screamed, "Someone get a doctor! Help."

Within minutes, a guard arrived, followed by other circus employees.

"Get my father! Tell him to hurry!"

***

Horace Chatfield was a busy man. From morning to night, overseeing the circus and the performers, livestock, supplies and all the other organizations and duties of an owner and administrator was overwhelming. He had help, his brother-in-law and business partner, Ivan Bowry, had his responsibilities that helped a lot. His daughter Nancy managed the sideshow, which also helped a lot, but one thing that no one else could do was be a father to David.

Horace had raised him as his son.

Horace dropped what he was doing and went to David. "Get a wagon. I have to get him to a doctor. Gerry, get a wagon!" he shouted urgently. "Steve, take as many people as you need to track down the town doctor. Hurry! He's in shock and losing blood." Horace began to break down much as his daughter did. "Hang on, son. I'm going to get you some help."

Chapter 25

"The circus? You're leaving?" Ollie Hoffman asked Nick, stunned. Nick had just arrived at the dance in the city park.

"I am. I'm going to work my way to being a clown or something."

"A freak more than likely," Ollie teased. "I'm going to miss you. You're my best friend."

"I know. I'll miss you too, but it's a good way to see the world and make money. What's the best I could do around here? The sawmill like my pa? No thanks."

"What did your pa say? Is he glad to see you go?"

"He doesn't know and I'm not telling him. I'll write him a note when we leave. Tomorrow is just packing everything up and we're leaving at daybreak on Sunday morning. I guess they stop around noon and have a church service during lunch and then we'll be moving again. I told Mister Chatfield that I wasn't a churchgoer, and he said that was fine.

It was for those who were. I think I'll like it. Besides, now that you're courting Rosey, I'd probably never see you anyway."

"That's not true," Ollie grinned. He was saddened to hear his friend was leaving him.

"Hey! There you two are," Tad Sperry shouted as he joined them. "I was hoping to run into my Branson pals."

"How are you?" Nick greeted Tad with a firm handshake. He and Ollie had met Tad months before while Tad was in town and became fast friends. Unlike Ollie, who was more easy-going and cautious about things, Tad was more like-minded to Nick. They had a lot of fun together when Tad was in town.

Tad answered, "I'm bored to death. I was just on my way to Rose Street to see if I couldn't find something more fun to do than watching my uncles dance. Do you want to join me?"

Nick nodded. "Yeah, I wasn't so fond of going to the dance anyway. Do you have any money?"

"No, but I'm sure we can rob a drunk and get some."

Nick slowly smiled. "Yeah, I'll go with you. Ollie, are you coming with us?"

Ollie answered, "No. If Rose is here, then I want to dance with her."

Nick chuckled. "See? I told you I wouldn't be missing anything by leaving. You're already whipped by her."

"Ollie has a girl?" Tad questioned. "I might need to spend more time in Branson if he has a girl already. Where are you going anyway?" he asked Nick.

"I joined the circus. I was hired as a setup and take-down man. I'll be leaving for good day after tomorrow. And I'll tell you right now; I'm not coming back."

"Are they still hiring? I haven't got a dang thing happening for me over in Natoma, except farm work or the stinking tannery. I've been chopping wood with my uncle, but there is nothing there. I thought about starting my own gang, but everyone is too cowardly to join me. They're afraid of my uncles. There can be only one Sperry-Helms Gang, and they're not doing much."

"I think the circus might hire you. It would be great if so. Come with me in the morning and ask."

"I might. For now, let's go cause some trouble on Rose Street," Tad said. "I haven't had fun in a while."

Once they left, Ollie continued to look for Rose Fowler among the crowd. A square section in the center of the park was roped off as the dancing area. All around it, people gathered while the orchestra played. Ladies from the dance hall enjoyed dancing for fun instead of business. They were causing quite a scene, socializing and meeting men they never really got to meet in the dance hall business. Some unwise men made the stupid decision of flirting with the ladies in front of their wives. To see an angry wife, whisper a few choice words, followed by a repentant man, was becoming a common sight.

Christine danced with a few men that asked, but

for the most part, she remained beside Matt. They danced a few times, but Matt was not in a dancing mood. Though he tried to be joyful, the burden of Hannie's death was a sadness that he could not hide. He was aware there were no other family members at the dance. They were either with Jim and Karen or staying home out of respect for them. He was the only one enjoying the day's activities and the guilt of doing so while they mourned was beginning to weigh him down.

"Ollie," Matt called. "Excuse me, my dear," he said and left Christine to approach Ollie. He immediately noticed the black obsidian arrowhead necklace with sinew cordage and colorful beadwork around Ollie's neck. The same necklace Avery Gaines had worn and said was given to him by the Sioux Chief, Red Shirt. "I wanted to ask you about last night. Did you see the leather man around there at all? Was he swimming by chance when you left the falls area?"

Ollie furrowed his brow. "I didn't notice him. But, Marshal Bannister," he hesitated to continue, "I was kissing on Rose. Don't tell her parents, though. Please."

"You were kissing Rose and walking too? The whole time?" he was skeptical.

"Well, no. But my arm was around her and she's all I noticed."

The youthful days of the first love came back to Matt's mind like a fleeting breeze that lasts a moment and is forgotten in the business and concerns of adult life. He remembered the excitement, passion and all-consuming possession of youthful romance and how it put a spell on him. "Lovesick," his uncle Charlie called it. That state of being where work ethic, whether in the hayfield or schoolwork, was overshadowed by thoughts of a girl. In Matt's youth, it was Elizabeth. However, that first crush became love, and he loved her all his life until he came to terms with losing her to Tom Smith. There was something about youth and being lovesick, or in Ollie's case, love blind, that Matt understood and accepted with a degree of respect. He knew precisely what Ollie was meaning.

"Rose could vouch for that?" Matt asked.

"Probably not in front of her parents," Ollie answered quickly. "She's only fourteen, Marshal. I don't think they'd be happy about her kissing me."

Matt grinned. "Probably not. Did Nick make any threats towards Hannie?"

Ollie shook his head thoughtfully. "No. Hannie was real quiet. I don't think he spoke to her at all. He was mad at Elizabeth. I think he hoped to steal her away from her fiancé, but he wasn't mad at Hannie. He didn't hurt her, Marshal. There is no way."

"Were they friends?"

"Not really. Hannie wasn't invited. Hannie was spending the night with Rose, and they followed Linda to the island."

"Did Nick give you the necklace?" Matt asked knowingly.

Ollie touched it with his fingers. "Yeah."

"Do you know where he got it?"

Ollie's head lowered as he nodded.

"That man's family will want that back. How about you hand it over?"

Ollie removed it and handed it to Matt. "We saw that man earlier yesterday on Rose Street. Nick harassed him some. I told the man it was a nice necklace. Nick gave it to me last night," he explained.

"Where is Nick tonight?"

"He just left. We ran into Tad Sperry from Natoma. They went to Rose Street for something to do."

"Ollie, in my opinion, you're a good kid. You would be wise to pick better quality friends. Come to church sometime and I'll introduce you to some new friends."

"Marshal, I'm not good at making friends. Besides, Nick is leaving. He got a job with the circus today."

"Really? Well, that's interesting. I kind of thought he was a clown." Matt smiled at his own joke. Ollie didn't.

Matt continued, "I haven't seen the Fowler family here, which isn't surprising. I had to tell Rose's parents everything I knew. She might be in trouble for a while yet. Parents finding out their girls were not where they were supposed to be, kissing boys and drinking throws a damper on the celebrating mood."

Ollie's head lowered sadly. "She probably hates me now."

"I doubt it. Have a good night, Ollie." Matt walked away with a sense of urgency brewing in his chest. He needed to arrest Nick before the circus left, but he could find no evidence that would prove Nick strangled Hannie. If Nick's story were true, his killing of Avery or Napoleon, whatever his name was, would be justified. There was more evidence for that being true than not. It was strange that Nick would have the calmness to take a man's necklace that he had just killed. Most people would have been too shaken up emotionally to consider taking a necklace as a gift for a friend unless it wasn't the first person they had killed. Eyes reveal a lot, and Nick had cold eyes. He was the perfect candidate to commit murder and not have it bother him, except for the fear of getting caught.

The circus was the perfect opportunity for a young man to escape town and see the country under usual circumstances. But these were not ordinary circumstances. Nick was beginning to crack under pressure and would make a mistake before long. If he was with Tad Sperry on Rose Street, it was only a matter of time until they broke the law.

Christine noticed the necklace in his hand. "Did you get me a present to go with the Indian dress Chusi gave me?"

He answered plainly, "No, my dear, this is evidence."

"Oh. A brick in the foundation?"

"One of them."

Chapter 26

"Where's a doctor? We need a doctor fast!" a man yelled as he half walked and half ran down the center of Rose Street. "Where can I find a doctor?" he shouted.

Nick figured the man was with the circus and felt a rush of urgency as the cry for help meant the monkey boy was still clinging to life. "Hey, sir, go back to First Street and go past the livery stable. It's the very last house on the right as you leave town." Nick answered. He had no idea who lived in the house, but the longer it took to get the doctor, the less chance of survival the freak had.

"Thank you!" the man said and ran the other way.

Nick watched him run. He spoke to Tad with an ornery grin, "I hope it's not an emergency. That's not where the doctor lives." He laughed.

"Do you know where the doctor lives? He's probably not at home and I'll bet he has some nice stuff in his house," Tad said, hinting toward breaking in.

"I'm sure he does have nice stuff, but I don't know where the doctor lives."

"Too bad. Well, there are a lot of empty homes tonight. We could make a fortune," Tad said.

Nick wasn't interested. "I'm starting a new job tomorrow and don't want to risk any trouble. I killed a man last night, Tad. He was strangling a girl and I stabbed him a few times. She died too. I think the marshal is trying to blame me for killing her."

"What?"

"I'm not breaking into any houses. I'm not giving the marshal any reason to arrest me or be suspicious of anything I do. I have a new job and I'm leaving town. I just want to get out of town as fast as possible."

"Why? Did you do it?"

"Do what?"

"Kill the girl."

"No! She was a friend of mine."

"I haven't killed anyone yet. But when my uncle Alan gets the gang moving and robbing again, I will. Uncle Alan says he is going straight, but I think he will go back to robbing once he gets sick of shovels, dirt, and farming. And when he does, I'm joining the gang. I've been practicing my shooting with my rifle and revolver. Uncle Alan will teach me how to draw fast if I ever need to. I'm getting pretty handy with a revolver."

"My Pa has a revolver, but I prefer my knife. It doesn't invite much trouble. I went to the circus today to apply for a job, and they didn't even ask me to take it off or question me about it. But you can't take a gun in there. A knife works just as well if you want to kill someone. It's just a lot quieter."

"If you can get close to them," Tad added, "but if not, a gun works best."

"That is true," Nick agreed. His attention was on the Green Toad Saloon. "My pa's friend is the barkeep in here. Let's go in and see if we can get a drink on my pa's tab."

"I hate not having money when I come here," Tad huffed.

They walked into the Green Toad Saloon and neared the busy bar. "John, I'm Leonard Griffin's son. Can my friend and I get a drink on my pa's tab?"

John Riggs looked at the boys and then hollered across the bar, "Leonard, can your boy and his friend buy a drink on your tab?"

"My boy? Nick…" Leonard said, standing from a gaming table with a noticeable stumble. He was intoxicated, but the stumble was from his foot catching the table leg as he stepped. "My boy, the hero! Give him and his friend a drink. A hero deserves a drink!" He put his arm around Nick. "John, my boy is a hero! He killed the rat that murdered that girl last night. He stabbed him to death. I'm downright proud of him for trying to save her. That's what heroes do."

John was interested in hearing the story and it showed in his expression as he handed two glasses of cheap liquor to the boys. "I heard about that.

What happened?"

Nick shrugged as he raised the glass. "It just happened. I heard her scream and saw him strangling her and reacted. He bit me pretty good," he showed John his hand with the bite mark pierced his skin. "I stabbed him and kept stabbing him."

"Show him the knife you used," Leonard encouraged. "I bought the knife for him when he was a kid. It's pretty handy to have."

"No, it's just a knife," he declined to show the blade. Nick was afraid it might have moist blood from the freak on it.

Leonard argued, "It's not just a knife, son. It's the knife that killed that crazy child killer. That knife's worth more than just a knife."

John refilled Nick and Tad's glasses. "This drink is on the house. We don't always get real heroes in here very often. Say, I'll give you two dollars for your knife. I'll hang it behind the bar with a note stating this is the knife that killed the famous child-murdering leather man."

"Leather man?" Tad asked questionably.

"It's the only name he has, isn't it?" John replied. "Two dollars?" John offered Nick.

Nick tapped the handle of his knife. He was afraid to reveal the blade because fresh blood on it might be suspicious when news of the circus stabbing made its way to the saloon. "No, sir, it was a gift from my father."

John Riggs squinted his eyes thoughtfully. "I'll tell you what. Five dollars? I'll give you five dollars for it. It would be a good conversation piece." Interesting conversations at the bar meant more time talking, which led to buying another drink.

The wheels in Nick's head were turning and he had an idea. "Let me think about it." He had another knife at home that he never used with about the same length of the blade and a slightly different handle that he would sell John and say it was the one.

"Fair enough."

Leonard glanced at Tad. "I'm Leonard, Nick's father." He shook Tad's hand.

"Tad Sperry, sir. It's nice to meet you and thanks," Tad said, raising the glass.

"Sperry? You're not related to the Sperry boys, are you?"

"Why yes, sir, they are my uncles."

"Well, where are they? They usually come in here when they are in town."

"They're at the dance. Uncle Jack is fawning over a dance hall girl. She's very pretty, though. Uncle Vince is not having such good luck with the ladies, Uncle Morton is watching over Grandma to make sure we don't come home with a new Grandpa, and Uncle Alan went to the brothel. He just got out of prison. They'll probably show up here eventually."

"Let's go," Nick said without warning. "I'll see you later." He said to his father.

"You don't want to sell your knife? For five dollars, you could buy a new one or a bottle of whiskey for us to drink," Tad replied.

"I'm thinking about it. Let's go."

"I can't believe you're not selling your knife. He

offered you five dollars for it. I would have sold it for two." Tad said as they walked out of the saloon.

"I have a knife at home that I never use. I'll put it in my sheath and trade it to John for a bottle. What do you think of that idea?"

Tad chuckled. "I think it's brilliant."

Chapter 27

Lee and Regina Bannister had to leave the Longo home to attend the community dance and be present at the fireworks display, as it was Lee's work throughout the year to organize it. Having two daughters himself, the shock and anguish of Hannie's death hit hard. He had watched her grow up and she was a welcomed guest and babysat his girls many times. It wasn't in him to set her death off to the side and enjoy the day's events like it didn't happen. He had been questioned more than a few times about why Matt had allowed a crazy man to roam the city during the most celebrated day of the year. Lee didn't have an answer, and quite frankly, he questioned that himself the more he thought about it.

Coming to the dance, it irritated him to see Matt dancing with Christine as if nothing had happened. Their cousin, Karen's little girl, was murdered and while the family was grieving, Matt seemed to be enjoying himself. It put a sour taste in Lee's mouth, and it showed in his eyes as the two brothers walked across the park and around the corner of the court-house to talk privately away from the large crowd.

"What do you want me to do, Lee?" Matt asked sharply. "Jim asked me to leave; you heard him! I'm not wanted there. Would you rather me be sitting at home crying?" Matt asked irritably.

"Yeah, I would!" Lee snapped. "Showing some emotion or that you care would be a good start. Jim and Karen are going through hell and you're down here dancing. William wanted to bet that you were at the circus, and sure as hell, you were! Are you enjoying the day, Matt? I knew that you were a callous man, but even with family? What if it was my daughter? Would you still be at the circus or dancing? Damn it, Matt, it was Hannie!" Lee's eyes were harsh.

Matt's voice grew deeper as he spoke slowly, "I know who she is. It wasn't you that saw her lay-ing there. It wasn't you at her autopsy. You didn't have to tell Karen that her daughter was murdered. *I had to*. Don't stand here and tell me I don't feel anything." He paused as his lip twitched and his eyes filled with liquid. "You're not the one being condemned while investigating her death and os-tracized by your family because of it."

Lee was unmoved. "You should never have stopped Bob from arresting that man. You knew he was crazy and a vagrant. You, of all people, should have had the foresight to know he was dangerous."

"How?" Matt asked. "Tell me, Lee, what indication was there that he was dangerous? You know so much about him; give me a sign he displayed that I should have recognized."

Lee raised his voice, "He was crazy! Steven told us about him a month ago at my house. Tim was in the right trying to protect this community. Hannie would be alive enjoying this dance if it wasn't for you stopping Bob. Vagrancy is not permitted within city limits and Bob had every right to arrest that insane man. You overrode him and set the murderer free. You never answered my question, Matt. Would you still be here dancing if it was Clarissa he murdered instead of Hannie?"

Matt was angry. "No, Lee, I wouldn't be. But I'd also hope you'd give me some credit beyond the words of Tim Wright. Maybe even listen to my side of the story before condemning me. But you're not. Yes, I released that man knowing he was crazy as a loon, and maybe I should not have, but I did! Let me tell you this; there was no indication that he was violent, and I still don't know that he did it…"

"Of course, he did it!" Lee shouted. "I don't know what's wrong with you, but you need to accept the fact that you made a mistake, and our family is paying for it. Unfortunately, I don't know how this will affect our family from here on out. You caused a rift that's torn the fabric and I doubt it can be mended because that side of the family wants nothing to do with you now."

Matt sighed heavily. "I did what I thought was right and I stand by it. They can hate me for the rest of their lives if they want to, but I did what was right," he said with finality.

Lee's eyes burned into his little brother fiercely. "No, you didn't. I just told you vagrancy is a crime in this city and Tim was doing what was right. Tim has jurisdiction within the city limits, not you! You have smacked him around so much that he is intimidated by you, but you had no legal responsibility or right to interfere with his duties. I'm telling you that right now, as a city of Branson and a Jessup County official, stay out of Tim's business. Your jurisdiction is outside city limits. Tim should be investigating Hannie's death, not you!" Lee finished firmly.

"Tim can't solve how the dog crap got in the yard without help and you know it. He's not a lawman. He's a politically appointed puppet for you jackasses in city government to order around."

"You heard me," Lee warned.

"I'm not giving up on Hannie's murder."

"What's there to give up?" Lee shouted. "It's solved! The man you released killed her. Get that through your head. Apologize to Jim and Karen. Maybe someday they'll forgive you."

"Who said it was solved? I never said it was," Matt argued.

"The Branson City Sheriff, Tim Wright! He's the lawful authority in charge, not you. It happened within city limits, Tim is the sheriff, and he has the authority to say when the investigation is over, not you. Hannie's murderer is dead, and the young man who tried to save her should be rewarded for his courage. And he will be in a couple of weeks."

"You have to be kidding me," Matt replied with scorn.

"You don't have any children that you raised, Matt. You have no idea what kind of grief Karen and Jim are going through. Hannie was as close to a daughter as William will ever have and she's gone because you had to do *what was right*," he mocked Matt. "It makes me wonder how you can sleep at night."

"I sleep just fine," Matt replied coldly.

"I bet," Lee said bitterly. "Her being family doesn't mean a damn thing to you, does it?"

"It means a lot to me! You and them can sit on your asses and mourn, but I don't have that luxury. I have a murder to figure out and you don't know half of the crap I'm dealing with and trying to sort out..."

"Like what circus act you liked best?" Lee chided.

Matt took a deep breath and exhaled to calm the fury that he was feeling. He spoke in a low, quiet voice, "Lee, you better walk away from me because we will not be getting along much longer."

"Are you going to try to hit me if I bring up the fact that your investigation sure looks like a lot of fun? The circus, dancing, what's next, a romantic dinner with Christine? This might just be the most fun day of your..."

"Lee," Regina interrupted as she walked around the courthouse corner with a man and a young woman. "Mister Chatfield and his daughter would like to speak with Matt. I would not interrupt, but it's urgent. His son was stabbed at the circus."

Horace Chatfield babbled, "Marshal, my son was stabbed several times. We don't know by who or why. Nancy heard him yell for help, and as she approached his cage, she was hit in the head and knocked out. David, my son, was stabbed."

"Is your son alive?" Matt asked.

"At the moment. The doctors have him in surgery. He was stabbed four or five times and it's serious, but he is alive at the moment. We just left the doctor's office."

"You didn't see who hit you?" Matt asked Nancy.

She shook her head to answer as she wiped her tears away.

Matt was still angry. "Lee, is that my jurisdiction or Tim's? It's right on the borderline of town. You know, I don't want to cross over into our sheriff's business or jurisdiction." His bitter sarcasm was plain to hear.

Lee scowled. "It's yours, obviously."

Matt answered his brother heatedly, "It would be my business if it happened in the middle of town too! Stay out of my way."

Horace spoke desperately, "Gentlemen, I understand you're having a tiff of some kind, but please keep that to yourselves. My son's life is endangered, and I need help." The hostility between the brothers was as visible as the large moon in the sky.

"I apologize," Matt said, ashamed of himself for letting his emotions get the best of him. "Tell me about your son. Does he have anyone with a grudge against him? A lady in his life with an unknown jealous beau or any other suspects that you know of?"

"No," Nancy said thoughtfully. "David is a very kind and loving sixteen-year-old boy. My parents adopted him when he was three and he's been a part of our sideshow all his life. He has no enemies. Everyone loves him."

"Sideshow?" Lee asked curiously.

"Yes. You saw him today, Marshal. He was born with a disease called hypertrichosis. He is the Tasmanian Wolf Boy."

"Him?" Matt asked. "He was staring at Christine and me."

"I'm not surprised," Nancy said. "You are a hero of his. No one in the circus would hurt him, Marshal Bannister. No one person would."

Matt said thoughtfully, "A lady drawing him said she had been there for a while, and he had not done that before. The stopping and staring, I mean."

"That's part of the act. Stop and stare at people once in a while to freak them out," Horace answered.

"Yeah, but he's been acting weird today," Nancy replied.

"How so?" Matt asked.

"Hmm, anxious. He didn't eat at suppertime and normally he does because he is so active. I went to see him, but he wouldn't tell me what the matter was. He was troubled about something."

"Where was he stabbed?"

"In the abdomen," Horace answered.

"No. Where was David found?" Matt asked.

"The end of his performing wagon."

"No other performers saw anything or anyone suspicious lurking around the area?" Matt asked.

"To be honest, we haven't talked to anyone. We got David to the doctor's office and prayed he'd survive until we could locate the doctor in time. A note on the door helped a lot, and we've been there since. We found the sheriff dancing, but he told us to find you."

Matt cast an irritated glance at Lee before replying to Horace, "I need to talk to your people. Someone has to know something. If you have all of your employees gather in your circus tent, I'll be there shortly." Small details were essential and the sooner he questioned the circus employees, the better any memory of any details would be.

Horace shrugged helplessly while raising his palms. "Most of our employees were going to go up on a nearby hill to watch the fireworks show. They probably already left, but I don't know since we haven't been back."

"Right after the fireworks then," Matt said. "I need them all there."

"I can't promise they'll all be there, but I'll do my best to have them there. It's the last night of the circus and a holiday; some of our people are already out and about getting drunk around town," Horace said.

Chapter 28

Matt had been able to watch the fireworks with Christine, but he didn't have the time to walk her back to the dance hall. He told her what had happened to the Tasmanian Wolf Boy, and together they prayed for him and his surgery. They also prayed that the person who did it would be brought to justice.

Matt stopped by the doctor's office and waited to speak with Doctor Mitchell Ryland, a more experienced surgeon than Doctor Bruce Ambrose.

He entered the large circus tent and found the bleachers full of employees waiting for him. Some he recognized from the circus and sideshow, but the majority worked behind the scenes. They all appeared to be tired and concerned for their friend.

Matt walked in front of the bleachers and the talking amongst the employees came to a stop as they put their attention on Matt.

"My name is Matt Bannister. I'm a U.S. Marshal.

I apologize for interrupting your Independence Day celebrations, but David Chatfield was stabbed, as you know. I'm here to collect any information you can give me. I assure you I will do my best to find the person or persons involved. I stopped by the doctor's office and spoke with the surgeon. If I can offer any comfort, it is we have a fantastic surgeon here; David is in good hands, despite our rural city. David lost a lot of blood and Doctor Ryland can't promise David will survive the night..."

The collective sigh of lost hope and the sound of sobbing from four or five people sounded.

"He's not going to survive?" one of the employees asked, heartbroken.

"Doctors Ryland and Ambrose are doing their best. The best we can do is pray for him to be strong enough to survive surgery and recovery. David isn't going anywhere for a while if he does survive. His wounds are serious and whoever did it intended to kill him. I'm here with you to find out why."

"Who would do that?" The Ugliest Woman in the World asked while weeping.

"That's the question I intend to find out. What I need from you folks is for you to tell me anything that might help. Do you know of any disagreements among your co-workers? Any relationships? Any debts? Any arguments? Anything at all might be important. Have you seen him or heard him argue with anyone?" Matt scanned the crowd for any faces that appeared more anxious than any others. Not one person seemed to be guilty or stuck out as suspicious.

"No," answered one of the cooks.

"We're all family," another answered.

It was quiet while many heads shook, and others shrugged unknowingly.

Matt questioned, "Nothing?"

"Nothing," answered one of the employees with a shrug.

"No," said another.

"Okay. Well, that doesn't help much," Matt said simply. "What about odd? Have you seen anything odd lately? You've only been here for a few days, so either it has been brewing for some time with one of you or it was a stranger from our town."

One of the most recognizable people was the Human Camel Spider, Susie Durden. She could not sit on the bleachers as an average person would. Instead, she sat on the lowest bench seat with her legs sticking straight out and her feet pointing toward the floor. She wiped her tears and sniffled. "Lord Jesus, please be with my friend. Help him to survive this." Her voice was as soft, emotional and pleasant as any Matt had heard before.

Theodore the Giant spoke sincerely, "He came to his bunk really late last night. He woke me up."

"I saw him sitting under a lantern last night reading a book about 2:00 a.m." one of the security guards offered. "I didn't talk to him, but he was sitting outside for a while."

No helpful answers were coming from the circus employees as Matt had hoped there would be. In the momentary silence, Matt said, "Nancy Chatfield mentioned David appeared anxious today. Did anyone else notice that or know why he might be?" Matt asked.

Head shakes and shrugged shoulders answered him.

Susie Durden spoke, "David didn't say. I could tell he was afraid of something, but he never told me what." She turned her head to look at Nancy Chatfield, who stood beside her father not too far from Matt. "Maybe that man he went to meet did something?"

"Oh yeah," Nancy said as if the thought had not occurred to her. "Matt, I took a few of our younger sideshow people to the river to swim yesterday and met a man who said he was a journalist from New York. He took an interest in David and they had plans to meet about midnight after the dance ended. The man said he wanted to write an article about David. I told David he could go see him."

"You did what?" Horace Chatfield exclaimed loudly. "By himself, Nancy?"

"I'm sorry, Father. I thought it would be fine and David really wanted to talk to him," Nancy began to weep.

"You let him go alone to meet a stranger at midnight? What were you thinking?" Horace was furious.

Matt sighed and dropped his head, dumbfounded. "That's important information to know. Was he dressed in leather clothing and named Avery Gaines or Napoleon?" Matt asked knowingly.

Nancy answered after a short hesitation, "He was naked, but yes, that was his name. Do you think he stabbed David?" Nancy asked with a whimper.

Horace was appalled. "You let him converse with a naked man and meet him alone at midnight? For crying out loud, Nancy!" He addressed Matt. "Is he a local pedophile? Did he harm my son?" Horace questioned emotionally. He turned back toward his daughter. He shouted, "You don't let anyone in our care wander off alone to meet a stranger! Ever! You know that!"

Nancy covered her face with her hands and cried. "I'm sorry."

"Is he the town pedophile?" Horace asked Matt again.

"No," Matt answered Horace. "Nancy, what name did he use? Avery Gaines or Napoleon?" Matt asked curiously.

"Avery Gaines."

"Is he a criminal?" Horace asked.

"No," Matt answered Horace. He asked Nancy, "Did David say anything about last night?"

"No. He didn't want to talk about it."

"Was he afraid or anxious before going to meet Avery Gaines?" Matt asked intentionally.

"No."

"Just today?" Matt questioned intently.

"Yes. Did Avery do something to him?" Nancy asked. Her shoulders began to shake emotionally in fear of the answer.

Matt shook his head. "I doubt it. The man called Avery Gaines told me he was a reporter doing a story about how he was treated as a crazy person in Branson. He dressed in rawhide and told me and others that he was from the middle earth. As of right now, I don't know who he was. A reporter or a crazy man pretending to be a reporter."

"Was?" Horace asked.

Matt nodded. "He was killed last night. I doubt he met with David, but I think David may have witnessed something bad. There were some teenagers down near Avery's camp drinking and being loud. Do you think the sound of laughter and arguing would draw David from Avery's camp through the woods?"

"Yes," Horace answered. "David is sixteen and like other boys, he longed to have friends. But because of his appearance, those friends outside of the circus are hard to find. If there were pretty girls there, they had his attention."

Nancy asked, "Avery was killed? You think David witnessed it?"

"He may have. It happened a few hundred yards directly across the woods from Avery's camp. I think I have all the information I need. If anything comes to mind, please let me know. A deputy will be in the office tomorrow if you need to get a hold of me."

Susie Durden dropped down to all fours and approached him. She stood at an awkward forty-five-degree angle on her feet and raised a hand to shake Matt's. "I'm Susie. I want you to know David would have been so excited to meet you. I am too, but him more so."

Matt shook her hand. She stood no more than four and a half feet tall with the angle of her body.

"It's nice to meet you, Susie. Can I ask you something rather personal?"

"Sure."

"My fiancée and I came through the sideshow today and heard some awful things people said. It broke my fiancée's heart to hear such mean-spirited words being spoken to you. It broke my heart too. Does it bother you to hear crap like that?"

Her smile had a humility to it. "I remember your fiancée and you being there, Marshal Bannister. In truth, I'm used to it. Words only hurt if you let them inside. I figure it's stupidity on their part, not mine. Like the young man you told to knock it off, I scrape comments like his off as easily as wiping dust off my sleeve."

Matt was interested in talking to the young lady. "My fiancée was very sad."

"Your fiancée told me I was beautiful," Susie said with a small smile. "I think she is gorgeous. She started crying when she saw me, didn't she?"

"Yes. She felt very sorry for you."

Susie offered a content smile. "Please tell her for me that the circus sideshow is a blessing because I come from a poor family and I can help them financially. If it wasn't for the circus, what else could I do? I can't stand for too long and walk on my hands and feet. I would starve to death or be forced into an asylum to be studied. I don't want to be studied or treated like I'm helpless. I want to be independent and live my life as fully as anyone else. My knees and feet are backward, but I am just as human as you and your fiancée are. I have dreams of a better future for myself. I can cook and clean, but I can't chop wood or carry groceries. The circus gives me the means to buy my own house and pay others to do what I can't do. So no, what people say doesn't bother me because this is a means to an end. I was born this way and learned to live just like this. What job can I get to support myself and who would hire me? If I was a waitress and brought you a plate of food, could you eat it? I get paid very well for abnormalities that I was born with, and I'll retire better than most of the people who make fun of me. Someday, I hope to get married and have children. It is only my knees and feet that are different. Other than those, I'm just like any other young lady, including your fiancée. Helen, our quote, Ugliest Woman in the World, is one of the most beautiful souls you will ever meet. It's not all as it appears and we are well taken care of. We're not being exploited; we are making a good living with what we were given. And in this world, you have to make a living, or you die. Tell your fiancée I don't want or deserve her pity. I'm better off than many people she probably knows."

"You're a bright young girl," Matt said with admiration.

"I have no choice but to be with Mister Chatfield and Nancy mentoring me. Now, can I ask you a personal question?"

"Sure."

"Are you and your fiancée seriously engaged or is there some wiggle room for me to steal you away from her?" Her expression revealed it was asked in jest.

Matt couldn't help but smile appreciatively. "Miss Durdin, you are a beautiful lady. Unfortunately, we're seriously engaged."

"I was joking. Seriously though, David has a dime novel about you. Can I have you sign it for him?"

Matt gave a hesitant exaggerated grimace. "You know...I'd hate to do that because those are mostly fiction, if not all fiction. And I can't stand those. I'll tell you what, David's going to get to know me over the next weeks that he is recovering, so I don't think he'll mind me not signing that."

She nodded with understanding. "If he survives," she said with a heavy burden crossing her expression.

"How about you and I pray right now that he does."

She nodded and stood awkwardly again to take his hands in hers. Matt reversed it and took her hands in his. "Jesus, you created the heavens and the earth and all humanity. You are the Lord of our lives and judge of our souls. Your power and goodness are far above our understanding and Susie, the others and I come before you in prayer to ask you to spare David's life. Please help him to survive the night and the long recovery. We ask for your power to intervene and keep his heart pumping and restore the blood from his blood loss. We ask for your blessing upon the doctor's hands and David's strength to be strengthened by you. In your name, Jesus, Amen."

Susie stared into Matt's eyes as he held her hands. "Thank you."

"You're welcome, sweetheart. If you'll excuse me, I have some business to take care of before the night is through."

"Matt, before you go, can I write to you sometimes after we leave?"

"I hope you do. I'd love to hear from you."

"Matt, one more thing. Catch the person that hurt my friend."

His slight smile faded to a stern expression of determination. "I will. You have my word on that."

Chapter 29

Nick Griffin, Ollie Hoffman and Tad Sperry stood in the courtyard of the Dogwood Shacks drinking from a bottle of whiskey while they laughed over something Tad said.

It had been a disappointing night for Ollie. Rose never showed up at the dance and Ollie assumed Matt was right; she and her sister were probably in a great deal of trouble at home. He watched the fireworks feeling more alone than a young man should in the middle of a large crowd. Ollie longed to see Rose while he watched the illumination of colors bursting in the sky; how he wished she was beside him. Oddly, he had never been too attracted to Rose or considered her a potential prospect for being his one and only, but after last night, he could not get her off his mind. He loved her.

"Love?" Nick questioned, "That's the foulest four-letter word in the human language. It has destroyed more lives than any other four-letter word in the world. Ten times over. It's been one day, Ollie, just one day and you're already consumed by Rose Fowler. Why?" He shrugged with a disapproving grimace. "She's not even pretty. She's cute, like a dog is cute, but she's not pretty. You could do better."

Tad Sperry took a swig of the bottle. "Cute is good enough. At least you two have options. Where I live, it's cousin number one or cousin number two!" he laughed.

Ollie asked Tad, "Aren't your uncles going to wonder where you are?"

"No! They're at the saloon or dance hall and Grandma's sleeping by now. I have all night. Shall we go to Rose's house and play Romeo and Juliet? You can throw a rock at her window and serenade her while Nick and I sneak in to see her sister."

"No! Her father would be mad. Besides, I don't know where they live," Ollie admitted.

"Not here," Nick replied, looking around the Dogwood Shacks apartments. "You know when you see Rose again, she's going to ignore you. You know that, right?"

"No," Ollie argued, "we are a couple now."

Nick scoffed doubtfully. "Her father won't allow her to be courted by you. She probably got whipped and will still have a sore hind end when she sees you again. I'll bet she will walk right past you like kissing you was the worst mistake of her life so far, maybe ever."

"I don't think she will," Ollie replied with a touch of doubt in his voice.

"Wait and see. Oh...crap. Here comes the mar-shal," Nick said with a touch of frustration. "Hello, Marshal Bannister. What can I do for you now?"

"You can hand me your knife," Matt said bluntly.

"My knife? For what?" He felt a chill race down his spine. He did not expect to become a suspect for stabbing the freak. Panic began to seize him, and his hand slowly reached for his knife, but the sheath was not on his belt. The moment of panic dropped like a granite block off the granite pit's wall and a comforting sense of relief surrounded him like the soft cushion of an extra-filled feathered mattress. "Actually, I can't give you my knife because I don't have it."

"Where is your knife?" Matt demanded with no patience in his voice.

"I sold it to John at the Saloon."

Matt was skeptical. "Let's go into your apart-ment and get your knife."

Nick laughed uneasily. "I just told you I sold it to John at the saloon."

Ollie added, "It's true, Marshal."

Nick chuckled. "Marshal, you can check with John Riggs at the Green Toad. He offered me five dollars for the knife that killed the leather man. I traded it for this bottle. If I'm lying, you can come back and arrest me for lying to you, but that's the honest truth. If you want my knife, that's where it is."

Matt took a step forward and stared at Nick with a hardened glare. "If you are lying to me, I will come back and arrest you. Don't bother running.

My career and reputation were made from tracking men down, men much smarter than you. Where were you earlier tonight, around 7:00 p.m. or so?"

"Here, I think. I don't carry a watch, so it's hard to tell, but I was all over town. There's a celebration going on and a lot to see. Ollie and I went to the circus this afternoon and then around town, and we were going to the dance when I ran into Tad. He and I went to Rose Street and spoke with my father and that's when John offered to buy my knife. Tad and I started drinking here and then Ollie came home. Why?"

"Is that true, boys?" Matt asked the two others.

"Yeah," Ollie agreed. Tad nodded his head.

Though it was dark, the moon was bright, and the boys had a lantern burning on the ground in front of them. Matt could see no visible blood stains on Nick's clothing. The clothes he had on the night before were splattered with Avery Gaines' blood, but the clothes he presently wore didn't have a drop of blood on them that could be seen. His yellow long-sleeved shirt would have revealed any blood spots and the tan-striped pants would have been discolored enough for Matt's keen eye to spot any discolored blotches, even in the dim light.

"You better hope I don't have to come back," Matt said before leaving the boys to walk to Rose Street.

"I'll hope you don't come back," Nick laughed as Matt turned the corner.

"I hate that man," Tad said.

Ollie spoke to Nick, "He asked me if I saw the leather man swimming last night while at the dance and then he took that necklace you gave me."

Nick glanced at Ollie quickly. "You told him I gave the necklace to you?"

"Yeah, he asked. He said the leather man's family would want it back."

Nick asked, "You saw him in the water, didn't you?"

Ollie shook his head. "No, I didn't see him. But like I told the marshal, my attention was on Rose."

Nick exhaled with a twisted grin. "That's alright." Silently, he thanked any god there was that he had decided to sell John his spare knife and not the one that he killed the leather man and stabbed the monkey boy with. Luck was on his side; it was pure coincidence that he got the lucky break.

"I don't think he'll be coming back," Nick said. He held the bottle up to his mouth and took a drink. The whiskey was watered down and of poor quality, but it was suddenly well worth the price of a spare knife.

***

Matt held the knife in his hands and looked over the blade, spine, edge, butt and black stacked leather handle for bloodstains. There was no trace of blood visible or a single hair from Nancy's head on the butt of the knife from the blow to her head. He took a damp white rag that John had and ran it along the base of the blade and handle guard and collected barely more than dust. There was no evidence of it being used to stab David or Avery, for that matter.

There was a good possibility that Nick had washed the blood off the knife, but the tight black leather grip was perfectly dry. If it had been washed the night before, it would be dry, but not just an hour before selling it to John.

"The handle was dry when you bought it?" Matt asked.

"Yes, sir. It was just like it is now," John answered. "I asked Nick why there was no blood because that would have been nice to have on the blade." He added quietly, "I may even put some red paint on there and let it dry for a bit before wiping it off to give it a red shimmer. I thought it would be a good wall decoration. You know, the knife that killed the murdering leather man." He nodded his head with a wide grin.

"What did Nick say when you asked about the bloodstains?"

"He said he washed it off. He didn't want the man's blood on his knife."

"Hmm," Matt grunted. It was another trail that led to nowhere. "Alright, thank you, John."

"Do you want a drink?"

"No. I'm calling it a night."

Matt turned to leave and saw Leonard Griffin standing close behind him with a scowl on his intoxicated face.

"You're still at it trying to prove my son's a killer?" Leonard accused loudly. "My boy's a hero! A hero, do you hear me?" Leonard Griffith shouted. "What are you trying to prove?"

Matt had no desire to deal with an angry drunk man. "Excuse me," he said as he tried to step around him.

Leonard pushed Matt with both hands as he passed, and Matt fell against a table where four men were seated. Leonard shouted, "I asked you a question, boy! What are you trying to prove?"

Matt pushed himself off the table and back to his feet. There was no consideration; he drove a hard right fist into Leonard's abdomen, just below the sternum, knocking the breath out of the man. The glass fell from Leonard's hand and hit the floor simultaneously with Leonard's knees. He fell forward, gasping for a breath.

The crowded saloon of men grew quiet, and many stood to get a better view of what had happened.

Matt dropped his left knee on the upper back of Leonard and forced him flat on the floor. He grabbed Leonard's chin with his right hand while his left hand held a handful of hair and twisted Leonard's head until it stopped. Now having the man's full attention, Matt spoke fiercely, "You're playing with fire, Mister Griffin! I'm not someone you push and get away with it. I'm investigating your son. Yes, I am! If your son is guilty, he will hang. I'll gladly put the noose around his neck myself. If he's not guilty, then all is well. Whether I like your son or not is not part of the equation. Are we clear on that?"

"Argghioe," Leonard grunted out an unintelligibly while rapidly slamming the floor with his hand.

Some of the men nearby chuckled.

"I assume that's a yes."

A stream of warm vomit spewed out of his mouth across Matt's hand. Matt released him and stood quickly while shaking the vomit off his hand with a disgusted grimace. Leonard got to his hands and knees, vomiting until nothing was left in his stomach. The constricting muscles of his abdomen refused to quit convulsing and Leonard's face turned red as he strained involuntarily to vomit up an empty stomach.

"Here," John tossed Matt a towel.

"Thanks," Matt said as he wiped off his hand.

"No, thank you for the mess I have to clean up," John complained.

"I think he might have been trying to tell me that he was going to puke, but I mistook it for understanding that we were clear," Matt said with a humored chuckle. "I think we're clear, though."

Matt stepped outside the saloon and heard a commotion as the Sperry brothers led their brother Alan down the street. Alan Sperry was stumbling and fighting with Jack and Vince to let him go. He wanted to go back and kill a man. Alan was upset, crying and shouting, "I'll kill him! Let me go; I'm going to kill him!"

Matt paused to watch. Morton Sperry saw him and approached with a half-grin. "Hello, Matt. My brother drank too much. We're taking him back to our camp before he gets in trouble."

"Good idea," Matt said as he watched the two

Sperry brothers leading Alan away. He had met Alan Sperry that day, but Matt had heard a lot about Alan. It would be wise to know who he threatened if that man ended up dead. "Who angered him?"

Morton pressed his lips together tightly. "I'm sure you know Cliff Jorgeson from Willow Falls?"

"Of course. Why is your brother threatening him?"

Morton raised his eyebrows with a shrug. "When Alan was sentenced to prison, his wife left him. Racheal took their kids and slipped away to somewhere, but nobody knows where. We couldn't find her, though we searched to bring her and the kids home. They're Sperrys, you'll understand."

"What does that have to with Cliff?"

Morton chuckled. "She's Cliff's sister."

"Racheal Jorgeson? Alan married Racheal?" Matt asked. The surprise in his voice was not hidden.

"Yeah. You didn't know that?"

"No. When I left here, she was Lee's sweetheart. I had a bit of a crush on her myself when I was young."

"Yeah," Morton said slowly. "She's part of the friction between Alan and Lee."

"I didn't know there was any friction between them."

"I don't know about now, but before Alan married Racheal, there was. You know, Alan and Lee fought together in a war. They were all pretty close, but after coming home, your brother and mine fought over Racheal, which separated their friendship a

269

bit. Alan married Racheal and they had a couple of kids. After he went to prison, Racheal and the kids disappeared one day. The last we have heard of her was the divorce papers Alan received in prison." He pointed down the street. "Cliff is down there and refused to tell Alan where she is. Cliff says he doesn't know and wouldn't tell Alan if he did. I'll admit, Alan wasn't the best husband. Short temper and all, you know."

"Tell Alan I overheard him. I understand he is drunk and upset, but if anything happens to Cliff. He will be my first suspect. Morton, I should tell you I got a letter from the prison warden stating that Alan was coming home and would probably cause trouble before long. He is suspected of killing another prisoner not long ago. The warden said Alan is a dangerous man."

"He can be," Morton admitted. "Matt, this is the first time he's acted like this since coming home. The drinking sparked him. He believes Cliff snuck Racheal out of the area and is protecting her, which he may be. We searched for her, Matt, the whole Sperry-Helms Gang did, and we didn't find her. I'll admit we nearly beat Cliff to death, and he didn't say anything. I honestly don't think Cliff knows where Racheal is. Alan, on the other hand, he's not convinced."

"Well, let Alan know I'm aware of his threats and will come looking if anything happens to Cliff. Speaking of the Sperry-Helms Gang, any good robberies you fellows are planning?"

Morton laughed. "Yeah, the Branson Bank on Monday, 2:00 p.m. sharp." He looked at Matt appreciatively. "I told you, I'm trying to change my life. And I have you to thank for that. Spending time with you has opened my eyes to a few things and I'll be honest, I don't like cutting wood for a living, the tannery or farm work, but I'm trying to go straight."

Matt hesitated. "Run for sheriff. Your sheriff, Zeke Jones, may be a nice old man, but he is worthless as a lawman. If you run for sheriff, I'll help you."

"Ole Zeke is a good-hearted man. That office is all he has, Matt."

"Keep him as your deputy if you want. I'll talk with the town council to approve it if you're up to it."

"Can you imagine me as a lawman?" Morton asked doubtfully.

"I can. If you wore the badge with honor, you'd do well."

"I'd be fighting my relatives most of the time," he said with a grin.

"Or maybe they wouldn't cross any lines because of you. Think about it carefully because if you do, I'll be the one that holds you accountable for enforcing the law. Your sheriff now can't do that. You could."

"I'm an outlaw, Matt. Everyone knows that."

"There comes a time when you have to decide if you want to change your life or not. You can't go straight if you continue to call yourself an outlaw.

You either ride with your brothers and cousins or stand alone. The choice is yours, Morton. But someday, if the Sperry Helms Gang starts robbing again, we will square off. I might lose some men, but so will your family. But if you were the sheriff and a *just* sheriff, that may never happen. In a town of gunmen, it takes a gunman to keep the peace. You could do that if you wear the badge with honor."

***

Cliff Jorgeson was a good-sized man. He was broad-shouldered and muscular in his early thirties with short light brown, almost blond hair and a clean-shaven face. It wasn't that he could not grow a mustache or beard, which he would have preferred, but his wife refused to kiss him if he had either. It was the only downfall he could think of for being in love with his wife.

He was a family man, happy at home and work and perfectly content with the life he and his family were living. He wasn't wealthy by a mile, but wealth doesn't have to be financial. He was wealthy where it mattered the most, in his family relationships, friends, and soul. He had brought his family to Branson to enjoy the festivities and, after the fireworks, decided to go to the saloon with his friend, Johnny Barso.

Johnny Barso was another man that had grown up in Willow Falls and was now the deputy sheriff under Sheriff Tom Smith. Both men were surprised to see Alan Sperry out of prison and by the altercation that followed. If it wasn't for Big John Pederson interfering and the Sperry boys grabbing Alan and hauling him out of Ugly John's Saloon, Alan would have physically assaulted Cliff. Cliff was no weak link to deal with by any means, but he didn't have the killer instinct that Alan was known for.

Cliff was relieved to hear Matt say he had overheard Alan yelling threats about him. Alan knowing he would be the number one suspect if anything did happen to Cliff might be just enough to persuade Alan to leave Cliff alone. He hoped anyway. The boys from Willow Falls were not cowards, but it didn't take courage to carry a fresh bloody steak through a hungry wolf pack; it took the wisdom not to try it.

Matt Bannister joined the two friends at their small table in Ugly John's. He yawned. "I didn't know Racheal married Alan."

"Yeah," Cliff said. "About thirteen or fourteen years ago. Alan was mean to her right from the start; he's a horrible man. My parents tried to help her get away from that family, but we couldn't do anything to help her. The Sperrys kept her prisoner in their home. I think worrying about her led to my parents' early grave."

"I'm sorry to hear that. How did you get Racheal out of there?"

Cliff raised his hands to reflect emptiness. "I didn't. I don't know where she is. I get letters from her, but there is no address. She's too afraid of Alan finding her. They have two little girls and Racheal doesn't want them growing up around that family."

"You don't know where she is?"

"No. And she won't tell me. I don't know how she got away from there either."

"Morton said he didn't think you knew."

Cliff chuckled. "Well, they whipped me over good. But I can't tell them what I don't know and that's why she has never told me. For my safety and her girls."

Chapter 30

On Saturday morning, the sun broke over the horizon to the unusual sound of an elephant's trumpeting echoing off the mountain. For those who worked for the circus, it was a familiar sound, but for the people of Jessup County, it was the first time an elephant had ever been in town and cause for excitement. For Nancy Chatfield, it was a sad sound on a gloomy morning. The glorious sunrise, by all appearances, promised to be a bright and sunny day, but even the beauty of a sunrise couldn't lift her heavy heart.

It had been a long night of praying, waiting, trying to sleep, waking after an hour perhaps, and seeking the newest update on David's surgery. Was the surgery over? Did David survive it? Was her little brother still alive? Prayer was the most she could do, and she prayed earnestly often during the night. She could do nothing at the doctor's office any more than she could at the circus grounds, but at least among her traveling family, she was comforted by their love and shared concern.

David was far more than the Tasmanian Wolf Boy; he was an ordinary human teenage boy. It never occurred to Nancy that David may have been scared to death by something terrible he may have witnessed. It was the only explanation of why anyone would want to kill him. David was a well-behaved, sensitive and kind young man who may have looked quite different from most people and perhaps even scary to some, but he wouldn't harm a person and hated to scare children. Fortunately, children were not allowed into the sideshow to protect their eyes from disfigurements that might cause them nightmares and anxieties.

Nancy sat alone at a folding table in the cookhouse, merely a large canvas tent with two dozen folding tables surrounded by folding canvas seats, drinking a cup of coffee. She yawned as she rubbed the cut on her head gently. It was going to be a long day with little sleep. Tiredness was part of the circus life.

"Have you heard anything about David yet?" Susie Durden asked. She had entered the cookhouse on her gloved hands and feet. Her reddened eyes from a lack of sleep and worry watched Nancy with concern for her friend.

Nancy rested her head against a propped-up arm. "Father's at the doctor's office now and will return to let us know. As they say, no news is good news. The doctor didn't come during the night to say he passed away."

"That's good news," Susie said without any comfort in her voice. "You didn't sleep well either, did you?"

"Hardly at all."

"Me neither. I doubt any of us did. Do you want me to pack up David's things for you?"

Nancy answered slowly. "No. Alice's feet are hurting her today. Why don't you help her and let her rest her feet? I want to pack David's things because he's not coming with us, and he'll want his stuff with him here while he recovers. I believe he'll recover. I have to believe that," she said more to herself than to Susie.

"He can't stay here alone, Nancy. This town will harass him and make his life terrible. You should have heard some of the people here yesterday."

"I'm staying with him. I don't know how long we will be here, Susie."

"Don't worry about us, we'll be fine. I just worry about David and how this town will treat him. And if Matt doesn't find the person who did this to him, there is a chance David might not be out of danger."

"I know. But I think the marshal will keep him safe. He seems like a very nice and caring man."

"Handsome too! I'd marry him," Susie offered.

Nancy chuckled. "He is handsome."

"If you stay here and steal him from his fiancée and bring him along with the circus, I will be very jealous."

"I doubt I could get him to quit his job to join the circus, but if I could, I'd have to fire you, Susie, because I know you'd steal him away from me."

Susie laughed. Her laugh was a delightful sound of youth, innocence and joy. "I'd definitely try!"

The tent flap opened, and a young stranger

peered inside. "Excuse me," he asked with a smile. His eyes stared at Susie while his expression transformed into disgust.

"Yes?" Nancy asked impatiently. Her tolerance for rude people wasn't at its acceptable level that morning.

"Um...ah..."

"Spit it out or I might bite," Susie said, not surprised by his reaction. She recognized him from the day before. He was one of the rudest and most cruel of all the customers with his words to all the other sideshow exhibits.

"I'm new. I'm Nick Griffin, a new employee. I was told to find someone named Jeff? I don't know who he is or where to find him." His eyes shifted from Nancy back to Susie.

Nancy spoke candidly, "It's not nice to stare at people around here, Nick. Her name is Susie. She's not really a camel spider; she's a very normal seventeen-year-old girl. You can say hi to her. She doesn't bite."

"Sometimes I do," Susie replied to Nancy. "Especially when boys are mean to my friends and me. Like a certain boy yesterday with black hair who made some vulgar comments about me of the sexual nature that I recall. That was you, wasn't it? I never forget a face that I would prefer to forget."

"Huh? Um..." His face began to blush. The teasing and making fun of her the day before were now coming back to haunt him. He never expected to see the freaks outside of their cages, let alone ever have to talk to one. He was suddenly alarmed that his actions the day before in the sideshow would interfere with his new job.

"Answer her question, Nick," Nancy urged.

"Yeah, that was me," he admitted awkwardly. "Sorry. It didn't mean anything. I was just joshing with my pal."

Nancy spoke firmly, "My name is Nancy Chatfield, the circus owner's daughter. That means I can fire you before you even get started if I want to. And if I don't like you, I will. Nick, we are family around here, and you do not impress me so far. Why were you being mean to my friends yesterday?"

"Um...I was just playing," he shrugged uneasily.

Nancy looked at Susie curiously, "Did Nick make fun of Bigfoot Alice's feet yesterday?"

Susie nodded. "Of course. He and his friend laughed at her, but I don't recall exactly what they said. Something about not needing snowshoes for hiring her as a pack mule over the mountain in the winter or something." She looked at Nick, "What was the joke you made about her feet?"

Nick closed his eyes, annoyed by the interrogation. "I said we could make a fortune strapping supplies on her back to cross the mountain when the snow gets too deep. She wouldn't need snowshoes."

Nancy sighed. In truth, it wasn't the worst remarks she had ever heard. "Nick, Alice's feet hurt today. How would you like to rub them for her to make up for being mean to her?"

He was horrified by the thought. "I was hired to help break down the tents and stuff."

Nancy and Susie laughed. "I'm teasing. But if you join up with us, you will get to know Alice and the others and before long, you won't even notice that they are different. They'll just be part of the family and then you will get angry when you hear other young men like you speaking to them as you did. You'll realize how stupid you were to say things like that."

"Yes, Ma'am, I imagine so."

Nancy noticed the knife sheath on his belt. It wasn't uncommon to see a young man carrying a knife. Little did she know it was the knife that stabbed her brother and hit her over the head. "You'll find Jeff in the big tent."

"I looked there," Nick said.

"Did you look up? Before anything else, the trapeze equipment and all of that needs to come down."

"No. I didn't."

"Go look there and if he's not there, wait for him. He'll put you to work."

Susie watched him leave. "He was mean to David too."

"A lot of people are. He's your age, Susie, and kind of handsome. Maybe love is calling your name next? Hmm?"

Susie grinned uneasily. "I doubt it. He gives me the heebie-jeebies."

***

Nancy went to David's bunk area and sat down on his cot. Like all of them, personal belongings were limited by space, and a canvas bag or case was about all the personal belongings they could carry. The basics, three pairs of clothes, a hat or two, shoes, a coat, and a slicker for the rain. David was a reader and had a few books. Nancy picked up what was lying on the floor and stowed them in his canvas bag. A thin wooden board and a leather-bound book caught her attention. It wasn't a reading book but a journal with a buckle and leather strap to keep it bound shut. On the front cover stamped into the leather were the words:

This book belongs to Avery Gaines.
If found, please return for a reward.

Nancy pulled the leather tab from a loop and opened the journal. She read the first page and skipped through the pages until she gasped.

Chapter 31

Matt did not mind waking up in a quiet house or being alone. It was relaxing and he enjoyed it. Truet was his best friend, but it was nice not to have him home sometimes. Matt made a fire in the cookstove to heat water for coffee and fried up a quick breakfast of bacon and eggs. He sat at his dining table and ate in the quiet while his mind went back to the night before. He had been so busy over the past two days that it was nice to sit down and eat quietly with no one around him. A moment of silence was a moment to himself.

Now that Independence Day was over, he planned to speak to each of the teenagers on the island Thursday night. They might offer more information now that they had a day or two to settle their nerves and speak freely to him. He hoped to learn more than he knew and, Lord willing, offer a key to determining once and for all who killed Hannie.

Hannie's parents, William and even Lee and Regina, had already accepted that the stranger referred to as the leather man did it and blamed Matt for allowing him to roam free. The close relationships he once had were troubled and if the leather man did kill Hannie, they may never be mended. It was an odd sensation knowing if he went to his relative's homes for a friendly visit, he would not be welcomed. He didn't know if he would be welcomed to Albert and Mellissa's or even the Big Z Ranch at the moment. He had become the family's black sheep and felt like a calf with scours separated from the herd and alone for the first time since coming back home.

He hadn't had the time to mourn for the pretty young girl that just started calling him Uncle Matt. He didn't watch her grow up as the others had, but he had gotten to know her enough to know she was beautiful and a shining light that brought so much joy to their family. Her uncle, William Fasana, had a strong relationship with her, and Matt knew he was hurting deeply. If the leather man did kill her, Matt doubted William would ever forgive him for letting that man roam free. It would be the end of their close-knit family as it was stitched together now. One frayed stitch can loosen others and soon, the seam of the fabric comes apart. The idea of the family drifting apart because of him was a depressing thought.

A knock on his door brought him out of his thoughts. People have specific patterns of knocking where it becomes automatic to hear the knock and know who is knocking; such was the knocking pattern of Nate Robertson.

Matt unlocked the door and opened it without asking or worrying about who was there. Nate was with Nancy Chatfield.

She held out a leather-bound journal. "Read this. David wrote in it too. It was in his stuff," she said simply.

Matt's brow lifted to see the journal. He recognized it immediately. "I will, thank you. How is David?" he asked.

"I'm not sure, but no news is good news. I just wanted to get that to you. Read it. I'm going to the doctor's office now. Your deputy was good enough to show me where you live."

"Thank you for bringing it. I'll read it right now."

"Matt, one more thing. Who would I talk to about staying with David while he recovers from surgery? If everything goes well, that is."

Matt raised a single finger. "Don't you worry about that. I'll take care of it. Let me read this and I'll find you later today."

Matt sat down on his davenport and opened the leather man's journal. He learned that the leather man was Avery Gaines, a reporter for the Monmouth Pointe Chronicle in New York. The journal explained Avery had been asked to hide his identity and live other lives in various cities to investigate what was happening under city officials' noses. He had written articles that came in four parts and were highly successful. Avery was asked by Robert Fairchild, the owner of the newspaper, to do a piece on Jessup County and Branson, particularly on how he was treated as a stranger on Independence Day.

To make the article more interesting, Avery decided to copy the leather suit to all aspects of the real Leather Man that roamed a three-hundred-mile route in upper New York and Connecticut every month for reasons no one understood. Avery had a rawhide suit made to appear old and dirty. To make the character even odder, Avery decided it would be fun to borrow from the book *Journey to the Center of the Earth* and make up a character who said he was from the middle earth. He thought the name Napoleon Pickle would get some laughs when the public read the article back in New York.

Avery wrote of Willow Falls and his first experience wearing the costume and using his awkward walk. He wrote about how the locals reacted. He mentioned Steven Bannister by name and the kindness of his wife, Nora. He wrote of his excitement to learn the famous U.S. Marshal Matt Bannister was in Branson and couldn't wait to meet him in July when he mysteriously reappeared.

He wrote about meeting the Branson Sheriff, how unfriendly Tim Wright was, and how polite and friendly Matt Bannister was to him, even though Matt's deputies laughed at him. He wrote about Bob trying to arrest him for vagrancy, but Matt rescued him from being detained and, in doing so, saved Avery's assignment.

Matt read page by page to when Avery was resting beside the river to update his journal. He wrote that he was naked when a small group of so-called freaks from the circus abruptly surprised him. Avery took great interest in the group and wanted to interview David, a young man with Hypertrichosis going by the stage name of the Tasmanian Wolf Boy. Avery had plans of going to the community dance in his leather suit, but afterward, he scheduled a meeting at midnight at Avery's camp to interview David. It was an interview that Avery looked forward to doing with great excitement by the words he had written.

Matt turned the page and there were the words:

> *My name is David Chatfield. I am known as the Tasmanian Wolf Boy in the Chatfield & Bowry Circus Sideshow.*
>
> *I have Avery's journal because I watched him be killed tonight. I am scared because the girl with blonde hair saw me in the brush and ran away screaming, she saw a werewolf. I'm the only one that looks like a werewolf. I heard her screaming after she ran away from me, but it was different, so I went to see why.*
>
> *Let me start at the beginning, I was waiting for Avery to meet me at his camp, but I heard laughter and people talking upriver. I was curious and found a group*

of teenagers drinking from bottles and having fun. I wished I could join them, but I have already written the response I would have been greeted with. I watched from the forest. One girl, a beautiful girl I would have loved to meet, was named Elizabeth. She kissed the pillow that the blonde girl, I believe, had brought. Some of the people were kissing, some not. Elizabeth showed how she would kiss someone. I could only wish it was me.

A drunk boy called Nick got into a fight with Elizabeth and kicked the fire onto her. Another boy jumped up, but Nick pulled his knife on him. Nick got mad and left carrying a bottle of something with him. The others decided to go. I watched them leave. I saw in the dim firelight that the pillow kissed was left behind. I wanted to grab it as a keepsake. Elizabeth was beautiful and it's as close to her as I'll ever be able to get. Or any girl, really.

I was going to go out and get it when the blonde girl with curly hair came back to get her pillow. She saw me in the moonlight and screamed. She ran away. I heard her screaming like she was being hurt and I went to see. I saw the boy Nick sitting on her chest, strangling her. I was frozen in fear. He killed her. He

287

looked around and frightened himself, I suppose, he dragged her onto the bridge and tossed her into the current. That is when Avery yelled and came down to help her. He stripped his leather clothing and went into the water to get her. He pulled her to the bank and told Nick to get help. Nick pulled his knife and began stabbing Avery. I could not look away and I was scared to death. I began to back away when Nick looked my way. I stepped on a twig, and it snapped. He knew I was there, and he started to come at me when he heard others coming. He went towards them. I heard him yell that Avery killed the girl as I ran back to Avery's camp as fast as possible. I don't know why, but I wanted his journal. So, I took it and the board he set it on to write with. It is working well.

I am afraid to tell anyone what I saw, so I am writing it. I plan on leaving this at the post office right before we leave town for the marshal Matt Bannister. I hope it helps.

I don't like to think I am a coward, but I am. I am scared that Nick will recognize me if he comes to the sideshow and want to kill me. I'm afraid he saw me and is around the corner even now. I can't tell anyone, though. I just want to get far away and stay away. Avery was going to do an article about me. He was the only friend I have made outside of the circus. That doesn't happen often.

So, Matt Bannister, I will be gone if you read this, but it is the truth.

P.S. – You are a hero to me.

Your friend,
David Chatfield, also known as the Tasmanian Wolf Boy.

Matt set the journal down. It was time to make things right.

Chapter 32

Matt entered the Monarch Hotel and was greeted politely by Pamela Collins behind the curved courtesy desk.

"Good morning, Pamela," he responded in kind. "Is William here?"

She narrowed her brow in thought. "He should be. He had to work last night. I don't think he wanted to, but it's the one night a year that we need him the most. He's pretty upset about Hannie, as you know."

Matt nodded while squeezing his lips together. "Can I get the key to his room?"

"Sure." She opened a locked cabinet under the counter and handed Matt a spare key.

"Thank you. And..." he added slowly, "in a few days, we will be transferring a young man who was stabbed at the circus over here to recover for a while. His name is David Chatfield. Did you go to the circus sideshow?"

She was repulsed. "No. I didn't want to."

"If you had, you would have seen him. He is the Tasmanian Wolf Boy. He has a disease where his whole body is covered with hair, including his face."

"A beard?" she asked skeptically. "You have a beard, Matt."

"Not exactly, no. I'm talking about long hair all over his face like a legendary werewolf. His sister will be staying with him as his caretaker, but we'll make the arrangements later. I just wanted to let you know you're going to have to move William."

"He's not going to like that."

Matt shrugged. "Convince Lee to build another downstairs room or, better yet, a hospital. There is nowhere else to put David that is convenient."

"Okay, we'll make it work."

Matt unlocked the door and entered William's dark room. William snored as he slept on his back with his blankets tossed off the bed. The bedside table was littered with glasses, a mixed bunch of water and stiff drinks. His room had a consistent stale aroma to it.

Matt grabbed a single wooden chair and set it beside the bed. He sat quietly. "William, get up and get your badge. I need your help."

William blinked his eyes a few times to focus on Matt. "What do you want?" he snapped.

"You to help me. Get up and get dressed."

"I don't want to help you. Just get out and let me sleep!" William shouted. He laid back down and turned away from Matt. "Get out and leave me alone."

"Yes, you do want to help me. We're going to arrest the person that murdered Hannie."

William quickly sat up and glared at Matt with a dangerous glare. "He's already dead! Don't forget, you let him go. Get out of here, Matt, before I change my mind and hurt you!"

Matt leaned forward on his knees to speak clearly, "He was trying to save her. The leather man did not kill her. He is the true hero that gave his life trying to save her. Nick killed Hannie. I found a witness that saw the whole thing. Nick stabbed my witness last night to kill him."

William's brow lowered questionably. "Nick?"

"Yes. Truet is at the ranch, Phillip has family plans, and we'll take Nate with us to arrest him. I thought you might like to help."

"Hell, yeah, I do." He put his feet on the floor on the other side of the bed and stood. He dressed quickly. "Who is your witness? Which one of her friends was stabbed? I can't say they didn't deserve it for not telling you sooner!"

"You didn't go to the sideshow…"

"Hell no, I didn't go to the sideshow! My niece was killed! We were mourning, Matt. Which is a lot more than I can say about you."

"William, you all made it very clear that I wasn't welcomed. Hannie may not have been my niece, but she was still family, and my heart is broken. I have nieces too, William. You can stay mad at me if you want, but I was asked to leave when I tried to be there with you. Remember? You should have known me well enough to trust my judgment. The leather

292

man's name was Avery Gaines. He was a reporter from New York doing an assignment dressed up as a strange vagrant with a crazy story to see how he was treated in our town. It was a ruse for a story. He wasn't a pedophile, and he wasn't a killer. He was a good moral man trying to save Hannie."

"Why was he naked then?" William asked.

Matt hesitated. He spoke softly, "So he wouldn't drown. Nick strangled Hannie when she put up a fight. He pulled her up onto the bridge and tossed her into the river. Avery saw her fall and ran down to the water, stripped and dove in to save her. That's when Nick stabbed him and cut his throat."

William sat down on the edge of the bed and emotionally covered his face with his hands. His breathing became erratic as he fought from sobbing. "You know I'm going to kill Nick. Is that why you came to get me?"

"No. I'm not close with Jim or Karen, but I am you. As a part-time deputy, I wanted to get you so that you can make the arrest and be involved in his hanging. I'll let you put the noose around his neck. But to assure that you don't kill him, I need you to leave your weapons here. You won't need them."

He looked at Matt callously. "I survived the Battle of Henry Creek and there was a hell of a lot more hand-to-hand combat there than I'll face with that twig. I don't need my guns to kill him."

"The object is to arrest him. You'll have your sense of justice when you put the noose around his neck. You can enjoy every minute of it, and I won't say a word. But I won't let you kill him today. Are we understood?"

William exhaled. "Understood. But I'm putting the noose on his neck and pulling the lever! That's the least I can do. I appreciate you telling me what happened to Hannie Bear. If you don't mind, I'd like a few minutes to myself to absorb it."

"Sure. I'll meet you out front when you're ready."

William shouted, "Close the door!" as Matt left.

***

"If Nick's working at the circus, shouldn't we be going there?" William asked irritably. Matt had led him and Nate Robertson to the Dogwood Flats apartments.

"We will. I have questions for Nick's friend, though." He knocked on Ollie's door.

Ollie's mother opened it. In her late thirties, she was a lady with long yellow hair and a thin narrow face that showed the aged weathering of a rough life. Her dark blue eyes were as blue as the ocean's depths and showed genuine concern when she saw the three lawmen at her door.

"Hello, Ma'am, I'm the U.S. Marshal Matt Bannister and these are my deputies. Are you Ollie's mother?" Matt asked. He had seen her working in the kitchen of Ugly John's saloon in the past, but he had never met her.

"Yes, I am. Can I help you?"

"Is Ollie home? We'd like to come inside and talk to him if we could."

She opened the door. "Sure. Is he in some kind of

trouble? He's right here."

"I'm not exactly sure," Matt responded. The small apartment had two bedrooms, a family room, and a small kitchen. Like the others, it contained an old beat-up davenport, ripped padded chair and a small round dining table with two chairs. Ollie was sitting on the davenport, staring at Matt anxiously.

"What did you do, Ollie?" his mother asked.

His cheeks and ears flushed.

"Ollie, do you know why I'm here?" Matt asked.

"No," he answered in a wavering voice. Matt's composure wasn't as friendly as it had been in the past. It scared Ollie.

"Nate, do you have those wrist shackles?" Matt asked with his eyes boring into Ollie.

"I do," Nate replied. He had no idea what Matt was doing or talking about, but he pulled the shackles out of his pocket. "I have them right here."

Ollie's mother gasped with emotion. "Ollie... what did you do?" Her bottom lip began to tremble.

"I didn't want to!" Ollie blurted out. "I didn't want to break in there. Nick said he'd be arrested if we didn't do it." He began to weep.

"Do what? Tell your mother what you did," Matt ordered.

Ollie sobbed.

"What did you do?" his mother shouted.

"We broke into the mortuary and I..."

"You what?" her kind blue eyes had become fierce.

"He wanted bite marks, so I..." he hesitated to speak, "I pulled the man's mouth closed." He covered his face with shame and sobbed.

"Bite marks? What are you talking about?" his mother questioned. She was easily confused by the answer.

Matt spoke, "I thought so. Ollie, I want a straight answer and I'll warn you I already know exactly what happened. Who killed Hannie?"

His mother began to shake. "Please tell me Ollie had nothing to do with that poor girl's death?"

William's patience ran out. He shouted gruffly, "Answer him or I'll pinch your little head off!"

Ollie looked into Matt's eyes, "The leather man did. I wasn't there, I swear it. Ask Rose."

Matt asked, "Why did Nick want the bite marks?"

"Because he was afraid you would arrest him for the scratches on him. He said he didn't want to be hung for a crime he didn't commit."

"What made you help him?"

"He's my best friend."

"Have you ever seen Nick get violent?"

He nodded. "His father beats him. They fight."

"Is there anything else I need to know before I find out about it myself? If you're hiding anything, it would be better for you to tell me now."

"He lied to you last night. Nick likes knives. He has several. He sold a spare knife to the saloon, not his. And he stole a table from the furniture store."

"Anything else?"

"No, sir."

"Be honest with him, Ollie," his mother said with concern.

"I am, Mother," he responded respectfully.

"Is Nick really planning to leave with the circus?" Matt asked.

"Yes, sir. He should be working there now."

"Ollie," Matt said, "I told you last night that I think you are a good young man. I'm not going to arrest you for breaking into the mortuary or stealing a table. But I will talk to my uncle Solomon and see if you can work off the cost of the broken window and table before you get paid. Do understand; I could arrest you for burglary, vandalism, theft and desecration of a corpse. You could face a year or two in prison."

"But we didn't do anything to that man! We just opened and closed his mouth," Ollie argued.

"His corpse was evidence in a murder investigation. I could toss in tampering with evidence as well. What I'm getting at is I could arrest you for some serious crimes that could put you in prison with some of the worst people you could imagine. Instead, I'm going to sentence you to work for my uncle Solomon all summer. Every day he wants you to work; you work in the furniture store or the mortuary. If he wants you to dig graves, then that's what you'll do. Understood?"

He nodded.

"If you quit, I will arrest you, Ollie. Is that understood?"

"Isn't that blackmail?" his mother asked.

"No, Ma'am, that is an agreement between Ollie and me, you of course, and my uncle if he agrees. If not, I'll find Ollie work elsewhere."

"But it was all Nick's idea," Ollie protested.

"You didn't have to follow him into doing things you knew were wrong. I'm helping you, and some-day you will understand that. This gives you a chance to learn a trade that you can use for the rest of your life to have a good future and earn some money now. For the first two or three weeks, you don't have a choice. You need to pay off what was broken and stolen."

"Is Nick going to work there too?"

Matt shook his head hesitantly. He spoke slowly, "Ollie, Nick is the one that murdered Hannie, not the leather man. Nick is going to jail. We are going to arrest him now."

Ollie's mouth dropped open. "He didn't kill her. He couldn't have. He wouldn't."

"There is no question about it. Nick did it. I'll let you know what my uncle says."

Chapter 33

Nick Griffin had to learn how to roll up a rope, fold a tarp and tie them into bundles for organized packing in the limited space of the wagons. Everything had a place, and it was a tight fit, but the entire circus fitted into the wagons. The wall of drapes, tents, posts and poles were all placed inside the cage wagon that promoted David in the sideshow.

What appeared to be an overwhelming job proved to be more efficient and easier than Nick expected. The first job he was given was to help break down the circle of drapes and posts around the sideshow. The work wasn't hard as labor went, but there was a lot of repetitive work, such as folding the drapes, disconnecting the framework, and pulling posts out of the ground.

Nick was told by his coworkers about the Tasmanian Wolf Boy being stabbed outside of his caged wagon the night before. The blood was still visible on the ground. Nick pretended to be stunned by such a random attack. The exciting news for his co-workers was that David Chatfield had survived the stabbings and a prolonged surgery but still had a long recovery ahead. For Nick, that meant two things: he failed to kill the freak and secondly, the longer the freak stayed in Branson to heal, the greater the chances that he would tell either the sheriff or the marshal who stabbed him. It wouldn't be hard to identify him now since Nick was the only person from Branson hired by the circus and planned on leaving with it. It would not be hard to describe him or find him if he stayed with the circus.

Plans change like a flash flood creating a twisting and turning path down across the valley. It didn't matter if he loved the circus, he could not stay with it. He would, however, leave Branson with the circus for a free ride with food and board to Walla Walla and then part ways. Perhaps he'd change his name and never be heard from again. He had no bond with his father, and Leonard's sudden fatherly pride was as temporary as a fleeting breeze. It wouldn't take but a day for Leonard to start throwing him around and hitting on him again. His best friend Ollie, he would miss, but friends were replaceable, and the world was full of potential friends. It was better to cut ties now and get away with murder than to stick around and be hung.

"How long until lunch, Roy?" he asked one of his fellow employees. "I haven't eaten since yesterday."

"You'll hear a bell when it's done. Smells good,

though, doesn't it? One great thing about working for the circus is getting three good squares a day. All you can eat. I worked doing just about everything, I even tried my hand at cowboying once, but no one ever treated me better than the Chatfields and the folks here. I'll even see the ocean when we get to San Francisco. What other job offers that, huh?"

"I don't know. The only job I've ever had was delivering groceries. This doesn't seem so bad."

"It's not. We set up the tents and things and have a day or two off to help around here and explore the town. It becomes routine and pays well for what we do."

"Where are you from?"

"Kansas. Where I'm from, it's just flat forever, and to see mountains like this," he waved at the mountain ranges that surrounded them, "is fantastic."

"Yeah, unless you live here. We're snowed in during the wintertime and there's not much to do. I'd rather live in a big city. All I know is I'm ready to leave and I wish we were leaving today."

"We are in the morning. And the sooner we get this place packed up, the sooner we are done for the day. The other men and I are heading back to the saloons for another fun night. You can come if you want."

"I need to pack."

The bell rang for lunch, and they walked to the cookhouse and got a tray of food. They sat at a table with a couple of other men to enjoy a good lunch. The cranberry sauce, salad and meatloaf sandwich with a glass of iced tea on such a warm day was paradise compared to the little he had to eat daily. Nick ate hungrily and paid little attention to his surroundings until he heard Matt's name.

"Did you find the person that stabbed David?" a woman asked.

Nick looked over and saw Matt and two of his deputies had entered the cookhouse. Matt's eyes connected with Nick's and he knew Matt was there to arrest him. Nick leaped from his chair and grabbed a young lady sitting at the next table with her back turned to him. He grabbed her from behind, ripped her off the stool to her feet, and held her in front of him as he faced Matt. He held his knife to her throat. A twisted scowl deformed his lips.

The young lady screamed in alarm as Nick's left arm wrapped around her body tightly and his right hand pressed the knife's sharp blade against her throat. "Shut up!" he snarled into her ear. She did as he ordered. She squeezed her lips tightly together while she wept fearfully. Nick stepped back towards the opposite entrance of the tent than the one Matt and his deputies entered.

"Stay back! I'll cut her throat!" he hollered to the surprise of the other employees.

Matt raised a hand to calm Nick down. "Nick, put the knife down and let her go. I'm just here to talk." He knew it sounded lame as soon as he said it.

Nick kept his face hidden behind her brown hair as best he could. She was a circus equestrian acrobat and not as tall as Nick but slightly broader with muscle tone. Nick knew Matt's words were a lie. "You always come alone to talk, don't lie to me. You stay back! I'll cut her head off and you know I will if you come out of this tent! Stay in here until I let her go." He backed out of the tent.

"I'll get him," William said and turned to leave through the entrance they had just come in.

Matt spoke urgently, "Wait! Do not confront him until he lets her go. He has no reason to harm her, so let's not give him a reason to. Nate, go with William." Matt looked at the anxious faces of those in the cookhouse. "You all stay in here and out of our way." He crossed the broad tent and peeked out of the entrance Nick went out. He stepped through the canvas flaps and disappeared outside the tent.

Outside, he could hear weeping and went around a decorative red wagon with painted clowns and gold molding on it and saw the young lady sitting on the ground sobbing. She was scared but unharmed. "Where is he?" he asked.

She sobbed uncontrollably.

William ran around the backside of the cookhouse tent and shouted urgently, "Matt, he went towards the livery stable! He's probably going to steal a horse. Nate's heading that way! Since I don't have a weapon, I'll go to the main road to head him off if he tries to leave town!"

Matt nodded and ran across the circus grounds towards the livery stable to catch Nick before he could steal a horse.

William watched Matt run to help Nate and chuckled to himself. He ran around the sagging big top tent where he had seen Nick run.

Nick sprinted to the animal pens and opened the gate to the four white horses the equestrians rode in the circus. To Nick's dismay, all the horses wore a halter, but none had a lead rope or reins connected to them. He ran into the fenced corral and the horses scattered; two ran out of the corral's opened gate while he tried to corner a horse. He grabbed the halter, and it darted for the gate dragging him to the ground in front of the gate. He rolled to a stop and stood in the open entrance. One of the beautiful white horses remained in the corral, trotting nervously in a circle. Anxious to get away and knowing time was short, Nick opened his arms wide and tried to calm the skittish horse as it pranced around the corral, avoiding him.

"Stop! You stupid horse!" he muttered angrily. "I said stop!" he swung a fist at the horse, missing it; he almost fell from the force of the swing. He ran and jumped across its back as it made a quick trot for the corral's exit. With his stomach over the horse's back, he flew off like he was lying on a box of dynamite when the horse crow hopped once and then lowered its head and bucked its hind legs up high, throwing Nick ten feet into the air. He landed face down against the hard ground with a hard thud. Unable to catch his breath, he groaned as he forced himself to his knees and slowly stood in the empty corral.

William Fasana walked into the corral with a cynical chuckle. "You're a stupid kid! You don't know much about horses, do you? Well, you learned a lesson, but just a little too late to do you any good. Stand up straight and try to kill me like you did my niece when you're ready. I'm not even armed. Feel free to try." He spread his arms out invitingly. "Go ahead, pull your knife and give it your best thrust."

Nick's knee and arm ached from the landing. He didn't have time for the pain and pulled his knife from the sheath. He had never had anyone invite him to stab them as William had. The confidence William had with his outstretched hands made Nick cautious. He hoped to make William angry enough to rush forward and attack him blindly. "Fine. Let's make this quick. Hannie put up a good fight. See? She scratched me up. Not before I forced a kiss, though." He grinned and stuck out his tongue and wiggled it. "I think she liked it."

It seemed to work. William's inviting half-smile slowly turned into a sour grimace. His right hand reached under his black jacket and pulled out a stainless-steel single-shot derringer with a pearl grip. He aimed it at Nick and pulled the hammer back. "Don't drop the knife like a coward. Die with your weapon in hand like a man. I can't tell you how excited I am to be the one that kills you. It just makes my day!"

Nick wasn't expecting to see a gun. A gun changes everything in a fight. His only hope was to attack and hope the bullet missed. He sneered furiously and ran forward to stab William.

William's lips twisted upwards as he pulled the trigger, but to his horror, the gun clicked. He pulled the hammer back in desperation and pulled the trigger again just as Nick reached him. The derringer misfired again. Nick swung the knife towards William's body as he ran by, William tried to dodge the blade, but the swinging motion sliced across William's belly, leaving a six-inch gash that began to bleed profusely. William dropped to one knee in disbelief. He could feel the burning of his wound and feel the blood seeping through the fingers of his left hand. William looked at the new derringer that he bought in Portland and shook his head at his bad luck. He lifted his head and laughed at himself. He had not replaced the spent cartridge after target practicing with Maggie on Portland's waterfront. William grinned at Nick. "Don't get mixed up with a woman. Take it from me; she's bound to get you killed somehow." He tossed the derringer aside.

Nick grinned with the evil glare of victory in his eyes. "I heard you tell the marshal I went towards the livery stable. I suppose you wish you hadn't done that now, huh?"

"Oh, yeah," William said, holding the gash firmly to keep pressure on it with his left hand. He could feel the blood running down his pant leg. "You killed me, kid. You flayed me open like a fish and cut my liver too. I'm bleeding out." He nodded with a clenched jaw. "You could give me my last five minutes, maybe six if I'm lucky."

"I don't have time to wait. The marshal will be coming, I'm sure. What was it you said to me? Oh yeah, be a man and die with your weapon in your hand." He kicked the single-shot derringer towards William. He grinned. "I killed William Fasana," he said proudly.

William exhaled with a grimace. The sliced flesh burned like hot coals. "Yeah, you did. I've bested some of the meanest and toughest men in the west and a herd of wild Indians during the war. I can *not* believe a teenage punk with no hair on his face killed me," he chuckled softly. "All these years and a stupid kid with enough acne to be a sideshow attraction killed me."

"I wish I could stay here and watch you die. But I have to get out of town."

"Listen, approach the next horse you intend to steal slowly, calmly and you'll have better luck," William advised.

"Say hi to Hannie for me," Nick turned away from William with a laugh.

To hear him joke about Hannie's death infuriated William. He chuckled forcefully. "Hey, Jackass, do you know what's funny?"

Nick turned around. "What?"

William raised his arms invitingly, exposing his blood-covered left hand. "I'm playing possum." He stood with a grimace. "You didn't come close to killing me. You need to learn that you don't walk away from an enemy without making sure they're dead. I still have one good hand to whip you with, even as I hold my wound. Come finish me off if you can," William challenged him, covering his cut again.

Nick drew his knife and came at William with a furious expression on his twisted face.

William's bloody left hand pulled out of his jacket, holding a double-barrel derringer from his right shoulder holster. He pulled the hammer back and pulled the trigger. The bullet struck Nick's right shoulder. Nick dropped the knife as he grabbed his shoulder.

"Ouch!" William shouted with a sarcastic laugh. "Come on, boy, you have one good arm left. Pick up the knife and finish me!" he called ferociously. "Do you want to live? Then grab that knife and come get me. You can't run away from me. I'll shoot you in the back of the head. You could surrender, but that's a guaranteed hanging. Matt already promised I could put the noose around your neck and trust me, I'll make it hurt. I promise! Pick up that knife and fight for your life, boy!"

Nick stared at William, unsure if he should or not. Nick's frightened eyes showed the pain and panic of being shot and bleeding. He didn't want to die, but he knew he couldn't afford to be arrested either. He spoke through a suddenly dry throat, "You have a gun."

"I do, don't I?" William said, gazing at his old reliable two-shot derringer. "Well, I don't need it to whip you." He returned it to his shoulder holster. "You better hurry and decide before Matt gets here. He wants to see you hang as bad as I do. I wouldn't mind watching the piss run down your frightened little leg when I put that black hood over your head. Do you know what I'm going to do? I'm going to make your hanging slow, painful and torturous. It only takes a half-inch turn of the rope to watch you slowly strangle to death. I'll enjoy that more than now. Or you can pick your knife and try to kill me. I'm already hurt; it shouldn't be that hard. I even put my gun away, so quit shaking like a frightened girl and do something!"

Nick reached down for the knife. He hesitated for a second and then ran towards William, keeping the knife low and wide to swing it from the outside inward to drive the blade into William's side.

William's quick left hand reached in, pulled out the derringer, and pulled the trigger. He had put it away with the hammer cocked. The bullet struck Nick in the center of his forehead. He dropped to the ground, facedown and dead. The knife was still clenched in his fist.

William grimaced. "Well, you might've lived a little longer if you surrendered." He chuckled lightly. He put the small derringer back in its holster and covered his bleeding belly.

"William, are you alright?" Morton Sperry called as he quickly crossed the field from the Sperry camp across from the circus. He hopped over the fence and came to William's side. "Are you shot? Where's Matt?"

"I got cut. Matt will be here momentarily. He's faithful for that."

"Who is the kid?"

"He murdered my niece. I guess he was dumb enough to think he could run ten feet before I could reach six inches."

"He thought wrong, didn't he?" Morton asked.

"William," Matt called as he ran into the corral. He was breathing hard from sprinting back after hearing the first shot. "How bad are you hurt?"

"It'll call for some mending, but I'm fine."

Matt sighed with a disappointed shake of his head. "You lied to me."

William snickered. "No, I was just wrong. He came this way."

"Self-defense, I presume?" Matt asked.

William raised his bloody hand. "I'm cut open, aren't I? It looks like he's holding a knife to me. What about you, Mort?"

Morton nodded in agreement. "I'd say so. I saw the whole thing from our camp across the way."

"Let's get you to the doctor." Matt looked at Morton. "Do you have a horse handy to help get him to a doctor?"

"I'll be right back with one."

Matt knelt beside Nick and turned the body over. He looked at William. "I should have known you were armed."

William raised his eyebrows with a cockeyed smile. "Yeah, you should've and I'm sure you did. At least I can tell my sister and Jim that justice is done. It won't help the pain, but at least now we know who did it and why. For what little that helps, it matters a lot. I have to be honest, Matt, I thought I'd feel better after killing him. But I feel just about as empty as I did before. Just as angry too."

"You killed a young man who surely would have killed you and others if he had gotten away. Unfortunately, it doesn't heal the pain or satisfy the grieving soul. Hannie will always be a missing part of your life, William. That doesn't go away. Over time, you might grow used to it, but that missing piece of your life will always be there."

William sniffled. "I apologize for all the things I said to you. I was wrong."

"You're forgiven. Let's get you to the doctor while you still have some blood left in you."

Chapter 34

Leonard Griffin was incensed. His son was a hero and not a murderer, as the marshal claimed. Nick was the only family he had left, and he loved his son. To see Matt Bannister stand in Leonard's own apartment and tell him that his son was killed justifiably was an outrage. To say Nick murdered the girl related to the marshal and then murdered the crazy man that did kill her was an insult that could not be accepted.

Leonard hadn't always been proud of his son. There were times when looking at Nick, Leonard felt resentful for losing his wife. Nick had cursed his mother and the day he did she died. It wasn't something that Leonard was proud of, but he could not let it go. For all these years, he resented the boy and treated him harshly. Nick never did anything to make Leonard proud of him until Thursday night, when he showed the courage to kill a man to save a girl's life. Leonard could finally announce with pride to his friends in the saloon and all over town that his son was the one that killed the child murderer. Killing the crazy leather man probably saved many other lives. Nick was a hero shot down by the marshal's office because Matt Bannister would not accept the evidence. He hounded Nick to the point of death.

Everyone knew there was corruption in Branson's elite and the marshal was just as corrupt as his brothers or anyone else. Nick had a mark on his head for no other reason than Matt protecting his reputation. Matt had let the crazy leather man go free and then the stranger murdered a young girl, who just so happened to be related to one of the more prominent families, the Bannisters. It was only reasonable to blame her murder on someone Matt released from the sheriff's custody, and the only other person to blame was Nick.

The marshal drew Griffin blood and now the city looked at Leonard as the producer of a monster instead of a hero. He could not escape becoming known as the father of a murderer. Leonard could argue his son was innocent and set up, but it was falling on deaf ears. The shame was overbearing. He still had a job, but even there, he was the black sheep and the men gossiped about his cold-blooded son like women chattering at a social event.

It had only been a day, and his life turned into a miserable existence of blame, gossip and shame. The anger building within him festered like an untreated infection. His life was empty, and he no longer had a reason to continue, except for one, to get even with Matt. Blood for blood and perhaps save another family down the road from being set up and condemned to protect the precious marshal's reputation.

He cleaned his old revolver and filled the cylinder with six bullets. The marshal was going to pay for his lies.

***

It was Monday afternoon and drawing near to the end of the day. Matt had spent the day writing a report on the weekend's events and notified the Monmouth Pointe Chronicle of Avery Gaines's death. It was a complicated and detailed report to write. His hand ached and his fingers were stiff from writing for so many hours. He was ready to go home.

The sound of the cowbell didn't arouse any interest, but the call from Phillip that Leonard Griffin wanted to talk to him, sent a wave of caution down Matt's spine. It wasn't that Leonard was such a frightening man, but more so a grieving man who blamed Matt for his grief. Grieving men could not be trusted when they carried a grievance.

"I'll be out there in a second," Matt called from his private office. He grabbed his gun belt from the peg on the wall and fastened it around his waist. He removed the thong from the hammer and flexed his fingers to loosen them up. Perhaps it was overly cautious, but it was better to be than not cautious enough.

Matt closed his eyes and took a moment to pray. "Lord, I pray he is just here to talk. If not, I ask that you will keep me safe and that I might be able to talk him away from violence."

He stepped out into the main office and approached Leonard Griffin carefully. He could see the hatred that burned in the man's face and recognized the coiled posture of a man ready to strike, though trying to appear casual. Matt stopped five feet away with his left foot slightly angled to the right in front of him to make exposing his profile quicker if need be. Side profiles were a smaller target to hit while shooting under pressure.

"Phillip, why don't you and Nate go check on the jails and make sure they are cleaned for the night. I want to talk to Mister Griffin alone." His eyes never left the man.

Phillip and Nate, recognizing the tension, agreed and left their desks without saying more than yes, sir.

"What can I do for you, Mister Griffin?" Matt asked.

"You can apologize for calling my son a murderer. We both know who killed that girl. You're just protecting your precious pride by blaming my son."

"Not so. There was a witness like I told you. Mister Griffin, I don't want any trouble, and quite frankly, what I told you is the truth. It may be hard for you to believe, but that's the way it happened."

A twisted snarl formed on Leonard's lips. "My son was only seventeen! He was not a killer, and you know it! You framed him! What kind of a man does that?" he yelled.

"You can deny it for as long as you want, but I'm not going to argue about it."

Leonard called Matt a few choice words and then shouted, "Fine! Your day is coming! It's not over, Marshal Bannister." He turned to leave.

Matt's fingers twitched. There was something about the turning away that seemed unnatural and tense. Matt knew it was coming.

Leonard spun around quickly and raised his revolver. Matt drew his Colt and pulled the trigger. He held the trigger down as he fanned the hammer twice more, sending three bullets into the chest of Leonard Griffin.

Leonard hit the wall behind him as the gun in his hand fired a shot into the floor before dropping from his hand. Leonard slid down the wall into a sitting position and fell to one side as he took his dying last breaths.

Both deputies came running out of the jail, Nate carried his revolver. "Are you okay, boss?"

Matt nodded. He holstered his revolver. "I'm fine," he said quietly. "Go get my uncle Solomon." He knew Leonard would try to kill him sooner or later due to his insistence that Matt had set up his son.

And now, it was over.

Chapter 35

William Fasana needed twenty-seven stitches to close the gash across his abdomen. It was a painful wound, but one that would heal. His injury would have been far worse if he had not twisted his body to miss the blade. If he had remained in place, the knife most likely would have plunged into his liver and killed him. He would have liked to have stayed in his own room, but he was moved to the second floor to make his room available for David Chatfield to recover from surgery.

David's wounds were much more severe than William's. It had taken surgery to suture the internal damage done. It was a miracle that he survived surgery and was still alive with the amount of blood loss that he experienced. He was moved to the Monarch Hotel, where he would be for a few weeks or until his body healed enough to leave. A secondary cot was placed in the room, for Nancy Chatfield to stay with David.

He wasn't the usual kind of guest and for his
safety, it was best for Nancy to be with him so that
curious thrill-seekers didn't try to sneak into his
room. He had been kept on a heavy dose of morphine to keep him sleeping and pain-free.

David opened his eyes slowly and blinked a few
times to get himself oriented. He had woken up a
few times but was generally given more morphine
to keep him down. Doctor Ryland wanted David to
wake up and be alert for a little while, so he was not
given an immediate dose. David knew he was in a
hotel sharing a room with Nancy. He remembered
the kind face of Doctor Ryland and took notice of
him as the doctor asked him questions. Once Doctor Ryland checked his wounds and knew David
was up to having visitors, he said, "I have someone
out in the lobby waiting to meet you. I'll go get
him."

Nancy took hold of David's hand. "I want you to
know that you worried all of us. I'm thankful you'll
be okay. I love you."

He smiled slightly. "I love you too."

The door opened and Matt Bannister entered
the room with his fiancée, Christine. He held out
a hand to introduce himself. "David, it is nice to
meet you finally. I'm Matt Bannister and this is my
fiancée, Christine."

David's eyes widened. He shook Matt's hand
wordlessly.

"Hello, David," Christine said, shaking his
hair-covered hand.

"Hi," he said weakly. Matt Bannister was one of

those names he never expected to meet in person, let alone be visited by the actual man. David didn't know anything about Christine, except she was the most beautiful lady he had ever seen. Her brown eyes gazed upon him affectionately.

Matt said, "David, I want you to know that I struggled with who killed Hannie. She was part of my family, and her death was quite a shock to all of us. I couldn't get the evidence that I needed to arrest Nick Griffin. Every time I thought I had him by the scruff of the neck, the evidence slipped away like a slippery eel right out of my hands. I was losing part of my family because they blamed me for letting the so-called leather man go. Everyone thought he was a crazy, murdering stranger. No one knew who Avery Gaines was. He told me, but in the midst of it all, I didn't know if he was a journalist or a crazy vagabond. Even after you were attacked, I still couldn't get any real evidence to arrest Nick. It wasn't until Nancy brought me Avery's journal and I read what you wrote. It told me everything I needed to know. In this particular case, I have you to thank for solving who murdered Hannie. I don't know if I could have done it without you."

"Did you arrest him?" David asked with a touch of anxiety.

Matt shook his head slightly. "My deputy shot Nick; he's dead. You have nothing to fear anymore. I want you to know that writing what you did in that journal helped me. If you had not, Nick would be with the circus right now and any one of your friends would be in danger. You, young man, are a hero. And I'm going to write up a letter stating so for you to keep."

David's lips rose slightly.

Christine added, "And I will make sure it is framed before you get it."

"Thank you," David said.

The door opened and William Fasana walked in and closed the door behind him. He moved slower than usual and wore an uncomfortable expression of the pain on his face. He nodded to Matt and Christine as he stood at the end of the bed staring at David. He carried a saucer and forked a piece of cherry pie.

"David, this is my cousin William. He is the deputy that shot Nick. He lives here and is here to keep you and Nancy safe. This is his room."

"Hi," David said. He appeared uncomfortable under the severe glare in William's eyes as he ate a bite of the pie.

Christine took hold of David's hand. "I want you to know I would like to be your friend. If you don't mind, when Doctor Ryland says it is okay, I will start making you treats and bringing them when I visit. Is that okay with you?"

"I'd like that."

"Do you have any favorite treats? Cake? Cookies?"

"I like it all," he answered.

Matt waved towards William. "William, have you met David?"

William swallowed his mouth full of pie. "We met a few times, but he was sleeping. David, I just want to say one thing to you. If you get hair in my bed, I will hunt you down!"

David grinned for the first time. "I don't shed a lot."

William laughed and grabbed his side. "Don't make me laugh, kid. It hurts."

"I know," David said with a grimace and touched his abdomen.

Matt said, "David, you're going to be here for a little while and we'll have plenty of time to talk and get to know each other. Christine and I would like to be your friend, so we will be coming by often to visit. We're going to leave to have dinner. But we'll talk to you soon. William, do you want to join us?"

William sat down on a wooden dining room chair next to the bed. "No. I think I'll sit here and talk to this animal about how he steals all the hearts of the pretty women. First, it's Nancy's heart and now Christine's." He looked at David curiously. "I've been trying to win Christine's heart for almost a year now, and you did it in five minutes! She's never offered to bring me anything, but she'll make cake, cookies and pies for you? What's your secret? And don't say it's your animal magnetism because I can't grow such a fine beard as yours."

David grinned and again held his side. "It must be my scent."

William grinned. "David, I don't know that you smell too good right now. But I will tell you this; we're blood brothers, Pal. Yeah, I was stabbed by the same knife you were, which means we're related by blood now. Do you think some of that wildness that drives the pretty girls crazy will be passed on to me? It's like being bit by a werewolf, isn't it? Trust me, Pal, I need it."

David had just met William, but he immediately liked the man. He was going to respond when the door opened.

Lee Bannister entered the room with an awkward nod towards Matt and Christine.

William spoke, "Lee, have you met my blood brother? He's the wildest man I've seen with the ladies yet. This beastly fellow is David. Dave, that's my cousin Lee. He's Matt's brother and owns this facility." William whispered to David, loud enough to be heard by the others, "He's got a pretty wife too, but don't steal her heart like Christine's, or you'll get us both kicked out of here. Okay? Try to restrain yourself to only one." He pointed at Christine.

David grinned. "I'll try. Hello, sir."

Lee stood by the foot of the bed. "I hope you enjoy your stay. If you need or want anything, just let William or Pam know. The kitchen staff will make anything you want. We're going to take good care of you here. I look forward to getting to know you, young man."

William covered his mouth and mumbled to David. "Tell him you're looking forward to knowing his wife, if you know what I mean."

The corners of David's lips rose. "I look forward to knowing your wife, if you know what I mean."

William grabbed his side with a hearty laugh. "You weren't supposed to actually say that, kid!" He laughed.

"Well, you said to!"

"We're going to have a lot of fun together," William laughed.

Lee's lips rose just a touch. "Yeah, I'll talk to you later, David." He turned to his brother. "Matt, can I talk to you in private for a moment?"

"Christine and I were just leaving to have dinner."

"It will only take a moment. Let's borrow Roger's office."

The two brothers entered the hotel manager's office and closed the door. Lee spoke sincerely, "Matt, I wanted to apologize for the other night in the park. Things got heated and I was wrong. I hope there are no hard feelings."

Matt leaned against the desk and crossed his arms. "I expected you to have enough faith in me to know what I'm doing. You heard Tim make an accusation at the Slater's Ball and you bought into it. I was the one investigating Hannie's death because Tim is incompetent, and you know it. Tim would have bought Nick's story hook, line and sinker. And down the road, Nick would kill again and blame someone else. Tim's mind was already made up that the so-called leather man did it without investigating and you all were quick to believe it too."

"That's true. But in my defense, his being nude did add some suspicion, And I remember what Steven told us a month ago about him showing up in Willow Falls. We knew he was crazy, Matt. There was some reasonable cause for us to believe he did it. And you have to admit, you have a weakness for trying to see the goodness in people even when there isn't any. That will be your fatal flaw one of these days if you're not careful."

"I'm not exactly sure what that means, but if you're talking about letting Avery Gaines go when Bob tried to arrest him. I looked Avery in the eyes and spoke with him. He seemed harmless and sure enough, he was."

Lee's brow furrowed. "Matt, we could discuss that whole subject for hours. Look, I was wrong, and I apologize. I am sorry. I should have asked you what was going on instead of getting caught up in the emotional side of it. I did want to apologize, but I also wanted to warn you about something. You have a problem of always trying to see the best in people, and that's not a bad thing, but it's not always wise. You can put a poodle's skin on a badger and call it your pet dog, but you're still going to get bit."

"What are you talking about?" Matt asked.

"Morton Sperry. You two seem to be becoming friends. I know you probably want to look for the best in him, but I'll remind you Jesse James might've been friends with Bob Ford too. Morton is the leader of the Sperry Helms Gang, Matt. He's not a good man. As I said, you have a fatal flaw: trying to see the best in people. That is going to get you killed," Lee said pointedly.

Matt hesitated thoughtfully. "Perhaps I have let my guard down with him a bit. I like to think we have made friends. He says he wants to change his life since meeting me and the Sperry Helms Gang is all but finished. They haven't caused any trouble. So maybe he is changing."

Lee snickered cynically. "Keep him at a distance and don't turn your back. When it comes to that family, there is no good. They are a wicked bunch." He lowered his head and added with a severe expression in his eyes, "It surprised me to see you having lunch with Morton on Saturday. I don't want to see it again."

"So that's where this is coming from," Matt said, understanding. He had lunch at the Monarch Restaurant with Morton Sperry after Morton helped take William to the doctor. "Lee, do you think people can change? Better stated, do you think the Lord can change people? Morton's whole life has been about crime and wickedness, but it's growing thin of meaning in his life. There is an emptiness inside him that can't be filled with money or drinks anymore. Something is missing in his life, and I know what that is; it's the Lord. He just hasn't accepted that yet, but I believe he will."

Lee picked up a hard candy from a candy dish and put it in his mouth. "I'd be surprised if Morton or any Sperry accepted Jesus as their savior. What would not surprise me is if they gained your trust and then shot you in the back like Bob Ford. Matt, take it from me, I know how bad they are."

Matt lowered his brow thoughtfully. "In the Bible, Jesus tells the Parable of the Sower. It must be an important parable because it is repeated in three of the four Gospels. You know it. The sower tosses seed out and some seeds land on the pathway and the birds eat those seeds up. Some seeds fell on rocky places that didn't have much soil, the seeds sprouted quickly and grew, but when the day's heat came, the plants withered and died because they had no soil for their roots. Other seeds fell among the thorns and although seeds grew, the plants were choked out by the thorns. Other seeds fell on good soil and those plants grew strong and produced a crop a hundred, sixty or thirty times what was sown. The parable is followed by a key sentence: "*Whoever has ears, let them hear.*"

Lee stopped him. "Matt, I don't want to hear a sermon. What are you getting at?" Lee asked with an impatient shrug and a roll of his wrist to speed it up.

"Bear with me. You'll understand why it is relevant in a minute." Matt continued, "The seed spoken about is the Gospel. The seed on the path are folks who hear the Gospel but don't want to hear it and the moment is snatched away. The seed in the rocky places are those who accept the Lord and for a short time relish in the joy and excitement, but when the heat of living life comes upon them and a prayer is not answered or the first disappointment happens, their faith is without roots, and they fade away and go back to their old life. The seeds that fall among the thorns are those who grow and appear to be doing well but then get wrapped up in the day-to-day life of business, money and the world's concerns until their faith is overrun by the pressures of life. You might also refer to them as the people who say they are Christians but want to live in the world's sins and say it's okay. They proclaim grace but neglect Biblical truth.

"And then you have the seed that lands on good soil. The Christian life is all about growing in Jesus and the Word of God. Our roots are the measurement of our faith and when our roots are firmly grounded in good soil, we can produce a crop. Faith is not wishing or saying. It is knowing that no matter whether our will is granted to us or not, God's purpose and goodness will be greater than ours and we trust it, even if it hurts. And often, the outcome is far more pleasing to us than what we wanted in the first place. That crop of hundred, sixty or thirty isn't about numbers as much as it is about planting seeds in good soil.

"Lee, I'm not looking for numbers and how many people I can tell the Gospel to. You can bring fifty people to Jesus, but if not one of those seeds lands on fertile ground and fails to grow in Biblical knowledge and strength, it's just tossing out seeds to be plucked by birds, scorched by the sun and choked out by the world. Some people come into our lives, and they see something in you that they are lacking. Whether it is peace, joy, kindness, love or something else, there is a light we Christians have that attracts others. Morton Sperry is taking notice of that, and I'm not going to push him away and keep him at arm's length because I'm afraid of being assassinated. He'll never grow in good soil if I don't welcome him and accept him for who he is. I believe Jesus is working on his heart and I pray he accepts Jesus, and the roots grow in deep soil because he'll need deep roots in his family. And when he stands, someone else in his family will take notice and want what he has. Do you understand? Beyond the Gospel, I believe in planting seeds in good soil and nurturing the roots to grow deeper in the faith. That means encouraging him and others to read their Bible every day. To keep their Bible open because an open Bible is very inviting. Reading the Bible keeps the world's weeds trimmed back so we can have the Light of the world in clear view. So yes, I do look for the good in people because I believe it is there. And that will never change because I am a Christian and that hope for others is the very essence of the Gospels of Jesus."

Lee twisted his lips cynically. "I hope you're right, but I don't have much faith in them. Maybe I just know more about them than you do. Just be careful and don't turn your back to them, for your own protection."

"Well, I have faith in Jesus, and I know he hasn't given up on anyone still alive today, so I won't either. Speaking of the Sperrys, I met your old friend, Alan Sperry, the other day. Alan had a confrontation with Cliff Jorgeson in the saloon. He apparently thinks Cliff knows where Racheal is. I understand she disappeared. Do you know anything about that? I just found out Alan was married to Racheal."

"Alan's back, huh?" Lee asked with an expanding chest. "He's no friend of mine. Yeah, I know of it." His jaw clenched noticeably. "Don't turn your back on him for sure. Matt, let me try to explain this in conjunction with your parable. If Morton is your potted plant project, Alan is the bird, weeds and heat all in one that will burn that seed up. That's one man with no good in him whatsoever. Take my word on that if nothing else."

"How well do you know him?" Matt knew Lee had a troubled past with Alan, but he didn't know much about it.

"Well, enough." Lee didn't seem to want to talk about Alan.

Matt opened his interlocked fingers curiously. "What do you think about him?"

Lee took a deep breath. He narrowed his eyes and tightened his lips. "I think the wrong Sperry brother was killed at the Battle of Coffee Creek. Dwight Sperry was killed; I should never have saved Alan. Listen, I have to run. We'll talk another time. Just watch yourself, little brother."

Matt found Christine waiting for him in the hotel lobby. She had a glowing grin on her beautiful face. She waved a hand towards the closed door of William's room. "I think those two will become good friends or burst their stitches laughing together. I can't hear what they are saying, but you can hear them laughing."

Matt paused to listen to William's laughter through the door. Hannie Longo's death hung heavily on the hearts of them all. Her funeral would be later in the week when her grandfather and other relatives came to town to be with the Longo family. Maybe William's laughter was overcompensation for the hurting in his heart, or perhaps he was just enjoying the moment. Either way, honest laughter is a pleasing sound to hear. The corners of Matt's lips lifted.

"Shall we?" Matt asked, extending his elbow to escort his future bride into the restaurant.

"Always," she replied as she took hold of him.

Acknowlededments

I offer my highest praise and appreciation to my family. It would be impossible to write this book if it wasn't for the understanding and support they give me. My wife, Cathy. My three beautiful daughters and two handsome son in laws, Jessica and Chris. Chevelle. Katie and Isaiah. and of course, my very helpful son, Keith. I appreciate you all and the encouragement you all give me. I love you all.

A Look At: The Demon Uprising

Demon Hunter Book One by Kerry Adcock

Almost 3,000 years ago, the Demon Uprising began. Only a handful of humans knew about it—until now.

Jacob "Jake" Taft is enjoying his time as a rancher after serving in the US Army as a covert ops Major. But strange happenings on his ranch and around the world have him questioning the story on TV. **That is—until an Angel shows up and gives Jake the ability to see demons.**

All around the world, chaos is ensuing—one event in particular being the abduction of The President of the United States' daughter, Ann Campbell. And when the FBI are called in to investigate, they are charged with bringing her back at all costs.

As people in various parts of the country continue fighting the demon known as Ghazi, they are all unknowingly led to the same place—where the demon's ultimate goal of supremacy and mass murder is discovered.

But can FBI agents who don't believe in God, believe that Demons really do exist?

Will Jake and his team be able to save the US and, eventually, the world from a demon who's been planning his takeover for nearly 3,000 years?

AVAILABLE ON AMAZON

About the Author

Ken Pratt and his wife, Cathy, have been married for 22 years and are blessed with five children and six grandchildren. They live on the Oregon Coast where they are raising the youngest of their children. Ken Pratt grew up in the small farming community of Dayton, Oregon. Ken worked to make a living, but his passion has always been writing. Having a busy family, the only "free" time he had to write was late at night getting no more than five hours of sleep a night. He has penned several novels that are being published along with several children's stories as well.

Made in the USA
Monee, IL
07 August 2022